Paul Doherty was born in Middlesbrough in 1946. He was admitted to Liverpool University where he gained a First Class Honours Degree in History and won a state scholarship to Exeter College, Oxford. While there he met his wife, Carla.

Paul worked in Ascot, Newark and Crawley, before being appointed as Headmaster to Trinity Catholic High School, Essex, in 1981. The school has been described as one of the leading comprehensives in the U.K. and has been awarded 'Outstanding' in four consecutive OFSTED inspections. All seven of Paul and Carla's children have been educated at Trinity.

Paul has written over 100 books and has published a series of outstanding historical mysteries set in the Middle Ages, Classical Greece, Ancient Egypt and elsewhere. His books have been translated into more than twenty languages.

Also by Paul Doherty

The Brother Athelstan Mysteries

The Nightingale Gallery
The House of the Red Slayer
Murder Most Holy
The Anger of God
By Murder's Bright Light
The House of Crows
The Assassin's Riddle
The Devil's Domain
The Field of Blood
The House of Shadows
Bloodstone
The Straw Men
Candle Flame
The Book of Fires

PAUL DOHERTY

The Nightingale Gallery

San Diego, California

Canelo US
An imprint of Printers Row Publishing Group
9717 Pacific Heights Blvd, San Diego, CA 92121
www.canelobooksus.com

Printers Row Publishing Group is a division of Readerlink Distribution Services, LLC. Canelo US is a registered trademark of Readerlink Distribution Services, LLC.

First published in Great Britain in 1991 by Headline Book Publishing, a division of Hodder Headline PLC. This edition originally published in the United Kingdom in 2021 by Canelo.

Published in partnership with Canelo.

Correspondence regarding the content of this book should be sent to Canelo US, Editorial Department, at the above address. Author inquiries should be sent to Canelo, Unit 9, 5th Floor, Cargo Works, 1–2 Hatfields, London SE1 9PG, United Kingdom, www.canelo.co.

Publisher: Peter Norton • Associate Publisher: Ana Parker
Art Director: Charles McStravick
Senior Developmental Editor: April Graham
Production Team: Beno Chan, Julie Greene, Rusty von Dyl

Library of Congress Control Number: 2022933881

ISBN: 978-1-6672-0230-3

Printed in India

26 25 24 23 22   1 2 3 4 5

In memory of Eric

Introduction

The old king was dying. The wind snatched up the rumour and carried it along the Thames. Boatmen whispered about it and the fat-bellied sea-going barges took the rumour further along the coast. Edward was failing; the great, blond-haired conqueror of France, the new Alexander in the West, was dying. Too late for those who had incurred his displeasure, their straggle-haired, blood-caked heads spiked over the gateway of London Bridge, marble white cheeks turning black as the ravens dug for juicier morsels.

The great king, or great bastard depending on your perspective, was reluctantly allowing the spirit to seep from his ageing, smelly body. The court had moved to Richmond in the early summer of 1377 as the winds swung south-west, blowing hard and hot from the dry deserts around the Middle Sea. The plague had appeared in London, with men and women dropping as the buboes swelled in their armpits and, bellies distended, they spat out their life's blood. The king was frightened as Death, assassin-like, crept into his court.

Edward braved it well. He tried to paint his sallow face and kept his mouth closed to hide his crumbling, blackened teeth. He dressed in silver and white taffeta trimmed with gold and primped his once golden hair, even though it hung in straggly, sweaty wisps to his bony shoulders. But Death was not appeased. The heat and evil humours from the river wrapped their cloying fingers around his decaying body, and still the king refused to give in. Had he not smashed the armies of France at Crécy and Poitiers? And taken their king captive to ride behind him as he, like a new Caesar, returned to London to glory in his prowess?

Edward sat on cushions in one of his great withdrawing chambers, refusing food and physic. A priest came scuttling round the walls like a small, black spider, a Job's comforter if there ever was one.

'Your Grace,' he insisted, 'you must go to bed.'

Edward turned like an old fox, his lips, twisted by a stroke, curled in displeasure.

'Go away, little man,' he hissed. 'Death will never take me!'

He stayed where he was, staring at his finger where the coronation ring, once so deeply embedded in his flesh, had recently been sawn off. His marriage to the kingdom was dead. He had held the sceptre for fifty years and now must hand it over to another.

He shook his head and glanced at his fingers. Rings of fire seemed to circle them. Death was coming, soft-shoed, shuffling along the corridors.

Edward's great heart lurched and fought back. He stood bravely as he had at Crécy thirty years before. He smiled to remember the way the wind had kissed his face as his captains had shouted 'Loose!' and the archers had sent their black clouds of living death into the advancing hordes of French. He would stand like he had then. Death would not take him if he stood. He did so for fifteen hours before sinking to the cushioned floor, his fingers clenched to his mouth. The priests carried him to his bed.

Hysteria gripped the court and the air was thick with gloom and terror. The gilded courtiers whispered about signs and portents; the River Thames, its waters swollen, broke its banks at Greenwich and flooded the palace. A huge, grey fish, the size of a Leviathan, was beached on the northern shores. The sky turned red at noonday and strange creatures were seen in the dark woods to the north. Voices were heard calling in the shadowy streets and ghostly trumpets brayed from the battlements of the Tower of London and Windsor Castle. One of the ladies-in-waiting saw a tarot card bearing the black figure of Death nailed to a royal chair. Another glimpsed the ghost of the dying king's power in the form of a mystic knight, marching along the moonlit gallery, down the stairs to the great palace doorway.

Edward III, the Lion of England, was dying. Old men recalled their grandparents telling them how the Lion, when young, had seized the throne from his mother Isabella and her lover, Mortimer. Now the Lion's day was done.

The king stirred himself. He asked for music, and a young girl in a tawny dress and lace-edged veil played the viol. The king went back in time as the ghosts gathered around his bed. His father, Edward II, done to death in Berkeley. His mother Isabella, beautiful and passionate. Philippa his wife with her dark skin and tender, doe-like eyes, dead these eight years. And one other ghost: his most precious son, Edward the Black Prince, leader of armies, a Pompey to his Caesar. The general who had taken the banners of England across the Pyrenees into Navarre but came back with nothing except a disease which rotted his body away. All gone! His son was gone.

They brought back the proclamations about the succession and the king knew he was dying. Seals were attached. He was leaving. His retainers melted away. 'Is there no faith left in Israel?' Edward whispered. The palace at Sheen became a mausoleum. The king was left to lie in his own sweat and dirt, alone except for Alice Perrers, his mistress. She swept into the death chamber, her fingers fretted with gold wire, her rich red dress engraved with precious stones. She, with her blandishing tongue and beautiful face, who cared for no one because no one cared for her, sat beside her dying lord and lover, hungrily watching him. The king woke from a dream and saw her hard black eyes and voluptuous lips.

4

'My Lady Sun,' he whispered.

Perrers smiled, her white teeth gleaming as she remembered how she had ridden in cloth of gold up Cheapside, her head held high, her ears closed to the shouts of "Whore!", "Bawd!" and "Harlot!" Now she sat near the king, like a lioness watching her prey. An old Franciscan priest, John Hoccleve, came in but Perrers hissed and drove him out. The king closed his eyes. His breathing was shallow; a dreadful rattle had begun in his throat. Perrers waited no longer but stripped him of whatever finery he had left and fled.

The old Franciscan came back, grasping the king's hand, holding a crucifix up before the fading eyes. He intoned the *Dies Irae* and when he reached the verse 'And what shall I, frail man, be pleading; When the just are mercy needing?' the king opened his eyes.

'Do you wish absolution?' Hoccleve whispered.

'Ah, Jesu!' the king muttered back, and weakly pressed the Franciscan's hand.

'I therefore absolve you…' the priest said, '…from your sins in the name of…' he continued, his voice growing louder as the death rattle sounded in the king's throat like the beat of a tambour. The king turned, his eyes open. One last gasp and his soul went out into the darkness. Hoccleve finished his prayer and looked down at the grey, emaciated face, remembering the golden days when the king had walked in all his glory. He bowed his head, pressing his brow into the dead king's hand, and wept for the sheer waste of it all.

5

A few hours later in Westminster Palace, John of Gaunt, Duke of Lancaster and eldest living son of the dead king, sat alone before a great, hooded fireplace. He squatted, jerkin open, legs apart, letting the flames of the heated logs warm the chill in his thighs and crotch. The duke had heard the news as he returned from hunting, drenched to the skin after a sudden storm. His father was dead and he was regent but not king. John groaned to himself, clenching a bejewelled fist. He should be king, a man born to the crown with claims to the thrones of Castile, France, Scotland and England. And the only obstacle in his path? A golden-haired ten-year-old boy, his nephew, Richard of Bordeaux, son of Gaunt's elder brother, the feared and fearsome Black Prince.

'A heartbeat away!' Gaunt murmured. Only a short breath between him and the diadem of the Confessor. Gaunt stretched his great frame, his muscled body cracking and straining at the fury within. Regent but not king! Yet the land needed a firm ruler. The French were plundering the southern coats. The Scots were massing on the northern borders. The peasants were surly, demanding an end to incessant taxation. And the Commons, led by their speaker, were abusive and strident when they met in the chapel of St Stephen's at Westminster. Gaunt stroked his neatly barbered moustache and beard. Could he take the step? Would he? He chewed his lip and considered the possibilities. His younger brothers would resist. The great lords of the council, backed by the soft but powerful bishops, would take up arms and call down heaven's anger on him. And Richard – pale-faced, blue-eyed Richard – what would happen to him? Gaunt shivered. He remembered the old prophecy – that when the old cat died, the mice must not rejoice for the new kitten would grow into an even more dreadful monster!

Gaunt, who feared nothing, admitted his silent, grave-faced nephew held special terrors for him, as if the age-old eyes in that ten-year-old face read and understood his most secret thoughts. The Commons, too, would watch him and Gaunt had been careless. He had tried to raise money and the proof was there for the asking. The Sons of Dives had him in their clutches. The secrets they held must never be revealed.

Gaunt shifted in his chair. What was he frightened of? The demons in his own private hell stirred and rose from the black pit of memory. Murder! He stared around. The long chamber was deserted, as only shadows danced silently against the arras-covered walls. Assassin! The accusation seemed to leap from the flames and Gaunt broke into a cold sweat. The demon rose, twisting in his heart, and the duke gulped greedily from his wine cup, hoping its purple juice would drown the demons in its heavy vapour.

Gaunt was right to be wary. After all, Murder was no stranger to London. It stalked the streets, its eyes blind as night as it sought out its hapless victims. Murder tripped along the shit-caked alleys and streets of Southwark, and slid like a cold mist through the half-open doorways of hot, stuffy taverns to squat cold-eyed as men hacked each other to death. Murder lurked in the doorway of the filthy apothecary's house where poisons could be bought: ratsbane, crushed diamonds, belladonna and arsenic. Sometimes Murder would come across the city walls, sneaking along the dark country lanes behind the Tower, but on that night it had chosen a juicier prey and set up camp in Sir Thomas Springall's fine mansion in the Strand: a veritable palace with its tiled roof, black-embossed timbers, gleaming white plaster and freshly painted shield bearing the goldsmith's escutcheon of silver bars, gold trefoils and clasps of gold and silk.

The house itself was silent. In the lofty banqueting hall, the fire had died to popping cinders and smouldering ash. The candles were long snuffed though the air still bore the fragrance of sweet-smelling wax. The tapestries, heavy and gold-encrusted, hung on the walls, shifting slightly in the cold night breeze which pierced the gaps in the mullioned-glass windows. The massive table bore the remains of a banquet and its white lawn cloth, grease marked and purple-stained, still shimmered in the fading light of the fire. The silver dishes had been removed but the platters remained, covered with the remnants of fricassée and jiggets of mutton, as well as the bones of goose, peacock and chicken. Next to these were the deep-bowled cups smattered with the dregs of malmsey, Bordeaux and sack. A stout, long-tailed rat prowled amongst the dishes, its red eyes gleaming, its belly full and heavy, so sluggish it hardly squeaked when the ginger house cat pounced and crunched the swollen body in its jaws. Down the hall a dog heard the sound and stirred, lifting its shaggy, sleep-laden head.

Below stairs the servants slept on, their stomachs gorged, their brains dull with the scraps of food and wine they had gulped. In one chamber lay a maid, the hem of her skirts pushed into her mouth, twisting in mute passion under the hot probing loins of a young groom. She need not have worried about uttering any cries. The wide stairs above were deserted, as was the wood-panelled gallery which swept past the master bedrooms. In one a man and woman lay entwined, their skin gleaming with sweat as they writhed and turned under the blue and scarlet canopy of the four poster bed. A silver candelabra, set on a red- and white-tiled tabletop, gave the room a golden glow which was reflected in the precious silver thread of the wall hangings as well as the costly silk and lace clothes scattered over the floor. Further along the gallery, in the great bedroom of the master of the house, Sir

Thomas Springall, Murder brooded from its ghostly corner. Sir Thomas did not expect it. Oh, no! He ignored the preacher's words: 'In the midst of life we are in death.' Like the rich man in scripture, Springall was planning on destroying his old barns and building new ones, as befitted a merchant who had fingers in every silver pie. Sir Thomas lay between his silken gold-fringed sheets and basked in his wealth. He was pleased the old king was dead. A young boy now wore the crown.

'Woe to the realm where the king is a child!' Sir Thomas whispered, and laughed softly. 'Thank God!' he muttered. The regent needed him and Springall would prosper even more for he knew Gaunt's secrets. Sir Thomas licked his thick red lips. He stared into the darkness, across to the table where the Syrians, his precious chess set, glowed in the moonlight streaming through the casement window. More wealth would come. Springall would have entry to the treasure chambers of the kingdom. And the keys to such riches? The Book of the Apocalypse 6, Verse 8. And the other? Genesis 3, Verse 1. Springall smiled, rolled on one side and stared down at the cleverly carved bed posts. He thought of his wife, she of the chestnut curls, golden skin and eyes blue as a fresh spring sky. But Springall desired other flesh. He gripped the bed clothes and, at that moment, knew something was wrong. He clutched his throat, but too late. Murder was upon him.

Chapter 1

Brother Athelstan sat on a plinth of stone before the rood screen of St Erconwald's church in Southwark. He stared despairingly up at the hole in the red-tiled roof then at the dirty puddle of rainwater which shimmered on the flagstones two yards away from his sandalled feet. He stroked his clean-shaven face and glared down at the small scroll of parchment in his hand.

'You know, Bonaventure,' he murmured, 'and I say this in the spirit of obedience, so don't repeat my words if he ever comes, but Father Prior's remarks about my past cut like barbs.'

He folded the parchment neatly into a perfect square and slipped it into the battered leather wallet on his belt.

'I daily atone for my sins,' he continued. 'I observe most strictly the rule of St Dominic and, as you know, I spend both day and night in the care of souls.'

God knows, Athelstan thought, tapping the flag-stones with his feet, the harvest of souls was great; the filthy alleyways, the piss-soaked runnels and poor hovels of his parish sheltered broken people whose minds and souls had been bruised and poisoned by grinding poverty. The great, fat ones of the land did not care a fig but hid behind empty words, false promises and a lack of compassion which even Herod would have blushed at. Athelstan stared around the empty church, noting the dirty walls, peeling pillars, and the fresco of St John the Baptist. Athelstan grinned. He knew the Baptist had been beheaded but not whilst he was preaching! Someone had scrubbed the painting, removing St John's head as well as those of his attentive listeners.

'You have seen my house, Bonaventure? It's no more than a white-washed shed with two rooms, a wooden door and a window which does not fit. My horse, Philomel, may be an aged destrier, but it eats as if there is no tomorrow and can go no faster than a shuffling cat.' He smiled. 'I mean no offence to present company, but he drains my purse. Now, I am not moaning, I am just mentioning these matters to remind ourselves of our present state, so I can advise my prior that his paternal strictures are not necessary.' Athelstan sighed and went over into the small carrel built into the wall near the Lady Chapel where he had been penning his reply to the Father Prior. He picked up his quill, thought for a while and began writing.

> *As I have said, Reverend Father, my purse is empty, shrivelled up and tight as a usurer's soul. My collection boxes have been stolen and the chancery screen is in disrepair. The altar*

is marked and stained, and the nave of the church is often covered with huge pools of water, for our roof serves as more of a colander than a covering. God knows I atone for my sins. I seem to be steeped in murder, bloody and awful. It taxes my mind and reminds me of my own great crime. I have served the people here six months now and I have also assumed those duties assigned by you, to be clerk and scrivener to Sir John Cranston, coroner in the city of London.

Time and again he takes me with him to sit over the body of some man, woman or child pitifully slain. 'Is it murder, suicide or an accident?' he asks and so the dreadful stories begin. Often death results from stupidity: a woman forgets how dangerous it is for a child to play out in the cobbled streets, dancing between the hooves of iron-shod horses or the creaking wheels of huge carts as they bring their produce up from the river; still a child is slain, the little body crushed, bruised and marked, while the young soul goes out to meet its Christ. But, Reverend Father, there are more dreadful deaths. Men drunk in taverns, their bellies awash with cheap ale, their souls dead and black as the deepest night as they lurch at each other with sword, dagger or club. I always keep a faithful record.

Yet, every word I hear, every sentence I write, every time I visit the scene of the murder, I go back to that bloody field fighting for Edward the Black Prince. I, a novice monk, who broke his vows to God and took his younger brother off to war. Every night I dream of that battle, the press of steel-clad men, the lowered pikes, the screams and shouts. Each time the nightmare goes like a mist clearing above the river, leaving only me kneeling beside the corpse of my dead brother, screaming into the darkness for his soul to return. I know, Reverend Father, it never will.

Athelstan scrutinised the words he had written, replaced the quill beside his letter and walked back to the chancel screen. He looked across as Bonaventure rose and stretched elegantly.

'I intend no offence, Bonaventure,' he said. 'I mean, Sir John, despite his portly frame, that plum-red face, balding pate and watery eye, is, you will agree, at heart a good man. An honest official, a rare fellow indeed who does not take bribes but searches for the truth, ever patient in declaring the real cause of death. But why must I always be with him?'

Athelstan went back to sit before the rood screen. What use was it to list the terrible murders and scenes of violence he had witnessed? What would Father Prior know of them? Souls sent out into the dark before their time, unprepared and unshriven.

Men with their eyes gouged out, their throats cut, their genitals ripped off. Women crushed beneath scaffolding or horribly murdered in some stinking alleyway. If Christ came to London, Athelstan thought, he would surely cross to Southwark, where poverty and crime sat like two ugly brothers or wandered the streets hand-in-hand spreading their stench. Bonaventure rose and padded gently over to him. Athelstan stared down at the cat.

'Perhaps I should tell Father Prior about you, Bonaventure,' he said, admiring the sleek black body of the alley cat he had adopted, noting the white mask and paws, the tattered ear, the half-closed eye.

'You're a mercenary,' he continued, stroking the cat gently on the top of its head. 'But my most faithful parishioner. For a dish of milk and a few scraps of fish you will sit patiently whilst I talk to you, and be most attentive during Mass.'

Athelstan jumped as he heard a sound behind him. He looked round the chancel screen and realised how dark it was in the church, the only light being that from a taper lit before the statue of the Madonna. He yawned. He had not slept the previous evening. He did not like to close his eyes on dreams where he saw his brother's marble-white and glassy face, the eyes always staring at him. So, instead, he had climbed to the top of the church tower to observe the stars, for the movements of the heavens had fascinated him ever since he had begun studying them in Prior Bacon's observatory on Folly Bridge at Oxford. He had been tired and slightly fearful as well, for Godric, a well-known murderer and assassin, had begged for sanctuary in the church. Since his arrival, Godric had lain curled up like a dog in the corner of the sanctuary, sleeping off his exhaustion. He had eaten Athelstan's supper, pronounced himself well and settled down to a good night's sleep. 'How is it,' Athelstan murmured, 'that such men can sleep so well?' Godric had slain a man, struck him down in the marketplace, taken his purse and fled. He had hoped to escape but had had the misfortune to encounter a group of city officials and their retainers who had raised the 'Hue and Cry' and pursued him to St Erconwald's. Athelstan had been trying to repair the chancel screen and let him in after he hammered on the door. Godric had brushed past him, gasping, waving the dagger still bloody from his crime, and ran up the nave, shouting: 'Sanctuary! Sanctuary!' The pursuing officials had not come into the church, though they expected Athelstan, as clerk to Sir John Cranston, to hand Godric over. Athelstan had refused.

'This is God's house!' he'd shouted. 'Protected by Holy Mother Church and the King's decree!'

So they had left him and Godric alone, although they had placed a guard on the door and swore they would kill the murderer if he attempted to escape. Athelstan peered through the darkness. Godric still lay sleeping.

Athelstan prepared the altar for Mass, laying out the rather tattered missal and two candlesticks so bent they could hardly stand straight. A chipped, silver-gilt chalice, paten and small glass cruets, containing water and wine, were placed on the spotless altar cloth. Athelstan went into the dank sacristy, put on the alb and scarlet cope, crossed himself and went out to begin the magic of the Mass, priest before God, offering Christ to the Father under the appearances of bread and wine. Athelstan blessed himself as he intoned the introductory psalm.

'I will go into the altar of God, unto God who gives joy to my youth.'

Godric snored on, oblivious to the drama being enacted a few yards away. Bonaventure sidled up to the foot of the altar steps. The cat licked its lips, swishing its long tail in anticipation of a deep bowl of creamy milk as his reward for attention and patience. Athelstan, now caught up by the music of the words of the Mass, swept through the readings of the Epistle and the Gospel, reaching the Offertory where he mingled the water and wine. At the far end of the church a door opened and a hooded figure slipped in, moving soundlessly up the darkened nave to kneel beside Bonaventure at the foot of the steps. Athelstan forced himself to keep his eyes down on the white circle of bread over which he had breathed the words of consecration, transforming it into the body of Christ. The consecration over, he intoned the Lord's Prayer: '*Pater Noster, qui es in caelis.*'

His voice rang loud and clear through the hollow nave. He paused, as the canon of the Mass dictated, to pray for the dead. He remembered Fulke the warrener, a member of his parish killed in a tavern brawl four nights earlier. Then Athelstan's own parents and his brother Francis... the friar closed his eyes against the hot tears welling there as the faces of his family appeared, clear and distinct in his mind's eye.

'God grant them eternal rest,' he whispered.

He stood swaying against the altar, wondering for the hundredth time why he felt like an assassin. Oh, in France he had killed men whilst fighting for the Black Prince, the old king's eldest son, who wanted to unite the crowns of France and Castile with that of England. Athelstan had shot arrows as good and true as the rest. He remembered the corpse of a young French knight, his cornflower blue eyes gazing sightlessly up at the sky, his blond hair framing his face like a halo, Athelstan's barbed arrow embedded deeply in his throat between helmet and gorget. The friar prayed for this unknown knight, yet he felt no guilt. This was war and the Church taught that war was part of man's sinful condition, the legacy of Adam's revolt.

'Oh, God, am I a murderer?' he whispered to himself.

Athelstan thought once again how, as a novice in Blackfriars, near the western wall of the city, he had broken his vows and fled back to his father's farm in

Sussex. His mind had been filled with dreams of war and he had encouraged his younger brother in similar fantasies. They had joined one of those merry bands of archers who swung along the sunny, dusty lanes of Sussex down to Dover and across a shimmering sea, to reap glory in the green fields of France. His brother had been killed and Athelstan had brought the grim news back to the red-tiled Sussex farm. His parents had died of sheer grief. Athelstan had returned to Blackfriars to lie on the cold flagstone floor of the Chapter House. He had confessed his sin, begged for absolution, and dedicated his life to God as reparation for the grievous sins he had committed.

'A guilt greater than Cain's,' Father Prior had declared to the brothers assembled in the Chapter House. 'Cain killed his brother. Athelstan is responsible for breaking his vows, and, in doing so, bringing about the deaths of his entire family!'

'Father!'

Athelstan opened his eyes quickly. The woman kneeling on the steps was staring up at him, her beautiful face drawn with concern.

'Father, is there anything wrong?'

'No, Benedicta, I am sorry.'

The Mass continued, the *Agnus Dei* followed by Communion. Athelstan took a host down to the waiting woman who tilted back her head, eyes closed, full red lips open and tongue out, waiting for Athelstan to place Christ's body there. For a second he paused, admiring the flawless beauty: the soft golden-hued skin now stretched across the high cheekbones; the long eyelashes like dark butterfly wings, quiveringly closed; the parted lips showing white, perfectly formed teeth.

'Even if you lust in your mind's eye...' Athelstan reminded himself. He placed the host gently in the woman's mouth and returned to the altar. The chalice was drained, the final benediction given and Mass was ended.

Godric, in his little alcove, belched, snorted and stirred in his sleep. Bonaventure stretched, miaowing softly. But the widow Benedicta still knelt, head bowed.

Athelstan cleared the altar. On his return from the sacristy, his heart skipped when he saw Benedicta still kneeling there. The friar went and sat next to her on the altar steps.

'You are well, Benedicta?'

The dark eyes were full of silent mocking laughter.

'I am well, Father.'

She turned, stroking Bonaventure gently on the side of the neck so the cat purred with pleasure. She glanced mischievously at Athelstan.

'A widow and a cat, Father. The parish of St Erconwald will never become rich!' Her face grew solemn. 'In Mass you were distracted. What was wrong?'

Athelstan looked away. 'Nothing,' he muttered. 'I am just tired.'

'Your astrology?' He grinned. They had had this conversation before. He edged closer.

'Astrology, Benedicta,' he began with mock pomposity, 'is the belief that the stars and the planets affect men's moods and actions. The great Aristotle accepted the theory of the ancient Chaldeans that man is a microcosm of all there is in the universe. Accordingly, there is a bond between each of us and the stars above.'

Benedicta's eyes rounded in sham admiration of his scholarship.

'Now astronomy,' Athelstan continued, 'is the study of the planets and stars themselves.' He stretched out his hands. 'There are two schools of thought.' He thrust forward his left hand. 'The Egyptians and some of the Ancients believe the earth is a flat disc with heaven above and hell below.' Athelstan now stretched out his right arm, his hand rigid like a claw. 'However, Ptolemy, Aristotle and the Classics believe the earth is a sphere within a spherical universe. Each star, each planet, is a world in itself.'

Benedicta leaned back on her heels.

'My father,' she answered tartly, 'said the stars were God's lights in the firmament, put there by the angels at the beginning of time.'

Athelstan knew she was teasing him.

'Your father was correct.' He shrugged sheepishly. 'At Exeter Hall in Oxford I studied the greatest minds. In the end their explanations pale beside the creative wonder of God.'

Benedicta nodded, her eyes serious now, her teasing over.

'So why do you spend so many hours there, Father? On top of the church tower at night? We see your lantern.'

Athelstan shook his head.

'I don't know,' he murmured. 'But on a clear summer's night, if you stare at the velvet blackness and watch the movements of the planets, the shimmering light of the evening star, you become lost in their vastness.' He looked sharply at her. 'It's the nearest man comes to eternity without going through the door of death. When I am there, I am no longer Athelstan, priest and friar. I am just a man, stripped free of cares.'

Benedicta stared down, gently touching the crumbling altar step with the tips of her fingers.

'Tonight,' she murmured, 'I will do that, Father. Stare up at the sky, and see what it is like to die without dying.'

She rose quickly, genuflected before the winking sanctuary lamp and walked quietly out of the church.

Athelstan saw the door close behind her and turned to where Bonaventure awaited his reward. The friar went into the sacristy and brought out the expected bowl of milk. He sat and watched the cat greedily lick the lacy white froth with its pink, narrow-edged tongue.

'Do you know, Bonaventure,' he muttered, 'every time she goes, I want to call her back. She comes here to pray for her husband's soul, another casualty of the king's war, but sometimes I deceive myself and believe she comes to talk to me.'

The cat raised its battered head, yawned and went back to the milk.

'The Master was right,' Athelstan continued. The friar suddenly remembered his old novice master, Father Bernard, who had been responsible for Athelstan's spiritual education in the novitiate at Blackfriars.

'A priest's life, Athelstan,' Father Bernard once began, 'has three great terrors. The first are the lusts of the flesh! These will plague your dreams with visions of soft bodies, satin-silk limbs, full sensuous lips and hair which gleams like burnished gold. Yet these will pass. Prayer, fasting and the onset of old age will drive this enemy from the field of battle.' The old novice master had leaned forward and grasped Athelstan by the wrist. 'Then comes the second terror, the sheer soul-destroying loneliness of a priest: no wife, no children, never the clasp of small warm bodies and clinging arms round your neck. But,' Father Bernard muttered, 'that, too, will pass. The third terror is more dreadful.' And Athelstan remembered the old priest's eyes brimming with tears. 'There's a belief,' the novice master whispered, 'that each person is born destined to love another. Now sometimes we priests are lucky – in our early pilgrimage we never meet this person. But, if you do, then you truly will experience the horrors of the dark night of the soul.' The novice master had paused. 'Can you imagine, Athelstan, to meet, to love, but be bound by God's law never to express it? If you do, you break your vows as a priest and are condemned by the Church to be buried in hell. If you remain faithful to your priestly vows, you bury yourself in a hell of your own making for you will never forget her. You search for her face in crowds, you see her eyes in those of every woman you meet. She plagues your dreams. Not a day passes without her appearing in your thoughts.'

Athelstan thought of Benedicta and knew what the novice master had meant.

'Oh, sweet Christ!' he murmured.

He rose and dusted down his robe. Bonaventure, his milk finished, padded across and stared up.

'Catholic or Catolic, Bonaventure?' Athelstan laughed at his feeble jest. 'Is Father Prior playing a joke on me?' he murmured. 'I am past my twenty-eighth summer and I go from pillar to post.' Perhaps his superiors were testing him, sending him from the rigours of the novitiate to the academic glories of Exeter Hall, then pulling him back to menial duties at Blackfriars and finally to work as the Lord Coroner's clerk and parish priest of St Erconwald.

The friar knelt, crossed himself, and began softly to recite a psalm when he heard a disturbance at the back of the church. He rose in alarm, thinking that perhaps the city authorities had sent retainers to take Godric.

Even in the slums of Southwark, Athelstan realised he lived in turbulent times. Edward III was dead; his heir, Richard II, a mere boy. The powerful, noble hawks still had their way in most matters. Athelstan took a taper, lit it from the candle burning before the Madonna and hurried down the church, splashing through the puddles left by the violent rainstorm a few days before. He opened the door, thrust his head out and smiled. The city guards, roused from their sleep, were now locked in fierce argument with Sir John Cranston, who boomed as soon as he saw his clerk: 'For God's sake, Brother, tell these oafs who I am!' Cranston patted the neck of his huge horse and glared around. 'We have work to do, Brother, another death, murder in Cheapside! One of the great ones of the land. Come on, ignore these dolts!'

'They do not know you, Sir John,' Athelstan replied. 'You go round muffled in cloak and hood, worse than any monk.'

The coroner blew his great cheeks out, pulled back his hood and roared at his tormentors, 'I am Sir John Cranston, coroner in the city, and you, sirs, are disturbing the king's peace! Now back off!'

The men retreated like beaten mastiffs, their dark faces glowering with a mixture of anger and fear.

'Come on, Athelstan,' Cranston bellowed. He looked down at the friar's feet. 'And put that bloody cat away! I hate it.'

Bonaventure, however, seemed to regard Cranston as its long-lost friend. The cat skipped friskily down

25

the steps to sit beneath the coroner's horse, staring up at the big man affectionately as if he was the bearer of a pail of thick creamy milk or a platter of the tastiest fish. Cranston just turned his head away and spat.

'Leave Godric be,' Athelstan warned the city guards. 'You are not to enter my church.'

They nodded. Athelstan locked the door and went over to his own house next to the church. He stuffed his battered leather panniers with parchment, quills and ink, saddled Philomel and joined Sir John. The coroner was in good spirits, thoroughly enjoying his altercation with the city guard as he hated officialdom. He damned the city guards loudly, along with goldsmiths, priests and, looking slyly at Athelstan, Dominican monks who studied the stars. Athelstan ignored him, urging Philomel on.

'Come, Sir John. You said we had business.'

But Cranston was thoroughly roused by now. He shouted abuse once more at the guards, kicked his horse forward and drew noisily alongside Athelstan.

'I suppose you had no sleep last night, Brother? What with your damned stars, your bloody cat, your prayers and your Masses!'

'Ever heavenwards,' Athelstan quipped in reply. 'You, too, should look up at the sky and study the stars.'

'Why?' Cranston asked brusquely. 'Surely you do not believe in that nonsense about planets and heavenly bodies governing our lives? Even the church fathers condemn it.'

'In which case,' Athelstan answered, 'they condemn the star of Bethlehem!'

Sir John belched, grabbed the ever-present wineskin slung over his saddle horn, took a deep gulp and, raising one buttock, farted as loudly as he could. Athelstan decided to ignore Sir John's sentiments, verbal or otherwise. He knew the coroner to be at heart kindly and well intentioned.

'What business takes us to Cheapside?' he asked.

'Sir Thomas Springall,' Cranston replied. 'Or rather, the late Sir Thomas Springall, once a powerful merchant and goldsmith. Now he is as dead as that rat over there.' Cranston pointed to a pile of rubbish, a mixture of animal and human excrement, broken pots, and, lying on top, a mangy rat, its white and russet body swollen with corruption.

'So a goldsmith has died?'

'Has been murdered! Apparently, citizen Springall was not beloved of his servant, Edmund Brampton. Last night Brampton left a poisoned cup in his master's chamber. Sir Thomas was found dead and Brampton discovered later hanging from a beam in one of the garrets.'

'So we are to go there now?'

'Not immediately,' Cranston retorted. 'First, Chief Justice Fortescue wishes to see us at his home Alphen House, in Castle Yard off Holborn.'

Athelstan closed his eyes. Chief Justice Fortescue ranked foremost amongst the people he did not want to see. A powerful courtier, a corrupt judge, a man who took bribes and ran errands for those more powerful than he, the Chief Justice's ruthlessness was a byword amongst the petty law breakers of Southwark.

'So,' Cranston interrupted jovially, 'we meet the Chief Justice and then go to examine death in Cheapside. Merchants who are murdered by their servants! Servants who hang themselves! Tut, tut! What is the world coming to?'

'God only knows,' replied Athelstan. 'When coroners drink and fart and make cutting remarks about men who are still men with all their failings, be they priest or merchant.'

Sir John laughed, pushed his horse closer and slapped Athelstan affectionately on the back.

'I like you, Brother,' he bellowed. 'But God knows why your Order sent you to Southwark, and your prior ordered you to be a coroner's clerk!'

Athelstan made no reply. They'd had this conversation before, with Sir John probing whilst he defended. Some day, Athelstan decided, he would tell Sir John the full truth, although he suspected the coroner knew it already.

'Is it reparation?' Cranston queried now.

'Curiosity,' Athelstan replied, 'can be a grave sin, Sir John.'

Again the coroner laughed and deftly turned the conversation to other matters.

They continued along the narrow stinking streets, following the river towards London Bridge, pushing across marketplaces where the houses reared up to block out the rising sun. Near the bridge they met others, great swaggering lords who rode about on their fierce, iron-shod destriers in a blaze of silk and furs, their heads held high – proud, arrogant, and as ruthless as the hawks they carried. Athelstan studied them. Their women were no better, with their plucked eyebrows and white pasty faces, their soft sensuous bodies clothed in lawn and samite, their heads covered with a profusion of lacy veils. He knew that only a coin's throw away a woman, pale and skeletal, sat crooning over her dying baby, begging for a crust to eat. Athelstan felt his own soul dim, darken with depression. God should send fire, he thought, or a leader to raise up the poor. He bit his lip. If he preached what he thought, he would be guilty of sedition and the prior had kept him under a solemn vow to remain silent, to serve but not to complain.

Cranston and Athelstan had to stop and wait a while. The entrance to the bridge was thronged with people preparing to cross to the northern parts of the city to the great marketplace and shops in Cheapside. Athelstan pulled his hood over his head and pinched his nostrils against the odour from an open sewer full of the turds of nearby households, dregs from the dye houses and wash houses, and rotting carrion which had been dumped there. The area was thick with the foul, tarry smell from the tattered cottages where tanners and leather workers plied their trade.

Cranston nudged him and pointed across to where an inquest was being held over a dead pig, and two constables in striped gowns were scurrying about trying to discover whether there were any bawds, strumpets or scalds in the area in order to arrest them.

'Are there hot houses, sweat houses, where any lewd woman resorts?' one of the constables bellowed, his fleshy face red and sweaty.

'Yes,' Athelstan muttered, 'they are all here. Most of them are my parishioners.'

He watched a milk seller, buckets strapped across her shoulders, come up hoping to ply custom, but turned away as Crim, son of Watkin the dung-collector, crept up and without being noticed spat in one of the buckets. The urchin suddenly reminded Athelstan of duties he had overlooked in his haste to join Sir John Cranston.

'Crim!' Athelstan shouted. 'Come over here!'

The boy ran up, his thin, pallid face grimed with dirt. Athelstan felt in his purse and thrust a penny into the boy's outstretched hand.

'Go tell your father, Crim, I am across London Bridge with Sir John Cranston. He is to feed Bonaventure. Ensure the church door remains locked. If Cecily the courtesan sits there, tell her to move on. You have that message?'

Crim nodded and fled, fast as a bolt from a crossbow.

The crowd eased and Cranston kicked his horse forward. Athelstan followed. They went down on to

London Bridge, weaving their way through houses built so close, the road was hardly a cart span across. Athelstan kept his head down. He hated the place. Houses rose on either side, with some of them jutting out eight feet above the river with its turbulent tide-water rushing through the nineteen arches below. Sir John began to tell him about the history of the old church of St Thomas Overy which they had just passed. Athelstan listened with half an ear. He crossed himself as they passed the chapel of St Thomas à Becket, and only looked up when Sir John ordered them to stop so they could stable their horses at the Three Tuns tavern.

'The crowd is too great,' Sir John commented. 'It would be quicker on foot.'

He paid for ostlers to take the horses away and, with Athelstan striding beside him, they made their way up Fish Hill past St Magnus the Martyr church and into Cheapside. The good weather had brought the crowds out. Apprentices and merchants, their stalls now laid ready for trade, scurried backwards with bales of cloth, leather pelts, purses, panniers, and jerkins. They piled their stalls high, eager for day's business. The ground underfoot was a mixture of mud, human dung and animal decay, still damp from the storm. They slipped and slid, each holding on to the other, Cranston mouthing a mixture of curses and warnings, Athelstan wondering whether to protest or smile at Sir John's purple countenance and violent imprecations. The dung carts were out picking up the refuse left the day before. The burly, red-faced carters, swathed in a collection of garish rags, shouted and swore, their oaths hanging heavy in the thick, warm air. As Cranston and Athelstan passed, they heard one of the dung-collectors give a cry for them to stop working as a corpse was rolled out from behind the buttress of an old house. Athelstan stopped. He glimpsed straggly, white hair, a face sunken in death, the skeletal fingers of an elderly lady. Cranston looked at him and shrugged.

'She is dead, Brother,' he said. 'What can we do?'

Athelstan sketched a sign of the cross in the air and said a prayer that Christ, wherever he was, would receive the old woman's soul.

They went down past the Standard and the Conduit gaol with its open bars where courtesans and bawds caught plying their trade at night, stood for a day whilst being pelted with dirt and cursed by any passing citizen. Cranston asked him a question and Athelstan was about to reply when the stench from the poultry stalls suddenly made him gag: that terrible odour of stale flesh, rotting giblets and dried blood. Athelstan let Cranston chatter on as he held his breath, head down as he passed Scalding Alley where the gutted bodies of game birds were being cleaned and washed in great wooden vats of boiling hot water. At the Rose tavern on a corner of an alleyway they stopped to let a ward constable push by, leading a group of night felons, hands tied behind their backs, halters round their necks. These unfortunates were bound for the Poultry Compter, most of them still drunk, half asleep after their late night revels and roistering. The prisoners slipped and shoved each other. One young man was shouting how the constables had taken his boots and his feet were already gashed and scarred. Athelstan pitied them.

'The gaol's so hot,' the friar murmured, 'it will either waken or kill them before Evensong.'

Cranston shrugged and pushed his way through like a great, fat-bellied ship. They walked on past Old Jewry into Mercery where the streets became more thronged. The women there moved gingerly, skirts brushing the mud, their hands on the arms of gallants who walked the streets looking for such custom, in their high hats, taffeta cloaks, coloured hose and dirty-edged lace shirts.

The paths became softer underfoot as the sewer running down the middle had begun to spill over, choked to the top with the refuse dumped there by householders cleaning the night soil from their chambers. The road narrowed as they passed Soper Lane. The heavy, tiered houses closed in. Dogs barked and frenetically chased the cats hunting amongst the piles of refuse heaped outside each doorway. The crowd now thronged into an array of colour; the blues, golds, yellows and scarlets of the rich contrasting sharply with the brown frocks, russet smocks and black, greasy hats of the farmers who made their way from city market to city market, pulling their small carts behind them. The noise grew to a resounding din. Apprentices were busy yelling and screaming as they searched for custom. The taverns and cook shops were open, the smell of dark ale, fresh bread and spiced food enticing the customers inside. Cranston stopped and Athelstan groaned softly.

'Oh, Sir John,' he pleaded, 'surely not refreshments so early in the day? You know what will happen. Once inside, it will take the devil himself to get you out!'

Athelstan sighed with relief as the coroner shook his head regretfully and they moved on. A party of sheriff's men appeared, dressed in their bands of office, carrying long white canes which they used to clear a way through the crowds. They circled a man in a black leather jerkin and hose. His hands were bound, the ends of the cord being tied around the wrists of two of his captors. The prisoner's jerkin was torn aside to reveal a tattered shirt. His unshaven face was a mass of bruises from brow to chin. Someone whispered, 'Warlock! Wizard!' An apprentice picked up handfuls of mud and threw them, only to receive whacks across his shoulders from the white canes.

'Make way! Make way!'

Cranston and Athelstan walked on, past the stocks already full with miscreants: a pedlar; a manservant caught in lechery; a foister; and two other pickpockets. At last they turned off the Holborn thoroughfare into Castle Yard. A pleasant place, the houses being fewer, better spaced, each ringed by sweet-smelling rose gardens and tree-filled orchards. Fortescue's house was the grandest, standing in its own grounds, a massive framework of black timber, thick and broad as oaks, gilded and embossed with intricate devices. Between the black beams the white plaster gleamed like pure snow. Each of the four storeys jutted out slightly over the one on which it rested and each had windows of mullioned glass, reinforced with strips of lead. Cranston lifted the great brass knocker shaped in the form of a knight's gauntlet and brought it down hard. A servant answered and, when Cranston boomed out who they were, ushered them through the open door into a dark panelled hall with woollen carpets on the floor and gold-tinged drapes on the wall.

Athelstan noticed how cool the place was as they were led up an oak staircase and into a long gallery, so dark the wax candles in their silver holders had already been lit.

The servant tapped on one of the doors.

'Come in!' The voice was soft and cultured.

The chamber inside was rectangular in shape, walls painted red with silver stars and the polished tile floor covered with rugs; candles also glowed here because the light was poor and the mullioned window high above the desk was small. The candles bathed the area round the great oak desk in a pool of light. Chief Justice Fortescue, enthroned behind it, barely moved as they entered. One beringed hand continued silently to drum the top of the desk while the other shuffled documents about. Like the rest of his kind, Fortescue was a tall, severe man, completely bald, with features as sharp as a knife and eyes as hard as flint. He greeted Sir John Cranston with forced warmth but, when Athelstan introduced himself and described his office, the Chief Justice smiled chillingly, dismissing him with a flicker of his eyes.

'Most uncommon,' he murmured, 'for a friar to be out of his order even, and serving in such a lowly office!'

Cranston snorted rudely and would have intervened if Athelstan had not.

'Chief Justice Fortescue,' he answered, 'my business is my own. You summoned me here. I requested no audience.'

Cranston belched loudly in agreement.

'True! True!' Fortescue murmured. 'But this meeting was arranged by someone more powerful than I.' He smiled mirthlessly and picked up a knife he used for cutting parchment, balancing it delicately between his hands. 'We live in strange times, Brother. The old king is dead and for the first time in fifty years we have a new king, and he is a child. These are dangerous times. Enemies within and enemies without!' He lowered his voice. 'Some people say that a strong man is needed to manage the realm.'

'Like your patron, His Grace John of Gaunt, Duke of Lancaster?' Cranston interrupted.

'Like His Grace the Duke of Lancaster,' Fortescue mimicked in reply. 'He is the regent, proclaimed so by the late king's will.'

'Regent!' Cranston snapped. 'Not king!'

'Some people say he should be.'

'Then some people,' Cranston barked, 'are varlets and traitors!'

Fortescue smiled as if he had tried to go down a path and realised it was blocked.

'Of course, of course, Sir John,' he murmured. 'We know each other well. But Gaunt is regent, he needs friends and allies. Other lords seek his head; the Commons mutter about conspiracies, expenditure, the need to make peace with France and Spain. They object to taxes which are necessary.'

'The Commons may be right,' Cranston tartly replied.

'About others,' Fortescue continued, 'they may be, but the regent is steadfast in his loyalty to the young king and looks for support from his friends and allies. Men like Springall, Sir Thomas Springall, goldsmith, merchant, and alderman of the city.'

'Springall is dead,' Cranston retorted, 'and so the duke has lost a powerful friend.'

'Exactly!'

Athelstan saw the obsidian eyes of the Chief Justice glare at the coroner and intervened before further damage was done. Sir John was a lawyer from the Middle Temple and appointed as coroner by the late king, an appointment confirmed by the Commons and the powerful Guildhall merchants, yet even he could go too far.

'My Lord of Gaunt must grieve for Springall's death?' Athelstan asked.

'He does.'

Fortescue rose and went to a small table in the corner where stood a number of cups. He filled them to the brim and brought them back. Athelstan refused his, as it was too early in the morning for such drink, but Cranston did justice to both of them, draining one goblet then the other down his cavernous throat in a long, gulping sound. After he had finished, Cranston slammed the cups on the table in front of him, folded his great thick arms and looked steadily back at the Chief Justice.

'Sir Thomas Springall,' Fortescue continued, 'was a good friend of the duke's. A close associate. Last night he held a banquet in his house in the Strand. I was there, together with his wife, his brother Sir Richard, and other colleagues. I left after sunset when the bells of St Mary Le Bow were ringing the curfew. A pleasant evening – the conversation, like the food, most appetising and titillating. From what Sir Richard Springall has told me, Sir Thomas retired just before midnight. Although married, he slept in his own bed chamber. He bade his wife, brother and associates good night and went upstairs to his chamber where, as always, he locked and bolted the door. Now Sir Thomas was a fleshly man. Like you, Sir John, he liked a good glass of claret. Every night he ordered his servant, Brampton, to leave one such cup on the table beside his bed. This morning, Springall's chaplain, Father Crispin, went to rouse him and received no answer. Others were called and, to cut a long story short, the door was forced. Sir Thomas Springall was found lying dead in his bed, the cup beside him half empty. The local physician was summoned. He examined the corpse as well as the contents of the wine cup and pronounced Sir Thomas had been poisoned. A search was immediately made.' Fortescue paused and licked his thin lips. 'Brampton's chamber was deserted but, when his chest was rifled, they found phials of poison hidden beneath garments at the bottom. Then an hour ago Brampton was found hanging in a garret of the house.' Fortescue heaved a sigh. 'It would appear that Brampton and Sir Thomas had quarrelled during the day and this reached a climax early in the afternoon. Brampton kept to himself in a sulk. He must have purchased the poison or had it ready, took the cup to his master's room, put the poison in and left. However, like Judas, he suffered remorse. He went up to the garret of the house and, like Judas, hanged himself there.'

'Strange,' Cranston mused, and pursed his lips.

'What is, Sir John?'

'We have a steward who has quarrelled with his master and stormed out. Nevertheless, he remembers his duty and takes up a goblet of wine.'

'If the wine had not been poisoned,' Fortescue replied sharply, 'it would have been a kindness. But, Sir John, a man who offers a poisoned chalice is no friend.'

'So what is the mystery?'

Fortescue smiled thinly.

'Ah, that is for you to discover. My Lord Gaunt thinks there is one. Remember, Springall lent the crown monies. There may be reason to see the merchant's death as a hindrance to the regent.' Fortescue shrugged. 'His Grace has not opened his secret thoughts to me, but he believes there is a threat to his rule here.'

The Chief Justice picked up a scroll tied with scarlet ribbon and handed it over to Cranston. Athelstan glimpsed the purple seals of the regent.

'Your commission,' Fortescue said drily, 'warrants, and permission for you to pursue this matter.'

The Chief Justice rose as a sign that the meeting was over.

'Of course, all expenses are to be handed over to the clerk of the Exchequer.' He rubbed his hands together dryly. 'Though the Barons will question any overindulgence in food or drink.'

Cranston rose.

'My bills will be fair, as they always are, and I will be taking constant refreshment. After all, My Lord, when you listen to some men, their lies stick in your throat and give you a terrible thirst.'

He picked up his cloak; Athelstan, clutching his leather bag of writing materials, followed Cranston's lumbering gait towards the door. The friar did not dare look up and fought to keep his face straight.

'Sir John!'

The coroner stopped.

'The Sons of Dives?' Fortescue asked. 'Do you know of them?'

Cranston shook his head. 'No, why should I?'

'They are a secret group,' Fortescue testily replied. 'Their nature and purpose a mystery. But Sir Thomas's name, so my spies relate, was linked to them. Dives means nothing to you?'

'He was a judge in the gospels, was he not? Rich and corrupt who let the poor starve outside his gates.'

Fortescue smiled and looked at Brother Athelstan.

'Is it true, Friar,' he said abruptly, 'that you atone for your brother's death? Is that why your Order has put you in St Erconwald's church and made you clerk to Sir John Cranston here?' The Chief Justice's grin widened. 'You should sit at his feet, Brother. Sir John will instruct you in the law. He will tell you all he knows. I am sure it will not take long!'

Cranston turned. His steel grey mop of hair seemed to bristle with anger, and his dark eyes held the ghost of malicious mockery as he stroked his beard and moustache.

'I will do that, My Lord,' he said slowly. 'I will instruct Brother Athelstan in what I know about the law and I am sure it will not take long. Then, of course, I will instruct him in what you and I both know, and I am sure it will not take any longer!'

Cranston spun on his heel and, with Athelstan scurrying behind him, choking on his laughter, swept out of Alphen House into Castle Yard and back to Holborn.

'Bastard! Varlet! Lecher! Arse pimple!' Cranston indulged in a succinct summary of what he thought of the Chief Justice. Athelstan just shook his head, caught between admiration of Cranston's honesty and a desire to burst into laughter at the way he'd dealt with the Chief Justice. They paused on the corner of Holborn thoroughfare to let an execution cart rattle by, its iron wheels crashing on the cobbles. Inside a black-masked hangman and a parson, his sallow face covered in sweat, were standing over a pirate caught, so the notice pinned to the cart said, two days ago off the mouth of the Thames. Despite the placard around his neck, the fellow was laughing and joking with the small crowd which followed on either side, chanting a song popular on execution days: 'Put on your smocks on Monday.' The condemned man did not seem to give a fig for his impending death. He was more determined to cut up his scarlet cloak and taffeta jerkin and distribute the pieces amongst the spectators. Every so often he would look up and grin at the executioner.

'You will take no share of my clothes!' he bawled. 'I came naked into the world and I will go out naked. And all the more merrily for knowing you got nothing from me!'

The crowd roared with laughter at this sally and, as the cart trundled up to the great three-branched scaffold at the Elms, broke into fresh chants and songs.

'More like a wedding than an execution!' Cranston muttered. 'The hangman will slip the knot. This fellow will dance for a long time before he dies.'

They crossed the rutted track leading to the shady side of the street for the sun now shone much stronger, beating fiercely down on them. Cranston mopped his sweating face and pushed Athelstan into the welcoming shadows of the Bishop's Pig tavern. The tap room inside was dark and cool with a high, black-timbered ceiling letting the air circulate as it poured through the great open windows at the far end. Cranston and Athelstan sat there, the friar silently wondering to himself about Sir John's constant need for refreshment; the coroner seemed to eat and drink as if there was no tomorrow. As usual Sir John did full justice to himself, ordering two large tankards of frothy dark ale, an eel pie and a dish of vegetables. All disappeared down his yawning throat as the coroner continued to berate Fortescue. At last, the rancour drained from him, Sir John wiped his lips, leaned back against the wall and glanced across at the friar. Athelstan, looking up from his own thoughts about his church, realised Sir John's good humour had returned and now they would concentrate on the matter in hand.

'Was the Chief Justice right?'

'About what?' Athelstan asked.

'About you and your brother?'

Athelstan made a face.

'To a certain extent he spoke the truth, but I do not think the Chief Justice was concerned with that. More with the malicious desire to hurt.'

Cranston nodded and looked away. Now, he did not like priests. He did not like monks. He certainly did not like friars, but Athelstan was different. He looked at the friar's dark face, the black hair cut neatly in a tonsure. More like a soldier, he thought, than a monk. He sighed, wiping the sweat from his throat; every man had his secrets, and Cranston had his own.

'This matter,' he said. 'Springall's death. Do you think there is a mystery?'

Athelstan leaned forward, resting his elbows on his knees.

'There is something strange,' he muttered. 'A merchant is murdered by his servant who then commits suicide. A very neat death, orderly. All the ends tied up like a parcel, a package, a gift for Twelfth Night. Surely two mysteries? The first one is the

44

neatness of the deaths, the second my Lord of Gaunt's interest in them. Yes, Sir John, I think there is a mystery but only the good Lord knows whether we will solve it!'

'There is more, isn't there?' Cranston said, pleased to have confirmation of his own thoughts.

'Oh, yes,' Athelstan replied, sitting up and stretching. 'Gaunt seems frightened that Springall has died, as if the death poses a personal threat. It must be so, otherwise why would he get the Chief Justice of the Courts to interview us? To impress upon us the importance of the task? To test our loyalty and give us a special commission?' He got up. 'If you are refreshed, Sir John, perhaps it is time we found out.'

Cranston rose, picked up his cloak and threw it across his arm. He adjusted his great sword belt round his girth. From it hung a long thin Welsh dagger shoved into a battered leather sheath and the broadest sword Athelstan had ever seen. Once again, he tightened his lips to hide his smile. Cranston waddled through the tavern, shouting goodbye to the landlord and his wife who were busy amongst the barrels at the far end of the room. The coroner's good spirits were restored and Athelstan braced himself for an exciting day.

They walked back up Cheapside. It was now early afternoon and the traders were busy.

'A fine hat for the French block!' one called. 'Pins! Points! Garters! Spanish gloves! Silk ribbons!' shouted another.

'Come,' a woman cackled from a doorway, 'have your ruffs starched, fine cobweb lawn!'

The cries rose like a demonic chorus. Carts rumbled by, now empty after a morning's trade, their owners desirous of getting clear of the city gates before the curfew tolled. A group of aldermen attired in long, richly furred robes were rudely mocked by a troupe of gallants resplendent in gold, satin garments and cheap jewellery, the air thick with their even cheaper perfume. A party of horsemen trotted in from the fields, hawks on their wrists. The fierce birds, their blood hunger satisfied, sat quietly under their hoods. Cranston stopped by a barber's shop, fingering his beard and moustache, but one look at the steaming blood in the bowls beside the chair changed his mind. They continued back up Cheapside.

'You know the house, Sir John?'

Cranston nodded and pointed. 'It is there, the Springall mansion.'

Athelstan paused and took Cranston by the elbow. 'Sir John, wait awhile.' He pulled the bemused coroner into a darkened doorway.

'What is it, Monk?'

'I am a friar, Sir John. Please remember that. A member of the preaching order founded by St Dominic to work amongst the poor and educate the unenlightened.'

Cranston beamed. 'I stand corrected. So what is it, *Friar*?'

'Sir John, the warrants? We should inspect them.'

The coroner made a face, then pulled out the scrolls handed to him by Fortescue. He broke the seals and opened them.

'Nothing much,' he muttered, reading them quickly. 'They give us full authority to investigate matters surrounding the death of Sir Thomas Springall and oblige all loyal subjects, on their loyalty, to answer our questions.' He looked sharply at Athelstan. 'I wonder if that includes the Sons of Dives?'

The friar shrugged.

'You know the city better than I do, Sir John. Every trade has its guild, every coven its patron saint. I suspect the Sons of Dives is a title fabricated to cover the less salubrious dealings of certain of our rich merchants. They do not plot treason but profit.'

Cranston grinned and stepped out of the doorway.

'Then come, trusty Dominican, let us discover more!'

Chapter 2

The house was a fine building, very similar to that of Lord Fortescue, though today great black banners of costliest lawn hung from the upstairs windows and the broad shield of the goldsmith above the main door was hidden under black damask. An old manservant, dressed like death itself, answered the door; his face was soaked with tears, his eyes red-rimmed from crying.

'Sir John Cranston, coroner, and Brother Athelstan,' the friar quietly announced.

The fellow nodded and led them down a dark passageway into the great banqueting hall, also hung in black. As they crossed the black and white chessboard floor, Athelstan felt he was entering the valley of shadows. Black cloths hid the tapestries and paintings on the walls. The air seemed thick and heavy, not due to the heat and the closeness of the day but to something else which prickled the hair at the back of his neck and made him shiver. Cranston, however, lumbered along, his bleary eyes fixed on a group sitting round the table on the dais at the end of the hall. In the centre a great silver salt cellar winked like a beacon light in the glow of the glittering candles. The small oriel window above the table let in some brightness but Athelstan could not make out the figures clearly. They seemed concealed in the shadows, talking quietly. All conversation ceased as they stared at Cranston's huge form stumbling towards them.

'Can I help you?'

Cranston stopped abruptly, almost colliding with Athelstan as they turned to look at the speaker. A young woman who had been sitting in the window embrasure inside the hall got up and came forward.

'You are?' Athelstan asked.

'Sir Thomas Springall's wife,' the woman replied coolly, stepping into the light.

Sweet God, Athelstan thought, she was beautiful. Her face a vision of loveliness with dark-ringed eyes and the face of an angel like those painted on windows in the abbey church. Her slender body was exquisitely formed, her skin burnished gold. She had dark, blood-red hair and lips as crimson and as lush as a spring rose.

'Sir Thomas's widow?' Cranston asked tactfully.

'Yes.' The voice grew harsh. 'And you, sirs, what are you doing here?'

Cranston glanced up at the group still sitting silently round the table on the dais, and drunkenly doffed his hat.

'Sir John Cranston, king's coroner in the city. And this,' he waved behind him, 'is my faithful Mephistopheles, Brother Athelstan.'

The woman looked puzzled.

'My clerk,' Cranston slurred.

'Madam,' Athelstan interrupted, 'God rest your husband's soul, but he is dead. Sir John and I have orders to examine the body to determine the true cause of death. We are sorry to intrude on your grief.'

The woman stepped closer and Athelstan noticed how pale her face was, her eyes red-rimmed with crying. He noticed that the cuffs on the sleeves of her black lace dress were wet with tears.

The woman waved them up to the dais and the group sitting there rose. They were all dressed in black and seemed to hide behind a broad-chested man, sleek and fat, with a balding head, fleshy nose, and eyes and mouth as hard as a rock.

'Who are you, sirs?' he snapped. 'I am Sir Richard Springall, brother and executor to the late Sir Thomas!'

Cranston and Athelstan introduced themselves.

'And why are you here?'

'At the Chief Justice's request.'

Cranston handed over his commission. Sir Richard undid the red silk cord, unrolled the parchment and gave its contents a cursory glance. He waved expansively to the table.

'You may as well join us. We have business to discuss. Sir Thomas's death is a great blow.'

Athelstan thought Sir Richard looked more the eager merchant than the grieving brother, but they took their seats and Sir Richard introduced his companions. At the far end of the table was Father Crispin, chancery priest and chaplain to the Springall household. He was a young man, gaunt-faced, dark-eyed, clean shaven, his hair not cut in a tonsure but hanging in ringlets down to his shoulders. His dark gown was expensive, tied at the throat with a gold clasp and silver white bows. On the other side sat Edmund Buckingham, clerk to Sir Thomas, about the same age as Father Crispin, but darker, sallow-faced, hard-eyed and thin-lipped. A born clerk or secretarius, a counter of bales and cloths, more suited to tidying accounts and storing parchment away than engaging in idle conversation. He drummed the table loudly with his fingers, showing his annoyance at what he considered an unwarranted intrusion. The two remaining members of the group, Allingham and Vechey, were typical merchants in their dark samite jerkins, gold chains and silver wire rings on fleshy fingers. Stephen Allingham was tall and lanky, with a pockmarked, dour face and greasy red hair. His front teeth stuck out, making him look like a frightened rabbit; his fingers, the nails thick with dirt, kept fluttering to his mouth as if he was trying to remember something. Theobald Vechey was short and fat; his face puffy white like kneaded dough, his eyes small black buttons, his nose slightly crooked and his mouth pursed tight with sourness.

After the introductions, Sir Richard ordered cups of sack.

Oh, God! Athelstan prayed. Not more!

Sir John, already heavy-eyed, beamed expansively. A servant brought a tray of cups. Sir John downed his in one noisy gulp and looked greedily at Athelstan's; the friar sighed and nodded. Sir John grinned and supped that one, impervious to the astonished looks of those around him. Athelstan emptied his leather bag, smoothing the creases out of the parchment and arranging the quills and silver ink horn in his writing tray. Sir John, refreshed, clapped his hands and leaned forward, glancing towards Sir Richard at the head of the table. Cranston's elbow slipped and he lurched dangerously. Athelstan heard the young clerk titter and glimpsed the silent mockery in Lady Isabella's beautiful eyes.

'Yes, quite,' Cranston trumpeted. 'Sir Richard, your account? Your brother has been slain.'

'Last night,' Sir Richard began, 'a banquet was held. All of us were present, together with Sir John Fortescue, the Chief Justice. He left about eleven, before midnight.' Sir Richard licked his lips and Athelstan wondered why the Chief Justice had lied about the hour at which he had left the house.

'My brother,' Sir Richard continued, 'bade us good night here in the hall and went up to his chamber.'

'Lady Isabella,' Cranston interrupted, 'you have your own separate room?'

'Yes.' The lady glared back frostily. 'My husband preferred it that way.'

'Of course.' Cranston beamed. 'Sir Richard?'

'I went to say goodnight to my brother. He was dressed for bed, the drapes pulled back. I saw the wine cup on the table beside his bed. He wished me a fair night's sleep. As I walked away, I heard him lock and bolt the door behind me.'

Athelstan put down his quill. 'Why did he do that?'

Sir Richard shook his head. 'I don't know, he always did. He liked his privacy.'

'Then what?'

'Next morning,' Father Crispin began, leaning forward, 'I went to wake...'

'No!' Lady Isabella interrupted. 'I sent my maid, Alicia. She tapped on my husband's door a few minutes after he had retired and asked if there was anything he wanted.' She smoothed the table in front of her with long, white elegant fingers. 'My husband called out that all was well.'

Athelstan looked sideways at Cranston. The coroner's heavy-lidded eyes were closing. Athelstan kicked him fiercely under the table.

'Ah, yes, of course.' Cranston pulled himself up, burping gently like a child. 'Father Crispin, you were saying?'

'At Prime – yes, about then – the bells of St Mary Le Bow were ringing. It was a fair morning, and Sir Thomas had asked to be roused early. I went up to his

54

chamber and knocked. There was no reply. So I went for Sir Richard. He also tried to waken Sir Thomas.' The young priest's voice trailed off.

'Then what?'

'The door was forced,' Sir Richard replied. 'My brother was sprawled on the bed. We thought at first he had had some seizure and sent for the family physician, Peter de Troyes. He examined my brother and saw his mouth was stained, the lips black. So he sniffed the cup and pronounced it drugged, possibly with a mixture of belladonna and red arsenic. Enough to kill the entire household!'

'Who put the cup there?' Athelstan asked, nudging Cranston awake.

'My husband liked a goblet of the best Bordeaux in his chamber at night before retiring. Brampton always took it up to him.'

'Ah, yes, Brampton brought a cup of claret!' Cranston smacked his lips. 'He must have been a fine servant, a good fellow!'

'Sir John,' Lady Isabella shrieked in fury, 'he poisoned my husband!'

'What makes you say that?'

'He took the cup up.'

'How do you know?'

'He always did!'

'So why did Brampton hang himself?'

'Out of remorse, I suppose. God and his saints,' she cried, 'how do I know?'

'Sir John...' Father Crispin raised his hand in a placatory gesture at Sir Richard's intended outburst in her defence. The merchant looked choleric, so red-faced Athelstan thought he might have a seizure. 'Lady Isabella is distraught,' continued the priest. 'Brampton took the cup up, we are sure of that.'

'Was he present at the banquet last night?' Athelstan asked.

'No.' Sir Richard shook his head. 'He and my brother had a fierce quarrel earlier in the day.'

'About what?'

Sir Richard looked nervously down the table at Vechey and Allingham.

'Sir Thomas was furious: he accused Brampton of searching amongst his documents and memoranda. There are caskets in my brother's room. He found the lid of one forced and, beside it, a silver button from Brampton's jerkin. Brampton, of course, denied the charge and the quarrel continued most of the day.'

'So Brampton sulked in his room, did not attend the banquet and retired for the night – but not before he had taken a goblet of wine along to his master's chamber?'

'So it would seem.'

Cranston had now gently nodded off to sleep, his head tilting sideways, his soft snores indicative of a good day's drinking. Athelstan ignored the company's amused glances, pushed away the writing tray and tried to assert himself. 'I cannot understand this,' he said. 'Brampton argues with Sir Thomas, who has accused him of rifling amongst his private papers?'

'Yes,' Sir Richard nodded, watching him guardedly.

'Brampton storms out but later takes up a cup of wine. A kind gesture?'

'Not if it was poisoned!' Allingham squeaked. 'The cup was poisoned, laced with a deadly potion.' Athelstan felt caught, trapped in a mire. The listeners around the table were gently mocking him, dismissing Cranston as a drunk and himself as an ignorant friar.

'Who was present,' he asked, 'when Sir Thomas's body was found?'

'I was,' Sir Richard replied. 'And course Father Crispin. Master Buckingham also came up.'

'As did I,' Allingham grated.

'Yes, that's correct,' Sir Richard added.

'So you sent for the physician?'

'Yes, as I have said.'

'And then what?'

'I dressed the body,' Father Crispin offered. 'I washed him, did what I could, and gave Sir Thomas the last rites, anointing his hands, face and feet. You may recall, Brother, there are some theologians, Dominicans,' the priest smiled thinly, 'who maintain the soul does not leave the body until hours after death. I prayed God would have mercy on Sir Thomas's soul.'

'Did Sir Thomas need mercy?'

'He was a good man,' Father Crispin replied sharply. 'He founded chantries, gave money to the poor, distributed food, and looked after widows and orphans.'

'I am sure the good Lord will have mercy on him,' Athelstan murmured. 'Now for Brampton. You made a search for him?'

'Yes,' Sir Richard replied briskly. 'We suspected he was involved so we searched his chamber. We found a small stoppered phial in a chest beneath some robes. A servant took it round to Peter de Troyes, who pronounced it held the same mixture found in my brother's wine cup. We then searched for Brampton.'

'I found the corpse,' Vechey interrupted. 'I noticed that the door leading to the garret was half open, so I went up.' He swallowed. 'Brampton was hanging there.' The fellow shivered. 'It was dreadful. The garret was empty and cold. There was a horrible smell. Brampton's body was hanging there like a broken doll, a child's toy, his neck askew, his face blackened, tongue lolling out!'

He gulped at his wine.

'I cut him down and loosened the rope, but he was dead, the corpse clammy and cold.' He looked pleadingly at Sir Richard. 'The body's still there. It must be removed!'

'Tell me,' Athelstan said, 'do you all live here?'

'Yes,' Sir Richard replied. 'Master Allingham is a bachelor. Master Vechey is a widower,' he smiled, 'though still with an eye for the ladies. This mansion is great, four storeys high, built in a square round a courtyard. Sir Thomas saw no reason why his business partners should not share the same house. Tenements, property, their value has increased, and with royal taxes...' His voice trailed off.

Athelstan nodded understandingly, trying to mask his frustration. There was nothing here. Nothing at all. A merchant had been killed, his assassin had hanged himself. At the same time Athelstan detected something. These people were pompous, arrogant, sure of themselves. They walked the streets like cocks, confident of their wealth, their power, and their friends at court or in the Exchequer.

'Sir Thomas treated Brampton well?' Athelstan asked. 'Was he a good lord?'

'A more courteous gentleman you could not hope to meet,' Allingham answered. 'Sir Thomas gave generously in alms to the poor of the parish of St Bartholomew's, to the Guild, and,' he ended contemptuously, 'to friars like you!'

'So why should he quarrel so violently with Brampton? Had he done it before?'

Allingham stopped, wrong-footed.

'No,' he murmured. 'No, he had not. There were just disagreements.'

'Lady Isabella,' Athelstan asked, 'your husband – was he anxious or concerned about anything?'

Sir Richard patted Lady Isabella's wrist as a sign that he would answer for her.

'He was worried about the war, and the increase of piracy in the Narrow Seas. He lost two ships recently to Hanse pirates. He resented the old king's growing demands for loans.'

'And Brampton, was he a good steward?'

'Yes,' Lady Isabella answered quickly, 'he was.'

'What kind of man?'

She made a grimace. 'Quiet, gentle, a loyal servant.' Her eyes softened. 'I saw him just after the quarrel with my husband. I have never seen Brampton in such a state, fretting and anxious, so angry he could hardly sit still.'

'Your husband, did he mention the quarrel?'

'He said he would investigate the matter later. He was surprised more than angry that Brampton could do such a thing. He said it was out of character.' She paused. 'At the banquet my husband broached a cask of his best Bordeaux. I sent up a cup as a peace offering to Brampton.'

'You are sure Sir Thomas thought highly of Brampton?'

'Oh, I am certain.' Lady Isabella shook her head and stared down at the table.

'Shall we move on to other matters? The banquet last night.'

Cranston farted gently. The sound, however, rang through the hall like a loud bell and Lady Isabella looked away in disgust. Sir Richard glared at the coroner whilst Athelstan blushed with embarrassment at the sniggering and laughter from Buckingham.

'Why was the banquet held last night?'

'The young king's coronation,' Sir Richard replied. 'Each guild must prepare its pageant. We were discussing the plans the Guild of Goldsmiths had for their spectacle.'

'So why was Chief Justice Fortescue present?'

'We do not know,' Allingham squeaked. 'Sir Thomas said that the Chief Justice would be coming. He often did business with him.' He smirked. 'Fortescue owed him money, like many judges and lords in the city.'

'Why all these questions?' Sir Richard asked softly. 'Surely the matter is clear. Even a child,' glancing contemptuously at Sir John, 'can see that! My brother was murdered, his assassin was Brampton. Why must we go over these matters, muddying waters, causing pain and grief? We are busy men, Brother Athelstan. Your friend may sleep but we have business to attend to. My brother's corpse lies cold upstairs. There is a funeral to arrange, matters to put straight, business colleagues to contact.'

'Strange!' Cranston stirred and opened his eyes. 'I find it very strange!'

Athelstan looked down the table and grinned to himself. One of the things he could never understand but most enjoyed about Cranston was how the big, fat coroner could doze and yet be aware of conversations going on around him.

'What is strange?' Lady Isabella snapped, her distaste for the coroner now openly apparent.

'Well, My Lady,' Cranston licked his lips, 'your husband has a servant, Brampton. Brampton is faithful and obedient, like the good steward in the gospel. Why should he wish to search amongst your husband's papers? What did your husband have to hide?'

Lady Isabella just glared back.

'Let us say he did,' Cranston continued, breathing in heavily. 'Just let us say he did and there was a quarrel – surely no cause for murder or suicide? You have said, Madam, how Brampton was a quiet, placid fellow. Not a man of hot humours or rash disposition who would commit such a dreadful act and then compound it by taking his own life.'

'How else did it happen?' Sir Richard asked stiffly.

'Well,' Cranston said, 'is it possible that Brampton took the wine cup as a peace offering to his master?' He ignored the sneer on Vechey's face. 'Placed it on the table and then left?'

'And?' Lady Isabella asked.

'Someone else went up those stairs during the banquet and put poison into the cup. Or,' Cranston rubbed his fat hands together, now warming to his subject, 'how do we know that Sir Thomas did not have a visitor after he retired? Someone who went up the stairs and along the gallery, slipped into Sir Thomas's room, perhaps engaging him in conversation and, while doing so, secretly poured the poison into the cup.' He held up a hand to still the murmur. 'I am just theorising, as the theologians say, speculating on the nature of things.'

'Then, Sir, you are a fool!'

Cranston, Athelstan and the whole company turned round in astonishment and looked down the hall. In the doorway stood an old lady dressed completely in black like a nun. Her head was covered by a thick, lawn veil arranged in the old-fashioned wimple which framed her sour lemon face in its black lace. She walked forward, her silver-topped stick beating loudly on the hall floor.

'You are a fool!'

Cranston rose. 'Perhaps I am, Madam, but who are you?'

Sir Richard darted forward.

'Lady Ermengilde, may I present Sir John Cranston, coroner of the city.'

The old lady glared at the coroner with eyes like two dark pools.

'I have heard of you, Cranston, your drinking and your lechery! What are you doing in my son's house?'

'Sir John is here at the request of Chief Justice Fortescue.' Sir Richard's voice was soft, almost pleading.

'Another rogue!' the lady snapped.

'I asked, Madam, to whom do I have the pleasure of speaking?' Sir John repeated.

'My name is Lady Ermengilde Springall. I am the mother of Sir Richard,' she stroked Springall's arm. 'My other son now lies dead upstairs and I come down to hear you chatter on about nonsense. Brampton may have been a good steward. He was also a varlet, a commoner! He had ideas above his station. Thomas rebuked him, and like many of his kind, Brampton could not take it. His heart was filled with malice. Satan whispered in his ear, and he carried out his dreadful deed.' The old woman crashed her stick to the floor and held it between her two hands, resting on it. 'At least Brampton did us all the courtesy of hanging himself and so sparing the public expense and the work of the hangman at the Elms!'

Athelstan watched Cranston. The coroner was now in one of his most dangerous moods. He smiled but only round the lips. His eyes were hard and fixed, watching the old lady as a swordsman might an opponent waiting for the next parry.

'Lady Ermengilde, you seem well appraised of what happened. I crave your indulgence. Can you explain more?'

'My chamber is close to that of my son,' she snapped. 'The staircase beyond,' she indicated with a nod of her head, 'leads up to two galleries, one running to the right. At the end was Sir Thomas's chamber and, next to his, mine.'

'Any other?'

Lady Ermengilde's eyes slid towards her daughter-in-law.

'That of the Lady Isabella. There is a gallery to the left, identical to the one I've described except for one thing.' She raised one bony finger. 'My chamber, as well as those of Sir Thomas and Lady Isabella, stands on the Nightingale Gallery.'

'The Nightingale Gallery?' Athelstan asked. 'What is that?'

Dame Ermengilde smiled and walked nearer, her face looking more than ever like a sour apple. Athelstan noticed she was not dressed in black but in the dark brown habit of a nun, though her scorn for the luxuries of this world must have been shallow for the rings on her fingers held jewels the size of birds' eggs. A worldly lady, Athelstan thought, for all her prim face, sour lips and arrogant eyes.

'It's well known,' she continued, her voice tinged with patronising arrogance. 'This house was built on a square, and on the opposite corner of the square are stairs to the second storey.' She waved her hand to the far doorway which stood slightly ajar. Through it, Athelstan could glimpse steep stairs. 'They will take you up to Sir Thomas's chamber,' she added. 'At the top are two corridors. The gallery to the right is the Nightingale Gallery because it "sings" when anyone walks through it.' She must have seen the disbelief in Cranston's bleary eyes. 'This house is very old,' she continued, looking up at the great blackened beams. 'It was built in the reign of King John.' She smirked. 'A time very like our own. A strong ruler was needed. Anyway, one of John's mercenary captains used this house as a base from which to control London. He trusted no one, not even his own men.' Her eyes drifted to Lady Isabella, who was standing behind Athelstan. 'Anyway, he had the floor of that gallery taken up and replaced with special boards of yew. No one can approach any of the three chambers on that gallery without making it creak, or "sing". Hence its name.'

'And the importance of this?' Cranston asked.

'The importance, my dear coroner,' she purred in reply, 'is that I was in my chamber all evening. I am old and banquets bore me. Oh, I heard the talk and the laughter from the hall below. It disturbed my sleep. Fortunately, I need very little.' She glared at Cranston. 'You will find out for yourself, Sir John, age makes you sleep lightly.'

'Just in case Death taps you on the shoulder!' he answered crossly.

'Quite,' she jibed back. 'But Death has a tendency, as you well know, Sir John, to take the heaviest first!'

'My Lady,' Athelstan intervened, 'the events of yesterday… you heard no one go up to Sir Thomas's chamber?'

'Before the banquet people were scurrying backwards and forwards,' she retorted. 'During the meal I heard the Nightingale sing once. I was surprised. I opened the door and saw Brampton, carrying a wine cup in his hand. I heard him open the door to my son's chamber and then go back downstairs again. I heard no other noise before Sir Thomas's footsteps when he

66

came up to his chamber. Sir Richard followed him and bade him goodnight, then Lady Isabella's maid made her inquiry. After that the house was silent till this morning. Father Crispin came up, I heard him knock on the door, then he went for Sir Richard and brought him back.'

Cranston nodded. 'I thank you, Lady Ermengilde. You have solved one piece of the puzzle. Brampton did take the cup up. Now,' he looked at Sir Richard, 'disturbing and painful though it may be, I must insist that I view the bodies of both men.' He bowed to Lady Isabella. 'Your husband first, My Lady. You have no objection?'

Sir Richard shook his head and led them out across the hall and up the broad sweeping staircase. As Cranston passed Lady Ermengilde, he belched rather noisily.

At the top of the stairs the passageway, or gallery, to the left was unremarkable. The walls were white-washed and coated with fresh lime, and the wood-work painted black. There were canvas paintings nailed there in between the three chambers, which were now covered in black gauze veils; the doors of each chamber were huge, heavy set, and reinforced with iron strips. The gallery running to their right, however, was different. The doors and walls were similar but the floor was not made of broad planks but thin bands of light-coloured wood. As soon as Sir Richard stepped on them, Athelstan realised the gallery was aptly named. Each footstep, wherever they stood, caused a deep, slightly melodious twang, similar to the noise of a dozen bowstrings being pulled back simultaneously. Immediately to their left was Lady Isabella's room, the central chamber was Lady Ermengilde's, and the last Sir Thomas's, now in utter disarray. The floor outside was gouged. The door, smashed off its leather hinges, stood crookedly against the lintel. Sir Richard dismissed the servant on guard and, with the help of Buckingham, pushed it gently to one side.

Athelstan looked around. The company from the hall had followed them up, making the Nightingale Gallery sing and echo with its strange melody.

'Where is Father Crispin?' he asked. 'Dame Ermengilde?'

'Down in the hall,' Allingham muttered. 'The priest has had a deformed foot since birth. At times he finds the stairs painful. Dame Ermengilde is old. They send their excuses!'

Athelstan nodded and followed Cranston into the death chamber. The room was a perfect square, the ceiling a set design, the black timber beams contrasting sharply with the white plaster. The walls were white-washed, and costly, coloured arras hung from each, depicting a number of themes from the Old and New Testaments. No carpets but the rushes on the floor were clean, dry, and sprinkled with fresh herbs. There was a small cupboard, a huge chest

68

and two small coffers at the base of the great four poster bed. Next to it stood a small table, a wine cup still on it, and over near the window, on a beautiful marble tabletop, was ranged the most exquisite chess set Athelstan had ever seen. Sir Richard caught his glance just as Father Crispin hobbled into the room.

'The Syrians,' Sir Richard explained.

Athelstan, a keen chess player, went over and looked down at them. The Syrians were resplendent in their beauty. Each figure, about nine inches high, was a work of great craftsmanship, fashioned out of gold and filigree silver. Athelstan whistled under his breath, shaking his head in admiration.

'Beautiful!' he muttered. 'The most exquisite pieces I have ever seen!'

Sir Richard, who had followed him over, nodded.

'A hundred years ago, a Springall, one of our ancestors, went on a crusade in the Holy Land with King Edward I. He won a name for himself as a great warrior. In Outremer there was a secret sect of assassins led by a mysterious figure called The Old Man of the Mountains.' He straightened and looked across to where Sir John was now swaying drunkenly in the middle of the room, the rest of the group watching him attentively, only half listening to Sir Richard's account. He smirked. 'Anyway, the members of this sect were fed on hashish and sent out to assassinate anyone their leader marked down for destruction. They had castles and secret places high in the mountains. Our ancestor found one of these, laid siege, captured and destroyed it. He seized a great deal of plunder and, as a reward for his bravery, the English king allowed him to keep this magnificent chess set. My brother,' he added softly, 'was a keen player.'

'He was in the middle of that game last night,' Father Crispin interrupted, coming up behind them. 'Sir Thomas was so angry with Brampton, I persuaded him that a game would soothe his humour.'

Athelstan smiled.

'Did you win, Father Crispin?'

'We never finished the game,' Father Crispin murmured. 'We broke off for the banquet. I was threatening his bishop.' The priest looked up, his eyes smiling. 'So easy to trap a churchman, eh, Brother?'

'Did Sir Thomas think that?'

'No, he was furious,' Lady Isabella interrupted. 'During the banquet he kept plotting how to break out of the impasse.'

Athelstan just nodded and went over to where Cranston was staring at the ruined door.

'Both locked and bolted?' the coroner murmured.

'Yes,' answered Buckingham.

Cranston bent down, crouching to look at it, nodded and rose.

'And the corpse?'

Lady Isabella gulped at his harshness. Sir Richard led them over, pulling back the heavy bed curtains. The huge four poster bed had been stripped as a pallet for Springall's corpse which lay rigid and silent under

70

a leather sheet. Cranston pulled back the cloth. Now Athelstan had seen many a corpse, male and female, with the most horrible injuries, yet he thought there was something nightmarish in seeing a man in his bed, dressed in his nightshirt, eyes half open, mouth gaping like a landed fish. When alive Sir Thomas must have been a fine-looking man with his tawny hair, sharp soldier's face and military appearance. In death he looked grotesque.

Cranston sniffed the man's mouth and gently pushed back the lolling head. Athelstan watched fascinated, noting the slight purplish tinge in the corpse's face and sunken cheeks. Someone had attempted to close the dead merchant's eyes and, unable to, had placed a coin over each of his eyelids. One of these had now slipped off and Sir Thomas glared sightlessly at the ceiling. Cranston turned, waving Athelstan closer to examine the body. He always did this. The friar suspected Cranston took enjoyment in making him pore over each corpse, the more revolting the better. Athelstan pulled back the nightshirt and examined the rest of the body, impervious to the groans and gasps behind him. He looked over his shoulder; Lady Isabella had walked back towards the door, Sir Richard's arm around her waist. Buckingham just stood with eyes half closed. Both merchants looked squeamish, as if they were about to be sick. Outside the Nightingale Gallery sang and Lady Ermengilde, her hands grasping a black stick, her face covered in a fine sheen of sweat, pushed into the room and glared at Cranston.

'Is this necessary?' she asked. 'Is it really necessary?'

'Yes, Madam, it is!' he barked in reply. 'Brother Athelstan, have you finished?'

The friar examined the corpse from neck to crotch. No mark of violence, no cut. Then the hands. They had been washed and scrubbed clean, the nails manicured. The body was now ready for the embalmer's, before being sheeted and coffined and the funeral ceremony carried out.

'Poison,' Athelstan confirmed. 'No mark of any other violence. No sign of an attack.'

Athelstan picked up the cup and sniffed it. The smell was rich, dark, dank and dangerous. It cloyed in his mouth and nostrils. He put it down quickly and bent over the corpse, sniffing at the dead man's mouth from which issued the same acrid, richly corrupting smell.

'Belladonna and arsenic?' Athelstan remarked.

Buckingham nodded.

'A deadly combination,' the friar observed. 'The only consolation is that Sir Thomas must have died within minutes of putting the cup down. Sir John, you have seen enough?'

Cranston nodded, straightened, and went to sit in a chair over near the chess table. Sir Richard came back into the room.

'You have found nothing new, Brother?'

Athelstan shook his head.

'I speak for Sir John. Sir Thomas's body may be released for burial whenever you wish.' He looked round the chamber. 'There are no other entrances here?'

'None whatsoever,' Sir Richard replied. 'Sir Thomas chose this chamber because of its security.' He pointed to the chests. 'They hold gold, indentures and parchments.'

'And have you been through these?'

'Of course.'

'Have you found anything which may explain Brampton's strange conduct in trying to rifle his master's records?'

Sir Richard shook his head.

'Nothing. Some loans to rather powerful nobles and bishops who should have known better, but nothing else.'

Athelstan took one look round the bed chamber, noting the exquisite beauty of the carved four poster bed, with its writhing snakes and other symbols. A luxurious chamber but not opulent. He tapped gently on the floor with his sandalled foot. It sounded thick and heavy. No trap doors.

'Did Sir Thomas have a...'

'A secret place?' Sir Richard completed his sentence. 'I doubt it. Moreover, Master Buckingham and I have been through the accounts. Everything is in order. My brother was a tidy man.'

'Sir Richard, we are finished here. I would like to view Brampton's corpse.'

'Brother Athelstan,' the merchant smirked and nodded towards where Cranston sat, a contented smile on his face, fast asleep. 'Your companion, good Sir John, appears good for nothing! Perhaps tomorrow?'

'Yes, yes,' Athelstan replied. 'But first I must see where Brampton killed himself.'

'I will take care of it, Sir Richard,' Buckingham murmured.

Sir Richard nodded and the clerk left the room, returning within seconds with a candle in its metal hood. He led Athelstan out of the bed chamber, back along the passageway and up to the second floor. Behind them the Nightingale sang as if mocking Athelstan's departure. At the bottom of the second gallery was a narrow, winding, wooden staircase.

'It leads to the garrets,' Buckingham said, sensing the friar's thoughts.

They went up. Buckingham pushed open a rickety wooden door and Athelstan followed him in. The garret was built just under the eaves of the roof. The wooden ceiling sloped high at one end and low at the other. Just inside the door stood an old table, a stool beside it. Buckingham held the candle up and Athelstan studied the stout beam directly above the table. A piece of rope hung from it, scarred and frayed. It swung eerily in the breeze which came through a gap in the roof tiles. On the table beneath, covered by a dirty sheet, lay Brampton's corpse. Athelstan took the candle off Buckingham and looked around. Nothing but rubbish: broken pitchers, shattered glass, a coffer with the lid broken, and a mound of old clothes. The garret smelt dank and dusty and of something else – corruption, decay, the order of rotting death. Athelstan went across to the table and pulled back the filthy sheet. Brampton lay there, a small man dressed in a simple linen shirt, open at the neck, and wearing dark green hose on his scrawny legs. He would have appeared asleep if it had not been for the curious lie of his head. The neck was twisted slightly askew to one side. The heavy-lidded eyes were half open, his lips parted in death, and a dark blue-purplish ring circled the scraggy neck. Athelstan peered closer. There were no signs of violence on the yellow, seamed face. The small goatee beard was still damp with spittle; the gash on the throat quite deep, with a large bruise behind the ear where the noose had been tied. He scrutinized the man's hands, long and thin, manicured like a woman's. Carefully he examined the nails, noticing the strands of rope caught there. Behind him Buckingham muttered darkly, as if resenting his scrutiny. There was a crashing on the stairs and Cranston burst in, the ill effects of the wine readily apparent. He slumped on the stool, mopping his sweaty face with the hem of his cloak.

75

'Well, Monk!' he called out. 'What have we?'

'Brampton,' Athelstan replied, 'bears all the marks of a hanged man, though some attempts have been made to redress the ill effects of such a death. The mouth is half open, the tongue swollen and bitten, the neck bears the sign of a noose. There is a bruise behind his left ear and Brampton apparently grasped the rope in his death agonies.' He turned to Buckingham. 'So Brampton came up here, intending to hang himself. There is rope kept here?'

Buckingham pointed to the far corner.

'A great deal,' he replied. 'We often use it to tie up bales.'

'I see, I see. Brampton therefore takes this rope, climbs on the table, ties one length round the rafter beam, forms a noose and puts it round his neck, tying the knot securely behind his left ear. He steps quietly off the table and his life flickers out like a candle flame.'

Buckingham narrowed his eyes and shivered.

'Yes,' he muttered. 'It must have been like that.'

'Now,' Athelstan continued conversationally, ignoring Cranston's glares, 'Vechey finds the corpse. He searches for a knife amongst the rubbish,' Athelstan tapped it with the toe of his sandal where it lay on the floor, 'cuts Brampton down, but finds he is dead.'

'Yes,' Buckingham replied, 'something like that. Then he came down and notified us all.'

Athelstan picked the dagger up from the floor. He had glimpsed it when he had first entered the room and could see why it had been discarded. The handle was chipped and broken, and there were dents along one side, but the cutting edge was still very sharp. Athelstan climbed on to the stool, then on to the table. He looked at the hacked edge of the rope. Yes, he thought, Brampton had been tall enough to fix the rope round the beam, put the noose round his neck, and tie it securely with a knot before stepping off the table.

'Master Buckingham,' Athelstan said, getting down, 'we have kept you long enough. I should be most grateful if you would present my compliments to Lady Isabella and Sir Richard and ask them to meet me in the solar below. I would like the physician present. I believe he lives nearby? The servants, too, should be questioned.'

Buckingham nodded, relieved that the close questioning of himself was over, and left Athelstan dragging a dozing Cranston to his feet. The coroner struggled and murmured. Athelstan put one of his arms around Sir John's shoulders and carefully escorted him downstairs. Thankfully, the gallery below was deserted. He rested the coroner against the wall, slapping him gently on the face.

'Sir John! Sir John! Please wake up!'

Cranston's eyes flew open. 'Do not worry, Brother,' he slurred, 'I won't embarrass you.' He stood and shook himself, trying to clear his eyes, jerking his head as if he could dislodge the fumes from his brain.

'Come,' Athelstan said. 'The physician and servants still await us.'

Athelstan was partially correct. The servants were waiting in the small, lime-washed buttery next to the flagstoned kitchen, but the physician had not yet arrived. Buckingham introduced them as Cranston went over to a large butt, ladling out cups of water which he noisily drank, splashing the rest over his rosy-red face. Athelstan patiently questioned the servants, preferring to deal with them as a group so he could watch their faces and detect any sign of connivance or conspiracy. He found it difficult enough with Buckingham lounging beside him as if to ensure nothing untoward was said, whilst Cranston swayed on his feet, burping and belching like a drunken trumpeter. Athelstan discovered nothing new. The banquet had been a convivial affair. Chief Justice Fortescue had left as the meal ended, whilst Sir Thomas had been in good spirits.

'And Brampton?' Athelstan asked.

'He sulked all day,' the young scullery maid squeaked, tightly clutching the arm of a burly groom. 'He kept to his chamber. He...' she stammered. 'I think he was in his cups.'

'Did any of you hear someone moving round the house?' Athelstan queried. 'Late at night, when everyone had retired?'

The maid blushed and looked away.

'No one came through the yard,' the young groom hotly stated. 'If they had, they would have woken the dogs!'

'Brampton – what was he like?' Cranston barked.

The old servant who had answered the door lifted his shoulders despairingly.

'A good man,' he quavered.

'So why should Sir Thomas be angry with him?'

The old man wiped his red-rimmed eyes. 'He was accused of searching amongst the master's papers. A button from his jerkin,' he stammered, 'or so I understand, was found near one of the coffers which had been tampered with.'

'What was Brampton looking for?'

A deathly silence greeted his question. The servants shuffled their feet and looked pleadingly at Buckingham.

'Good friar,' the clerk intervened, 'surely you do not expect servants to know their master's business?'

'Brampton apparently tried to!' Cranston snapped, going back to the butt for another cup of water.

'So it would seem,' Buckingham answered sweetly.

Athelstan gazed at the servants. 'These can tell us nothing more, Sir John,' he murmured.

'And neither can I!'

Athelstan spun round. A plump, balding pigeon of a man stood in the doorway. He was dressed in a dark woollen cloak which half concealed a rich

79

taffeta jerkin slashed with crimson velvet. Athelstan glimpsed the green padded hose and the silver buckles on the dainty leather riding boots. The little fellow exuded self-importance. He held his smooth, oil-rubbed face slightly tilted back. A nose sharp as a quill prodded the air like the beak of a bird. In one hand he held a silver-topped walking cane, in the other a pomander full of spiced cloves. Now and again he would hold it to his face.

'You are, Sir?' Athelstan asked.

'Peter de Troyes, physician.'

He looked distastefully at Cranston.

'And you must be Sir John Cranston, coroner of the city? Do you need my help?'

The arrogant physician sat on the corner of the table. Athelstan watched Cranston carefully and held his breath. From experience he knew that Sir John hated physicians and would like to hang the lot as a bunch of charlatans. Cranston smiled sweetly, ordering Buckingham to clear the buttery whilst he lumbered across to stand over the physician.

'Yes, Doctor de Troyes, I am the Coroner. I like claret, a good cup of sack and, if I had my way, I would investigate the practices and potions of the physicians of this city.' His smile faded as de Troyes stuck out his plump little chest. 'Now, Master de Troyes, physician, you inspected Sir Thomas's corpse?'

'I did.'

'And the goblet he drank from?'

'Quite correct, Sir John.'

'And you think it was a mixture of belladonna and arsenic?'

'Yes, yes, I do. The cadaver's skin was slightly blueish, and the mouth smelt rank.' He shrugged. 'Death by poisoning, it was obvious.'

Athelstan walked across to them. The physician didn't even turn to greet him.

'Would death have been quick?' the friar asked.

'Oh, yes, and rather silent. Very much like a seizure, within ten or fifteen minutes of taking the potion.'

'Master physician,' Athelstan continued, 'please do me the courtesy of looking at me when I ask you a question.'

De Troyes turned, his eyes glittering with malice.

'Yes, Friar, what is it?'

'Surely Sir Thomas would have detected the poison in the wine cup? You smelt it. Why didn't he?'

The fellow pursed his lips. 'Simple enough,' he replied pompously. 'First, Sir Thomas had drunk deeply.' He glanced slyly at Cranston. 'Wine is a good mask for poison, and if there is enough in the belly and throat the victim will never suspect. Secondly, the wine cup has stood all night.' He wetted his lips. 'The smell could become more rank.'

'And the phial found in Brampton's coffer was the same potion?'

'Yes. A deadly mixture.'

'Where can it be bought?'

The physician's eyes slid away. 'If you have enough money, Sir John, and know the right person, anything or anyone can be bought in this city.' De Troyes stood up. 'Do you have any more questions?'

Cranston belched, Athelstan shook his head and the physician swept out of the room without a backward glance.

They found Sir Richard's group still waiting in the solar. Athelstan gathered his writing tray, paper and quills, putting them carefully back into the leather bag. He had written very little, but would make a thorough report later. He hurried back to where Sir John, legs apart and swaying slightly, stood leering lecherously at Lady Isabella, who stared back frostily.

'I think,' Sir Richard said quietly, 'that Sir John needs a good night's sleep. Perhaps tomorrow, Brother?'

'Perhaps tomorrow, Sir Richard,' Athelstan echoed, and slipping his arm through Cranston's, turned him gently and walked him out of the hall. Sir John suddenly spun round and looked back at the company, his heavy-lidded eyes half closed. Athelstan followed suit and glimpsed Sir Richard's hand fall away from Lady Isabella's shoulder. Something in the merchant's face made Athelstan wonder if they were more than just close kin. Was there adultery here as well as murder?

'Oh, Sir Richard!' Cranston called.

'Yes, Sir John?'

'The Sons of Dives – who or what are they?'

Athelstan saw the group suddenly tense, their faces drained of that pompous, amused look as if they regarded Cranston as the royal jester rather than the king's coroner.

'I asked a question, Sir Richard,' Cranston slurred. 'The Sons of Dives? Who are they?'

'I don't know what you are talking about, Sir John. The ill effects of the wine?'

'The wine does not affect me as much as you think, Sir Richard,' Cranston snapped back. 'I will ask the question again.' He bowed towards Lady Isabella. 'Good night.'

And, spinning on his heel, Cranston lurched with as much dignity as he could muster through the door, Athelstan following behind.

Once clear of the house, Cranston waddled as sure as a duck to water towards the welcoming, half-open door of an alehouse across Cheapside. Athelstan stopped and looked up at the starlit sky.

'Oh, good God!' he groaned. 'Surely not more refreshment, Sir John?'

Nevertheless, he hurried after; the water had apparently revived the good coroner and Athelstan wanted to clear his own mind and define the problems nagging at him. The alehouse was almost deserted. Sir John seized a table near the wine butts.

'Two cups of sack!' he roared. 'And some——?' He glared at Athelstan.

'Watered wine,' the friar added meekly.

The sack disappeared down Sir John's cavernous throat. More was ordered, and the coroner clapped his podgy hands.

'An excellent evening's work!' he boomed. He nodded in the direction of the Springall mansion. 'A coven of high-stepping hypocrites.' He turned to Athelstan, bleary-eyed. 'What do you think, Monk?'

'Friar!' Athelstan corrected him despairingly.

'Who gives a sod?' Cranston snapped. 'First, I wonder why our good Lord Fortescue was there? I think he left a little later than he claims.' Cranston belched. 'Secondly, Brampton. They say he was rifling through his master's papers, and they have evidence of it, so it is easy to imagine the quarrel between him and Sir Thomas. Springall would feel betrayed, Brampton furious that he had been caught as well as fearful of dismissal.' Cranston drummed his stubby fingers on the wine-stained tabletop. 'But if Brampton was innocent,' he slurred, 'why was he made to appear guilty? There's no answer to that.'

'And if he was guilty,' Athelstan added, 'what was he looking for? What great secret did Sir Thomas Springall possess?'

Athelstan gazed across the tap room, watching two drunken gamblers shove and push each other over a game of dice.

'Even so,' he murmured, 'why should Brampton kill his master and take his own life? Revenge followed by remorse?'

A loud snore greeted his question. Cranston had now fallen back against the wall, his eyes closed, a beatific smile on his fat, good-natured face.

'Was Sir Thomas murdered because of the secret?' Athelstan muttered. 'Or was his wife an adulteress, playing the two-backed beast with her husband's brother?'

Some men kill for gold, he thought, others for lust. And Dame Ermengilde? Did she play a part in this charade, trying to advance the interests of her favourite son, Sir Richard? And the other two, Vechey and Allingham? Strange creatures, battening like fleas on the skill and acumen of Sir Thomas. And, of course, young Buckingham. Athelstan shuddered. He had met men like Buckingham, with their fluttering eyelashes and graceful, dainty gestures; men who preferred to be women but hid their natures under the cloak of darkness lest they be discovered and boiled alive at Smithfield. Finally, the good priest Crispin. Was his leg as malformed as he pretended? When he first met the priest in the solar Athelstan had noticed how ungainly he walked, but when later he had joined them in Springall's chamber, Athelstan had observed how the priest had changed into Spanish riding boots, the heel of one slightly raised to lessen his deformity. In these he moved quietly and quickly.

Sir John suddenly groaned and sat up.

'Oh, God, Athelstan,' he moaned. 'I feel sick!'

The coroner rose and staggered to the door.

Chapter 3

Outside the alehouse Sir John paused to vomit, afterwards loudly protesting he was all right. Athelstan linked his arm through that of the coroner and they carefully made their way down Cheapside. It was raining and had become messy underfoot. They were stopped by the Watch, a collection of arrogant servants and retainers from the households of some of the great aldermen. They would have arrested them both, delighted to pick on a friar. Athelstan, however, informed them his companion was no less a personage than Sir John Cranston, who was now ill, so they stepped aside, doing their best to hide their smirks. As Athelstan turned off Cheapside into Poultry, he could still hear their loud guffaws of laughter.

The coroner's house was a pleasant, two-storeyed affair in an alleyway off the Poultry. Athelstan hammered on the door until Sir John's wife appeared – a small, birdlike woman much younger than Cranston, who greeted her husband as if he was Hector back from the wars.

'The weight of office!' she shrilled. 'It's the weight of office which makes him drink.'

And, grabbing Sir John roughly by the hand, she unceremoniously pushed him upstairs.

Athelstan stood in the hallway looking carefully around, for this was the first time he had been to Cranston's house and met his wife. The room beyond the hall was cosy and comfortable with clean rushes on the floor and a large, high-backed chair before the fire. Athelstan caught a fragrant aroma from the kitchen, the supper Sir John had missed. The friar realised how hungry he was.

Cranston's wife Maude rejoined him, still behaving as if Athelstan had brought her husband home from a heroic field of battle rather than half drunk, his doublet stained with vomit.

'Brother,' she said, taking the friar by the hand, her bright blue eyes full of life, 'this is the first time I have met you. Please, you must stay.'

Athelstan needed no second bidding and sank gratefully into a chair, accepting the meat pastry, mince tart and cup of cold wine that Lady Maude pushed before him. After that, she showed him up into a chamber at the top of the house. Athelstan said his prayers, the *Dies Requiem* for Springall, Brampton, his own brother and others, made the sign of the cross on himself and thanked God for a wholesome day.

He slept like a babe and woke just after dawn. He felt guilty at not returning to his own church but hoped that his few parishioners would understand. Had Simon the tiler fixed the roof? he wondered. Would Bonaventure be fed? And surely Wat the dung-collector would make sure the door was locked and Godric safe? And Benedicta the widow who attended every morning Mass, whose husband had been killed in the king's wars beyond the seas...? Athelstan sat on his bed and crossed himself. Sometimes he would catch Benedicta looking at him, her lovely face pale as ivory, her dark eyes smiling.

'No sin!' Athelstan muttered. 'No sin!' Christ himself had his woman friends. He gazed at the floor. For the first time ever, he realised how he missed the woman when he did not see her. Every morning at Mass he sought her smiling eyes as if she alone understood his loneliness and felt for him. Athelstan shook himself, dressed, and went along to the kitchen to beg from a startled maid a bowl of hot water, a clean napkin and some salt with which to scrub his teeth. After his ablutions, finding the house still quiet, he left and went back down Cheapside to the church of St Mary Le Bow. The bells were clanging in the high tower which soared up to a steel blue sky. Athelstan saw the night watchman douse the light, the beacon which was lit every evening to guide travellers through the streets of London.

Inside, the dawn Mass was just ending, the priest offering Christ to God in the presence of three old women, a beggar and a blind man with his dog.

They all squatted on the paving-stone before the rood screen. Athelstan waited near the baptismal font. When the Mass was finished, he followed the priest into the vestry. Father Matthew was a genial fellow and cheerfully granted Athelstan's request, giving him vestments and vessels so he could celebrate his own Mass in one of the small chantry chapels built off the main aisle.

After Mass and the chanting of the Divine Office, Athelstan thanked the priest but refused his kind offer of a meal and wandered back into Cheapside. The broad thoroughfare was now coming to life. The cookshops were open, the awnings of the stalls pulled down, and already the apprentices were darting in and out, seeking custom for their masters. The friar walked back up to the Poultry and knocked on the coroner's door. Cranston greeted him, standing like vice reformed, sober, dour, and full of his own authority, as if he wished to erase the memory of the night before.

'Come in, Brother!' He looked out of the corner of his eye as he beckoned Athelstan into the parlour. 'I am grateful for what you did last night when I was inconvenienced.'

Athelstan hid his smile as Cranston waved him to a stool, sitting opposite in a great high-backed chair. In the kitchen Maude was singing softly as she baked bread, its sweet, fresh scent filling the house.

Strange, Athelstan thought, that a man like Sir John, steeped in violent bloody death, should live in such homely surroundings.

Cranston stretched and crossed his legs.

'Well, Brother, shall we record a clear case of suicide?'

'I would like to agree with your verdict,' Athelstan replied, 'but something eludes me. Something I cannot place, something small, like looking at a tapestry with a loose thread.'

'God's teeth!' Cranston roared as he rose and went to fetch the boots standing in the corner. He pulled them on and looked sourly across at the friar.

'I know you, Brother, and your nose for mischief. If you feel there is something wrong, there is. Let's be careful, however. Springall belonged to the court faction in the city, and if we put a foot wrong, well...' His voice trailed off.

'What do you mean?' Athelstan asked sharply.

'What I say,' Cranston caustically retorted. 'I stay out of the muddy pools of politics. That gives me the right to insult fools like Fortescue. But if I offend the court, its opponents think I am a friend. If I am partial to them, I am an enemy.' He buttoned up his doublet. 'God knows when order will be restored. The king is young, a mere boy. Gaunt is so ambitious. You know, through his wife he has a claim to the throne of Castile; through his grandmother to the throne of France. And between him and the throne of England

– one small boy!' Cranston closed the parlour door so his wife could not hear. 'There may be violence. For myself I do not care, but I do not want armed retainers terrifying my household by arresting me in the dead of night.' He sighed, and picking up his cloak, swung it about him. 'However, I trust your judgement, Athelstan. Something's wrong, though God knows what!'

Athelstan looked away. He had spoken largely without thinking. He thought back to the visit to the Springall house yesterday. Yes, there was something wrong. Oh, everything was neat and orderly. Springall had been murdered and his murderer had committed suicide, so everything was neat and tidied away. But it was all too clear, too precise, and death wasn't like that. It was violent, cumbersome, messy. It came trailing its blood-spattered tail everywhere.

'You know...' he began.

'What's the matter, Brother?'

'Oh, I'm just thinking about yesterday in the Springall mansion. A strange coven. The deaths were so orderly.' He looked up at Cranston. 'You felt that, Sir John, didn't you? Everything precise, signed, sealed, filed away, as if we were watching a well-arranged masque. What do you say?'

Cranston moved back to his chair and sat down.

'The same,' he replied. 'I know I drank too much, I always do. But I agree, I sensed something in that house: an evil, an aura, a dankness, despite the wealth.

Something which clutched at my soul. Someone is hiding something. Of course,' he smiled, 'you know *they* are the Sons of Dives? They must be. Some sort of coven or a secret society, and I believe they are all party to it. Did you see their faces when I asked the question?' Cranston threw back his great head and bellowed with laughter. 'Oh, yes, and that Dame Ermengilde – I have heard of her. A nasty piece of work, vicious and venomous as a viper! Well,' he smacked his knee, 'we shall see.' He went off into the kitchen. Athelstan heard Lady Maude squeal with pleasure. The coroner came back, grinned at Athelstan, belched loudly, and without further ado they went back into the street.

They were halfway up Cheapside when a small voice called out: 'Sir John! Sir John!'

They stopped. A little boy ran up, face dirty, clothes dishevelled, his breath coming in short gasps so he could hardly speak. Sir John stood back and Athelstan smiled. Cranston always seemed to have a fear of small boys. Perhaps a memory from childhood when a fat Cranston must have been mercilessly teased by others. Athelstan knelt before the child, taking his thin, bony hand.

'What is it, lad?' he asked gently. 'What do you wish?'

'I bring a message from the Sheriff,' the boy gasped. 'Master Vechey...' The child closed his eyes to remember. 'Master Vechey has been found hanged

93

under London Bridge. The Sheriff says it's by his own hand. The body has been cut down and lies in the gatehouse there. The Sheriff sends his com—'

'Compliments,' Athelstan interrupted.

'Yes.' The boy opened his eyes. 'Compliments, and wishes Sir John to go there immediately and examine the corpse.'

Cranston, standing behind Athelstan, whistled softly.

'So, we were right, Brother,' he said, tossing a coin to the boy who scampered away. 'There is evil afoot. One murder can be explained, one suicide can be accounted for, but another suicide?' His fat face beamed. 'Ah, no, Sir Richard may be pompous, Lady Isabella frosty, Dame Ermengilde may strike her cane on the floor in temper, but Vechey's death cannot be dismissed. There is evil here, and you and I, Athelstan, will stay like good dogs following the trail until we sight our quarry. Come! The living may not want to talk to us, but the dead await!'

And, without even a reference to refreshment, Cranston waddled off down Cheapside with Athelstan striding behind him. They pushed their way through the morning crowd: monks, friars, hucksters and pedlars, ignoring the shouts and screams of the city as they turned into Fish Hill Street which led down on to London Bridge. They stopped at the Three Tuns tavern to ensure their horses had been well stabled. Cranston paid the bill. Philomel, happy to see his master again, nuzzled and nudged him. The road down to the bridge was packed so they decided to leave their horses rather than ride.

At the entrance, just near the gatehouse door, Cranston stopped and knocked hard at an iron-studded door. At first there was no reply so, picking up a loose brick, Cranston hammered again. At last the door was opened. A small, hairy-faced little creature appeared glared up at Sir John.

'What do you want?' he roared. 'Bugger off! The gatehouse is closed on the king's orders until the arrival of the coroner.'

'I *am* the coroner!' Cranston bellowed back. 'And who, sir, are you?'

'Robert Burdon,' the dwarf retorted. He rearranged his cloak and stuck his thumb into the broad leather belt at his waist like a wrestler waiting for his opponent to attack. Sir John ignored him and pushed forward into the dank entrance of the chamber.

'We have come to view Master Vechey's body.'

Robert ran in front of Cranston, jumping up and down.

'My name is Robert Burdon!' he shrieked. 'I am constable of this gate tower. I hold my office direct from the king!'

'I don't give a fig,' Cranston replied, 'if you hold it direct from the Holy Father! Where's Vechey's corpse?'

He looked into the small chamber near the stairs where the dwarf probably ate, lived and slept. A small baby crawled out on its hands and knees, its face covered in grime. Robert picked it up, shoved it back in the chamber and slammed the door behind him.

'The corpse is upstairs,' he said pompously. 'What do you expect? I can't keep it down here with my wife and children. The cadaver's ripe.' He indicated with his thumb. 'It's on the roof. Up you come!' And, nimble as a monkey, he bounded up the stairs ahead of Cranston and Athelstan. He pushed open the door at the top and led them out on to the roof, a broad expanse bounded by a high crenellated wall. The wind from the river whipped their faces. Cranston and Athelstan covered their face and nose at the terrible stench which blew across.

'God's teeth!' Cranston cried as he looked around. Vechey's corpse lay in the centre of the tower near a rickety hut, formerly used by guards on sentry duty. The body lay sprawled, its face covered by a dirty rag. Athelstan thought the odour came from that but, looking around, he saw the rotting heads which had been placed on spikes in the gaps of the crenellated wall.

'Traitors' heads!' Cranston muttered. 'Of course, they spike them here!'

Athelstan looked closely, trying not to gag. Like all Londoners, he knew that once the bodies of traitors had been cut and quartered, their heads were sent to adorn London Bridge. He looked closer. Thick, black pools around the spikes showed some of the heads were fresh, though all were rotting, crumbling under the rain and wind which whipped up their oddly silken hair. Large ravens which had been busy, plucking out juicy morsels with their yellow beaks, rose in angry circles above them.

'Their hair,' Athelstan whispered. 'Look, it's combed!'

'I do that!' Robert cried. 'I always look after my heads! Every morning I come up and comb them, keep them soft, pleasant-looking. That is,' he added morosely, 'until the ravens start pecking them, though they usually leave that bit for the last. Oh, yes, I comb their hair and, when I am finished, I sing to them. I bring my viol up. Lullabies are best.' He looked up at Athelstan, his face beaming with pride. 'Never lonely up here,' he said. 'The things these heads must know!'

'God's teeth,' muttered Cranston. 'I need refreshment! But never mind that. This morning I swore a mighty oath not to touch the juice of the grape or the crushed sweetness of the hop. But first let's see Vechey's corpse.'

Robert skipped over to show them the unexpected addition to his ghastly collection. He whipped off the rag which the wind caught and blew against one of the spiked heads.

'You examine it, Brother,' whispered Cranston. 'I feel sick. Last night's wine.'

Athelstan crouched down. Vechey was dressed in the same clothes as yesterday. The soft face was now puffier, its colour a dirty white. His eyes were half open, mouth slack, lips apart, displaying rows of blackened teeth. Vechey seemed to be grinning up at him, taunting him with the mystery of his death. Athelstan turned his head slightly to one side. He caught his knee on his robe and slipped. He felt queasy as his hand touched the cadaver's bloated stomach and noted that the dead man's legs were soaking wet. He inspected the gash round Vechey's neck, which was very similar to that of Brampton; black-red like some ghastly necklace and the dark, swollen bruise behind the left ear. He held his breath and sniffed at the dead man's lips. Nothing but the putrid rottenness of the grave. Then he examined the corpse's hands. No scars, the nails neat and clean, shorter than Brampton's. There was no trace of a strand of rope caught there. Athelstan looked at the dwarf.

'Where's the noose?'

'I tossed it away,' the fellow replied triumphantly. 'I see'd him there, I cuts him down, I loosened the noose and it falls in the water.' His face grew solemn, his eyes anxious. 'Why, shouldn't I have done that?'

'You did well, Robert,' Athelstan replied quietly. 'Very well. You found the body?'

'Well, no, my children did. They were playing where they shouldn't, on the starlings under the bridge. You know the wooden barriers around the arches?' He shook his head. 'So many of them. Nine, I have,' he declared. 'Should be ten but the eldest got drunk and fell in the river!'

Cranston stared in utter disbelief at Robert's potency.

'So you cut him down?' he asked. 'How did you know it was Vechey?'

'I found coins in his pocket and a piece of parchment. It had his name on it. That and someone else's. Thomas...' He closed his eyes.

'Thomas Springall?'

'That's right. Look, I have it here. There's something else written.'

The little guardian of the great gateway dug into his wallet and brought out a greasy scrap of parchment. Two names were written on it: Theobald Vechey and Sir Thomas Springall. Beneath the latter's name, written in the same hand, was Genesis 3, Verse 1 and the Book of the Apocalypse 6, Verse 8.

'Here, Monk,' Cranston muttered. 'You are the preacher, what do you make of it?'

'First, Sir John, as I keep saying, I am a friar, not a monk. And, secondly, though I have studied the Bible, I can't recollect every verse.'

Cranston smirked.

'Was there anything else?'

The little man bobbed up and down.

'Yes, some rings and some coins, but the sheriff's men took them. I sent one of my boys to the Guildhall, they sent down constables of the ward. That must have been,' he sucked on his finger, 'just after dawn. I heard them say they had sent for you.'

'Well,' Sir John sighed, 'we have a corpse and a scrap of paper, and the sheriff's men have the valuables – and that's the last any one will see of them,' he added bitterly. He looked down. 'The man was just hanging, his hands were free?'

'Oh, yes,' the little fellow replied. 'Just hanging there from one of the beams, swaying as free as a leaf in the wind. Come, I will show you!'

He led Cranston and Athelstan downstairs past the closed chamber where the noise of his large brood sounded like the howling of demons in hell. They went back through the gatehouse, following the line of the riverbank down some rough-hewn stairs cut into the rock and beneath the bridge.

'Be careful!' the dwarf shouted.

Cranston and Athelstan needed no such warning. The Thames was flowing full and furious, the water greedily lapping their feet as if it would like to catch them and drag them under its swollen black surface. The bridge was built on nineteen great arches. Vechey had decided to hang himself on the last. He'd climbed on to one of the great beams which supported the arch, tied a length of rope round it and, fastening the noose around his neck, simply stepped off the great stone plinth. Part of the rope still swung there, hanging down directly over the water.

'Why should a man hang himself here?' Cranston asked.

'It's been done before,' the gateman replied. 'Hangings, drownings, they always choose the bridge. It seems to attract them!'

'Perhaps it's the span which represents the gap between life and death?' Athelstan remarked.

He looked at Cranston. 'Bartholomew the Englishman wrote a famous treatise in which he remarked how strange it was that people chose bridges as their place to die.'

'Give my thanks to Bartholomew the Englishman,' Cranston replied drily, 'but it doesn't explain why a London merchant came down here in the dark, fastened a rope round a beam and hanged himself.'

'Bangtails come here,' Robert piped up. 'Bawds! Whores!' he explained. 'They often bring their customers down here.'

'What does Bartholomew the Englishman say about that, Friar?'

'I don't know but, when I do, you will be the first to know!'

They examined the rope again and, satisfied that they had seen everything, climbed the stone steps back on to the track high on the riverbank. Cranston thanked the gatekeeper for his pains, quietly slipping some coins into his hands.

'For the children,' he murmured. 'Some pastries, some doucettes.'

'And the corpse?'

Cranston shrugged. 'Send a message to Sir Richard Springall. He has a mansion in Cheapside. Tell him you have Vechey's body. If he does not collect it, the sheriff's men who pocketed poor Vechey's valuables will find him a pauper's grave!'

'At the crossroads,' the fellow said, eyes rounded. 'What do you mean?'

'He means, Sir John,' Athelstan interrupted, 'that Vechey was a suicide. Like Brampton, a stake should be driven through his heart and the cadaver buried at the crossroads. They still do that in country parts. They claim it prevents the dead man's troubled soul from walking abroad. But what does it matter? It's only the husk. I will remember poor Vechey at Mass.'

They bade farewell to the gateman, collected their horses from the urchin and, seeing the busy crowds ahead of them, decided to walk up to Cheapside. The throng was thick, massing like a swarm of bees, the noise and clamour so intense they were unable to hear one another speak. In Cheapside, where the thoroughfare was broader and the houses did not press so close, they relaxed. Athelstan, patting Philomel's nose, stared across at a now perspiring Cranston.

'Why should Vechey kill himself?' he asked.

'Don't bloody ask me!' Cranston retorted crossly, wiping the sweat from his face. 'If it wasn't for that poor bugger, I would be getting as pissed as a bishop's fart in the Crossed Keys and you would be back in your decrepit church feeding that bloody cat or watching your bloody stars! Or trying to save the soul of some evil little sod who would slit your throat as quickly as look at you!'

Athelstan grinned.

'You need refreshment, Sir John. You have had a hard morning. The rigours of office, the exacting duties of coroner – they would break many a lesser man.'

Cranston looked evilly at the friar.

'Thank you, Brother,' he said. 'Your words of comfort soothe my heart.'

'Be at peace, my son,' Athelstan said mockingly and pointed. 'Over there is the Springall mansion. And here,' he turned and gestured to the great garish sign, 'is the tavern of the Holy Lamb of God. The body needs refreshment.' He grinned. 'And your body, great as it is, more than any other!'

Cranston solemnly tapped his bell-like stomach. 'You are correct, Brother.' He sighed. 'The spirit is willing, but the flesh is very, very weak.'

And there's a lot of weakness there, thought Athelstan.

'But not now,' he added hastily, catching the gleam in Cranston's eyes. 'Sir Richard Springall awaits us. We must see him.'

Cranston's mouth set in a stubborn line.

'Sir John, we must do it now!' Athelstan insisted.

Cranston nodded, his eyes petulant like those of a child being refused a sweet. They stabled their horses at the Holy Lamb of God and threaded their way across the noisy marketplace. A figure garbed in black, a white devil's mask on its face, was jumping amongst the stalls, shouting imprecations at the rich and the avaricious. A beadle in his striped gown tried to arrest him but the 'devil' scampered off to the cheers of the crowd. Cranston and Athelstan watched the drama play itself out; the beadle chasing, the 'devil' dodging. The small, fat official was soon lathered in sweat. Another 'devil' appeared, dressed identically to the first, and the crowd burst into roars of laughter. The beadle had been tricked, fooled by two mummers and their game of illusion.

'Like life, is it not, Sir John?' Athelstan queried. 'Nothing, as Heraclitus says, is what it appears to be. Or, as Plato writes, we live in a world of dreams. The realities are beyond us.'

Cranston gave one last pitying glance at the beadle.

'Bugger philosophy!' he said. 'I have seen more truths at the bottom of a wine cup, and learnt more after a good tankard of sack, than any dry-skinned philosopher could teach in some dusty hall!'

'Sir John, your grasp of philosophy never ceases to amaze me.'

'Well, I am now going to amaze Sir Richard Springall,' Cranston grated. 'I haven't forgotten yesterday.'

The same old manservant ushered them into the hall. A few minutes later Sir Richard came down, closely followed by Lady Isabella and Buckingham.

The latter informed them that Father Crispin and Allingham were working elsewhere.

'Sir John, you feel better?' Springall asked.

'Sir, I was not ill. Indeed, I felt better yesterday than I do now.'

Sir Richard just glared, refusing to be drawn into Cranston's riddle.

'You have heard of Vechey's death?'

Sir Richard nodded. 'Yes,' he said softly. 'We did. But come, let us not discuss these matters here.'

He led them into a small, more comfortable room behind the great hall where a fire burnt in the canopied hearth; it was cosier and not so forbidding, with its wood-panelled walls and high-backed chairs arranged in a semicircle around the hearth.

'Even in the height of summer,' Sir Richard observed, 'it's cool in here.'

Athelstan smelt the fragrance of the pine logs burning in the hearth, mixing with sandalwood, resin, and something more fragrant – the heavy perfume of Lady Isabella. He looked sharply at her. She had now donned full mourning weeds. A black lacy wimple framed her beautiful white face while her splendid body was clothed from neck to toe in a pure black silk gown, the only concession to any alleviating colour being the white lace cuffs and collar and the small jewelled cross which swung from a gold chain round her neck. Buckingham was paler, quieter. Athelstan noticed how daintily he moved. There was a knock at the door.

'Come in!' Sir Richard called.

Father Crispin entered, his thin face creased with pain at his ungainly hobbling. He caught Athelstan's glance and smiled bravely.

'Don't worry, Brother. I have had a clubbed foot since birth. You may have noticed a riding boot greatly eases my infirmity. Sometimes I forget my lameness, but it's always there. Like some malicious enemy ready to hurt me,' he added bitterly.

Lady Isabella went forward and grasped the young priest's hand. 'Father, I am sorry,' she whispered. 'Come, join us.'

They sat down. A servant brought a tray of wine cups filled to the brim with white Rhenish wine, as well as a platter of sweet pastries. Cranston lost his sour look and satisfied himself by glancing sardonically at Athelstan as he sipped daintily from the wine cup.

'So,' said Sir John, smacking his lips, 'a third death, Master Vechey's suicide.' He held three fingers up. 'One murder and two suicides in the same household.' He stared around. 'You do not grieve?'

Sir Richard put down his wine cup on the small table beside him.

'Sir John, you mock us. We grieve for my brother. His funeral is being held tomorrow. We grieve for Brampton, whose body has been sheeted and taken to St Mary Le Bow. Our grief is not a bottomless pit and Master Vechey was a colleague but no friend.'

'A dour man,' Buckingham observed, 'with bounding ambition but not the talent to match.' He smiled thinly. 'At least not in the lists of love.'

'What do you mean?' Cranston asked.

'Vechey was a widower. His wife died years ago. He saw himself as a ladies' man, when in his cups, a troubadour from Provence.' Buckingham grimaced. 'You met him yourself. He was small, fat and ugly. The ladies mocked him, laughing at him behind their hands.'

'What the clerk is saying,' Sir Richard interrupted, 'is that Master Vechey was immersed in the pleasures of the flesh. He had few friends. Only my brother really listened to him. It could well be that Sir Thomas's death turned Vechey's mind on to the path of self-destruction.' He spread his hands. 'I do not claim to be my brother's keeper, so how can I claim to be Vechey's? We are sorry for his death but how are we responsible?'

'Master Vechey left the house when?'

'About an hour after you.'

'Did he say where he was going?'

'No. He never did.'

Cranston eased himself in his chair, head back, rolling the white Rhenish wine round his tongue.

'Let me change the question. Where were you all last night?'

Sir Richard shrugged and looked around. 'We went our different ways.'

'Father Crispin?'

The priest coughed, shifting his leg to favour it.

'I went to the vicar of St Mary Le Bow to arrange Sir Thomas's funeral.'

'Sir Richard? Lady Isabella?'

'We stayed here!' the woman retorted. 'A grieving widow does not walk the streets.'

'Master Buckingham?'

'I went to the Guildhall, taking messages from Sir Richard about the pageant we are planning.'

'My brother would have liked that,' Sir Richard intervened. 'He would see no reason why we should not make our contribution to the royal coronation.' His voice rose. 'Why, what is this? Do you hold us responsible for Vechey's death? Are you saying that we bundled him down to the waterside and had him hanged? For what reason?'

'The coroner is not alleging anything,' Athelstan remarked smoothly. 'But, Sir Richard, you must agree it is odd, so many deaths in one household?'

'Does this mean anything to you?' Cranston took the greasy piece of parchment out of his wallet and handed it over. Sir Richard studied it.

'Vechey's name, my brother's, and two verses from the Bible. Ah!' Sir Richard looked up and smiled. 'Two verses my brother always quoted: Apocalypse 6, Verse 8 and Genesis 3, Verse 1.'

'You know the verses, Sir Richard?'

'Yes.' The merchant closed his eyes. 'The second one refers to the serpent entering Eden.'

'And the first?'

'To Death riding a pale horse.'

'Why did your brother always quote these?' Cranston asked.

'I don't know. He had a sense of humour.'

'About the Bible?'

'No, no, about these two verses. He claimed they were his key to fame and fortune. Sometimes, when deep in his cups, he would quote them.'

'Do you know what he meant?' Athelstan asked.

'No, my brother loved riddles from boyhood. He just quoted the verses, smiled, and said they would bring him great success. I don't know what he meant.'

'What other riddles did your brother pose?' Cranston asked.

'None.'

'Yes, he did,' Lady Isabella spoke up, pushing back the black veil from her face. 'You remember, the shoemaker?'

'Ah, yes,' Sir Richard smiled. 'The shoemaker.'

'Lady Isabella,' Cranston queried, 'what about the shoemaker?'

She played with the sparkling ring on her finger. 'Well, over the last few months, my husband used to make reference to a shoemaker. He claimed the shoemaker knew the truth, and the shoemaker was guilty.' She shook her head. 'I don't know what he meant. Sometimes, at table,' she smiled falsely, 'my husband was like you, Sir John. He loved a deep-bowled cup of claret. Then he used to chant: "The shoemaker knows the truth, the shoemaker knows the truth".'

Cranston watched her closely.

'These riddles your husband used, when did they begin?'

'The quotations from the Bible? About – oh, fourteen or fifteen months ago.'

'And the shoemaker riddle?'

Cranston noticed that Lady Isabella had become tense and anxious.

'Shortly after Christmas? That's right. He first made the riddle up during one of our mummer's games at Twelfth Night.'

Somehow Athelstan knew these riddles were important. The room had fallen deathly silent except for Cranston's abrupt questions, the equally abrupt answers and the snapping and crackling of the logs in the fire. What did this group fear? he wondered. What was the meaning of the riddles?

'Tell me,' Athelstan spoke up, 'did anything happen in the household to account for these riddles? Anything in Sir Thomas's life? Sir Richard, Lady Isabella... you were the closest to Sir Thomas.'

'I don't know,' Sir Richard muttered. 'My brother liked to speak in riddles, refer to shadowy things, lectures and parables. He was a man who loved secrecy for secrecy's sake and hugged such secrets to his chest like other men do gold, silver or precious stones. No, nothing special happened here.'

'Are you sure?' Cranston turned and looked at him, resting his cup on one large, plump thigh. 'Are you sure, Sir Richard? My memory fails me about specific details but was there not a death here eight months ago?'

Lady Isabella's face now paled and Sir Richard refused to look up.

'No!'

'Come, come, sir,' Cranston barked. 'There was something.'

'Yes,' Lady Isabella said softly, 'Sir Richard's memory fails him.' She looked at Sir John more guardedly, as if realising the coroner was not the fool he liked to appear. 'There was Eudo's death.'

'Ah, yes, Eudo,' Cranston repeated. 'Who was he?'

Sir Richard looked up. 'A young page boy. He fell from a window and broke his neck, out there in the courtyard. No explanation for the fall was ever given, though Sir Thomas believed he may have been involved in some stupid jape. The boy was killed outright, head smashed in, neck broken.'

Cranston drained his cup and beamed in self-congratulation, giving a sly grin at Athelstan, who glared back. He wished the coroner had told him about this!

'Yes, Eudo's death. I was ill at the time with the ague, but I remember the verdict being recorded. Poor boy!' Cranston murmured. 'This house has ill fortune.' He stood and took in his audience with one heavy-lidded stare. 'I urge you all to be most careful. There is a malignancy here, an evil curse. It may yet claim other lives! Lady Isabella, Sir Richard.' He bowed and stepped out of the chamber.

Athelstan stopped at the door and looked back. The group sat quite still as if bound by some secret.

'Sir Richard?' Athelstan asked.

'Yes, Brother?'

'May I have permission to visit the garret where Brampton died?'

'Of course! But, as I have said, his corpse has been sheeted and removed to St Mary Le Bow.'

Athelstan smiled. 'Yes. But there is something I must see.'

He asked Cranston to wait for him outside and went upstairs. On the first landing he stopped and stole a glance down the Nightingale Gallery, so engrossed he jumped when Allingham suddenly touched him on the shoulder.

'Brother Athelstan, can I help you?'

The merchant's long face was even more mournful and the friar was sure the man had been crying.

'No, no, Master Allingham, I thank you. You have heard of Vechey's death, no doubt?'

The merchant nodded sorrowfully.

'Poor man!' Athelstan muttered. 'You know of no reason why he should take his life?'

'His was a troubled soul,' Allingham replied. 'A troubled soul, vexed and tormented by his own lusts and pleasures.' He paused. 'The only puzzling thing was that he kept muttering, "There were only thirty-one, there were only thirty-one".'

'Do you know what he meant?'

'No. When we went into Sir Thomas's chamber yesterday, I heard him mutter.' Allingham screwed up his eyes. 'Vechey said, "Only thirty-one, I am sure there were only thirty-one." I remember it,' he continued, 'because Vechey was puzzled, upset.'

'Do you know to what he was referring?'

Allingham pursed his lips.

'No, I don't, Brother. But if I find out, I shall tell you. I bid you adieu.'

He proceeded down the wooden stairs and Athelstan went along the gallery and up to the garret. He pushed the door open and wished he had asked for a candle. The chamber was dark and dank. Athelstan shivered. There was a sinister atmosphere, a feeling of oppressive malevolence. Were the church fathers right, he wondered, when they claimed that the soul of a suicide was bound eternally to the place where he died? Did Brampton's soul hover here, as he would for eternity, between heaven and hell?

He stepped in and looked around. The table was now clear of its ghastly remains, and the floor had been swept clear of its litter. It looked tidier, neater than it had the previous day. What had he seen here that afterwards had jolted, pricked against his memory? Something which had been out of place?

He leaned against the wall desperately trying to clear his mind but the memory proved elusive. He sighed, looked round once more and went back to rejoin Sir John.

The coroner was fretting, hopping from foot to foot, standing close to the wall of the house, well away from the crowds which now thronged the entire thoroughfare of Cheapside. He pulled Athelstan closer.

'They are lying, aren't they, Brother? There's something wrong, but what?'

'I don't know, Sir John, but there may be many logical explanations. Something may be wrong, but they may not realise it. Something may be wrong but only one or two may know the truth. Or, finally, something may be wrong but known to someone outside the household.'

'Such as who?'

Athelstan looked round and lowered his voice. 'My Lord of Gaunt or even Chief Justice Fortescue. After all, he did lie; the Chief Justice said he left the house about curfew, but Sir Richard claims it was much later.'

Sir John rubbed the side of his face.

'Yes, Chief Justice Fortescue. We don't even have a good reason for his being there. Why should he be visiting a London merchant?' The coroner grinned evilly, biting his lower lip with his strong, white teeth. 'I look forward to putting that very question to our Lord Chief Justice, but now for refreshment. Oh!'

Cranston grinned and tapped his wallet. 'I've taken the small phial of poison Brampton's supposed to have used.' He tapped the side of his nose. 'I've an idea, but not now. What I need now is a drink!'

Chapter 4

Athelstan cringed. He had hoped Sir John's appetite had been curbed but he seemed both insatiable and unable to learn from previous experience. The friar followed him dolefully across the street as Sir John scampered direct as an arrow for the Holy Lamb of God. Cranston took to its dry, dark warmth as a duck to water. He waddled amongst the customers, using his not inconsiderable bulk to force a way through pedlars, tinkers, labourers and farmers fresh from the countryside, spending the profits of their produce on large stoups of ale.

Sir John commandeered a table in the corner, greeting the ale wife as if she was a long-lost sister. The lady looked like a female incarnation of Satan. She had a hooked, perpetually dripping nose, skin as rough as a sack and bleary, bloodshot eyes. She munched continuously on her lips and her fingers were dirty and greasy down to the knuckles. Her cloak of Lincoln green covered a red kirtle which hung a few inches above tallow-smeared shoes. Athelstan looked at her and prayed to God to forgive him for all he felt was disgust. She, with her wide hips, dirty grey hair and face as wrinkled as a pig's ear, looked as blowsy as any harridan from hell. Athelstan sat looking at her in wonderment, constantly marvelling at the difference in women, contrasting this hag to the beauty of Lady Isabella. He grimly reminded himself that his vow of celibacy had certain consolations.

Cranston, however, acted as if she was an old friend, flattered and fussed her. She winked wickedly back at him, slyly insinuating that she would satisfy all his wants.

'Enough of that, you wicked wench!' Cranston teased. 'Food and ale first, then other comforts perhaps.' He dropped one eyelid. 'Later.'

The ale wife went away cackling and came back to serve both of them huge tankards slopping over with ale and a shared platter of meat mixed with onions and leeks swimming in a sea of grease. Cranston stuffed his mouth. He downed one tankard and, when the friar nodded, helped himself to the second.

'You are not eating, Brother?'

Athelstan toyed with the food on the platter in front of him.

'I don't feel hungry. I am wondering what we do next.'

Cranston, his mouth full of food, stared up at the blackened ceiling, coveting the leg of ham hooked there to be cured in the smoke.

'There's nothing much to do,' he replied. 'We have our suspicions but no proof. Oh, there's something wrong, we all know there is. Two suicides, one murder… but no proof whatsoever, no evidence. We should file our record, send copies to the sheriff, go back and tell Chief Justice Fortescue that whatever secret Springall had died with him, and then return to our normal business.'

'There's something wrong,' Athelstan repeated. He peered across the tavern, watching a group of men busy baiting a relic-seller who claimed he had Aaron's beard in a sack and was prepared to sell it to them for a few coins.

'It's like grasping a slippery fish or a greasy pole. You think you have it, then it slips away.'

Cranston stuck his red, bulbous nose into a tankard, took one slurp and slammed it down on the table.

'Very well, Brother, what is wrong? What do you think?'

'I believe there were no suicides. I think all three deaths were murder, and I think the murderer still walks!'

'And your proof?'

'Nothing, just a feeling of unease.'

'Oh, for God's sake!' Cranston bellowed. 'What do we have here? A merchant who likes riddles is murdered by his servant, who later hangs himself; a small, fat, morose man who thinks he is a Hector with the ladies and, when he realises he is not, goes out and hangs himself. A few riddles written on paper. Let's face the truth. That group over there,' he nodded in the direction of the Springall mansion, 'do not mourn for anyone. I suspect they are glad Sir Thomas is dead! And Brampton! And Vechey! More money, less fingers in the pot and a larger portion of the spoils. All you can feel, Brother, is human greed. Look around, there's a whole sea of it lapping at us everywhere we walk, sit, eat, and pray!' He glared at the friar. 'Come, Brother,' he concluded wearily, 'let us tie the ends of this and call it suicide.'

'In a while,' Athelstan murmured.

He asked for a cup of water, finished it, and leaving Cranston to his drinking, went outside. It was now mid-afternoon. The stalls and booths along Cheapside were plying a busy trade, the shouts of their keepers and the bold imprecations of the apprentices creating an unbearable din. A knight broke through on his way to a local joust or tournament, his steel codpiece carved as large as a bull's whilst the helmet which swung from his saddle bow was fashioned in the macabre mask of a hangman. The helmet gave Athelstan an idea. He was curious and, shouldering his way through the crowd, made his way to St Mary Le Bow.

Father Matthew was resting. Athelstan suspected he was half drunk, but he welcomed the friar cheerily enough, trying to force a cup of Rhenish into his hand. Athelstan promptly refused, for the few mouthfuls of ale he had already drunk bit at his stomach. He also felt rather sick when he recalled how in the ale house he had just left he had seen a hen roosting on the brim of an uncovered beer tub. He just hoped the ale wife strained the ale before she served it to Sir John! Chicken dung would not do even the coroner's innards any good.

The priest listened to Athelstan carefully.

'Yes, yes,' he murmured. He knew the Springalls, a good but rather secretive family. They attended Mass on Sundays, they gave generously to the poor, and the chancery priest sometimes celebrated Mass at St Mary's. They were always generous at Christmas, Epiphany and Maundy.

'And the funeral of Sir Thomas?' Athelstan asked.

'It will take place tomorrow morning. Once the Requiem Mass is sung, the coffin will be buried here.'

'And Brampton, the suicide?'

The priest, lounging in his chair, shrugged, wiping his greasy hands on his gown.

'What can we do? Brampton has no relatives and he is a suicide. Canon Law has laid down…'

'I know what Canon Law says,' Athelstan snapped back. 'But for God's sake, man, Christ's mercy!'

The priest made a face. 'Oh, he will be given a burial.'

'Where is the body?'

'In the death house, a small hut behind the church near the graveyard.'

'May I have a look?'

'The man is sheeted already with a canvas cloth.'

Athelstan dug in his purse and took out a silver coin. 'If I rip the cloth open, you will have it resewn. Surely some old lady in the parish?'

Father Matthew nodded and the silver coin disappeared in the twinkling of an eye. 'Do what you want!' he muttered.

He leant over to where keys hung on hooks in the wall and took a huge, rusting one down. 'You will need this.' He went into the small scullery and came back with a pomander, a ball of cloth stuffed with cloves and herbs.

'Hold it to your nose. The stench will be terrible.'

Athelstan took the key and the pomander, left the priest's house and walked down the length of the church to the derelict hut beyond. The door was barred and bolted. The huge padlock seemed oddly out of place, for anyone could have broken in if they had wished. He inserted the key, released the padlock and the door creaked open. Inside it was dark and musty. A strange, sour smell pervaded the air. An ancient tallow candle stood fixed in its grease on one of the cross-beams, with a tinder beside it. Athelstan took it, lit the candle, and the room flared into life.

Brampton's corpse lay on the ground, covered in a dirty, yellowing canvas sheet, inexpertly sewed up. Athelstan carefully ripped the canvas open with the small knife he always carried. The stench was terrible. Putrefaction had already set in. Used to the sight and the smell of the dead, Athelstan did not feel queasy, though now and again he held the pomander to his nose for a welcome respite. Brampton now looked hideous. His face had turned a blueish-yellow and his stomach was swollen, straining against the thin linen shirt. The friar studied the body carefully; the shirt, the hose, but there were no boots. He looked at the soles of the feet, making careful note of what he saw. He then made the sign of the cross, said a Requiem for the poor steward's soul, re-locked the hut, returned the key to the priest and wandered back into Cheapside.

Athelstan stood there dreaming, wondering what was happening in St Erconwald's. Who would feed Godric? Would Bonaventure return or take offence at not being fed by him and disappear forever into the stinking alleyways? He wished he was free of Cranston and this matter; free of Cheapside, back at the top of his tower, staring up at the stars. He leaned against the wall and analysed his guilt-laden thoughts. He missed Benedicta the widow. Her face, innocent and angelic, was always with him. How long had he known her? Six months? He breathed a prayer. He had sinned. Yes, he wished he was back in his church with his beloved sky and charts, standing on the tower, letting the evening breeze cool him as he stared up, lost in the vastness. Was he breaking his vows by wanting that? Should he have become a friar or a student? An astrologer, one of those cowled, bent figures who haunted the halls of Oxford.

And what was the attraction of the planets in the sky? Athelstan bit his lip. There was order there. Order in time. Order in motion. Was Aristotle correct? he wondered. Did the planets and spheres give off music when they turned in the universe? A cart crashed by, its driver mouthing oaths. Athelstan stepped back, free from his dreams, and looked around.

There was no order here. A beggar, his face covered in sores, his legs cut off just beneath the knees, scampered about on wooden crutches. A whore tripped by, her eyes ringed with black paint, her thick painted lips lustrous and red like rotting fruit. She smirked and dismissed Athelstan with a flicker of her eyes. He walked across the thorough-fare. In the centre of Cheapside stood the stocks, empty except for one person, a large, fat man, his head securely clasped between the wooden slats. Beneath him were the charred remains of a small fire. Athelstan studied the notice posted above the prisoner's head and gathered that he was a butcher who had sold putrid meat. The friar stopped a water carrier, took his ladle and gave the fellow a drink. The prisoner slurped noisily, thanking him, bleary-eyed. A mounted soldier trotted by and Athelstan remembered the knight's helmet as well as something he had glimpsed in the garret and at the tower gate of London Bridge...

Athelstan made his way north to the Elms near Newgate where a great three-branched scaffold stood stark against the sky; each bore its grisly burden, a corpse swinging by its neck, head askew, hands and feet securely tied. The crowd had gone and a serjeant-at-arms, wearing the florid livery of the city, threw dice with his two companions, ignoring the grim carrion swaying just above their heads. The area around them was empty. Strange, Athelstan thought, how men liked to see their brothers die, yet feared the actual sight and stench of death. The serjeant looked up as he approached.

'What is it, Brother?'

Athelstan pointed to the three dangling figures, trying to ignore their empurpled faces, black protruding tongues, popping eyes and stained breeches.

'These men?'

'They were shriven this morning, Friar,' the soldier interrupted. 'Before we turned them off the ladder.'

'How long will they hang?' he asked.

The fellow shrugged and Athelstan tried not to concentrate on the great yellowing ulcer on the right side of his face, the pus now suppurating, bubbling out, staining his cheek. The soldier, his eyes dead and full of drink, shrugged and grinned at his two companions, sallow, pimply youths already much the worse for wine.

'They will hang, Father, till sunset. Why do you ask?'

'I want to look at them.'

'They are to hang until sunset,' the serjeant repeated.

'Their clothes and belongings are ours. There is a canvas sheet for each of them, a swift prayer, and then into some forsaken grave to meet their maker.' He tapped one of the swaying bodies. 'Don't feel sorry for any of them, Father. They murdered a woman and cut her throat, after they brutally sliced her breasts, raped and burnt her over a fire!'

'Sweet Jesus have mercy on them!' Athelstan whispered. 'But I am here on the orders of Sir John Cranston, coroner of the city. I want to see them.'

He felt in his purse and threw down a couple of copper coins. The serjeant rubbed his chin and looked at them and then at the friar, sucking in air noisily through his blackened teeth. At last he rose and barked an order at one of the young men who placed the ladder lying on the ground against the scaffold, then gestured dramatically at Athelstan.

'Brother, the ladder awaits. Do what you want!'

Athelstan climbed the ladder slowly. He studied each of the corpses, noting how the rope had been tied firmly behind one ear. He moved around, inspecting each body carefully, holding his breath against the sour smell of corruption. At last he came down. Another coin was thrown on the ground. The serjeant looked up.

'What now, Brother?'

'Who hanged these men?'

'Well, we all did.'

'No, I mean who tied the ropes around their necks?'

'I did!' One of the pimply youths got up. 'I did, Brother. I do it expertly.'

'Would you say,' Athelstan asked, trying to hide his distaste at the glee in the young man's face, 'that each hangman arranges the knot in his own way?'

'Of, of course!'

'And from the noose you could tell which man you'd hanged and which you had not?'

'Naturally. A goldsmith has his mark, leaves his insignia on a plate. An artist who sketches a painting can recognise his own work. The same with the hangman. My knots are unique. I place them carefully.' The young man beamed expansively. 'I am skilled in my trade, Brother. I always make sure they take a long time to die.'

'Why?'

The fellow shrugged. 'Why not?'

'Do you enjoy it?'

'Well, the bastards deserve to suffer long.'

'And how do they suffer?'

'Oh, they kick a lot. They always kick.'

Athelstan pointed to the feet of the corpses.

'So, you always hang them without their boots on?'

'Yes, of course. Otherwise they would kick them off and we'd lose them. Some thief from the crowd might steal them and we'd be all the poorer. Why do you ask, Brother?'

The friar smiled and sketched a sign of the cross in the air. 'Nothing, my son, nothing at all.'

Athelstan turned and left the grisly bodies and walked back up Cheapside towards the Holy Lamb of God. He was convinced that Brampton and Vechey had been brutally murdered, though by whom he could not say.

He found Cranston dozing, comfortably ensconced in the inglenook of the tavern, a number of large empty pewter tankards arranged on the table before him. The ale wife walked over. Athelstan tossed her a coin and asked her to bring a fresh tankard and some wine whilst he roused Sir John. The coroner woke like a child, mumbling to himself, wondering where he was. Athelstan told him of the visits to the death house and the gibbet. The coroner nodded off to sleep again so, crossing to a barrel of dirty water, Athelstan filled the ladle and splashed it over Cranston's face. This time Sir John woke, shaking himself like a dog, mouthing the most terrible curses. He was only placated by the ale wife placing a frothing tankard in front of him and throwing him the most longing and sly of glances, as if he was Paris and she Helen of Troy. In the presence of such flattery and with the taste of ale once more on his lips, Sir John regained his good temper and this time listened attentively as Athelstan spoke. He belched loudly when the account was finished and picked at his teeth with a sliver of wood. Athelstan thought he was going off to sleep again but the coroner took one further gulp from his tankard.

'Sir John,' Athelstan said testily, 'we must discuss matters!'

'Yes, yes,' the coroner bellowed. 'Buy me another one of these and I will listen to you again!'

Athelstan did so. Sir John, now fully awake but still in his cups, belched and gazed around the tavern, murmuring what an excellent place it was. Athelstan remembered the hen roosting over the beer barrel and kept his own counsel. He sipped slowly at a cup of watered wine and decided to return to his church. The roof might not have been repaired. Cecily the courtesan might still be plying her trade. And what would happen to Godric? Fleetingly, he wondered once again if Benedicta had missed him. He looked through the narrow tavern window. The sun was beginning to set. It was time he was gone. The Springall business was hidden by a tissue of lies. He was too tired to probe and Cranston too drunk.

Athelstan rose to his feet. 'Sir John, look!'

The coroner glanced up blearily.

'Sir John, I can do nothing with you. I must go back to my church. Tomorrow or the day after, when you are in a better frame of mind, join me there.'

Athelstan picked up his leather bag, marched out of the tavern, collected Philomel and made his way slowly through the empty streets to London Bridge.

Cranston watched him go, then leaned back against the wall.

'Christ!' he murmured. 'I wish you'd stay, Athelstan, just for once!'

He groaned and pushed the tankard away. He had drunk enough and wished he hadn't. But the friar was not the only one with secrets and Sir John drank to drown his. No one remembered, except Maude who kept her thoughts to herself, that seven years ago this week his little child, Matthew, died suddenly, the victim of the plague which stalked the alleyways and streets of London. Cranston tightened his lips, blinking his eyes furiously as he always did when the tears threatened to return. Every day he thought of Matthew, the small angelic face, the blue eyes shimmering with innocence. Christ could not blame him for drinking. He'd drink and drink until the memory was gone. And why not? Yet drink clouded his mind, and in his heart, Cranston knew that Athelstan was right to disapprove. His maudlin drunkenness was not helping matters. There had been murder, deliberate and malicious, perpetrated in the Springall household. But where was the proof? He vaguely tried to remember what the friar had told him. Something about neither Brampton nor Vechey killing themselves. But where was the proof? Cranston tried to clear his thoughts. He, too, knew there was something wrong. Something was bothering him, something he had seen this morning at the bridge... He looked at the half-empty tankard.

'Christ, Matthew, I miss you!' he murmured. 'Oh, let the world hang itself!'

He was about to order another when he thought of Maude and his promise to her. At least tonight he would return halfway sober. Cranston pushed the tankard away and waddled out of the tavern to collect his horse and return to his house in Poultry.

Two days after he returned from the city, Athelstan rose early and went to examine his small garden. Outside he glared angrily about. Someone's pig had been rooting amongst the cabbage patch. Athelstan cursed in some of the language Cranston used on such occasions. He felt angry, agitated. He had come back to find his church safe but Godric gone.

'You see, Father,' Watkin the dung-collector explained, 'the silly bastard thought he could slip out, so he did, through the sacristy door. Of course, they were waiting for him, the sheriff's men. They beat him up in the alleyway, tied his hands and led him off to the Marshalsea. He'll probably hang!'

'Yes, Watkin,' Athelstan replied, 'he'll probably hang.'

Apart from that, everything had been in order except for Bonaventure, who had slipped away and had not been seen since. Athelstan hoped he was safe and would come padding back when he was hungry, tail in the air, miaowing for food and comfort.

The friar looked up. The sky was still blue; the sun, growing in strength, promised a hot sweltering day.

He sighed. He'd said his prayers and celebrated Mass, Benedicta just slipping in at the door and kneeling next to the baptismal font instead of coming further up the nave. Athelstan wondered if there was anything wrong. He moved down the side of his church to see if Crim was waiting on the steps but they were empty. He went back, took a hoe from inside the door of his house and stabbed furiously at the cabbage patch, trying to rearrange the furrows in neat order. Once Crim had arrived, he would go and see Hob the grave-digger, dying they said after he had slipped and fallen under a cartwheel, which had crushed his ribs.

Athelstan tired of his task. He threw the hoe to the ground, hoped that at least the pig had had a good meal, and went back inside his church. He looked around and felt happier. Simon the tiler had done a good job. The roof was secure against the coming winter rains. Huddle the painter had scraped the wall and begun a new fresco, his first church painting. Athelstan had requested that Huddle should first draw charcoal sketches, from these giving the gifted young man scriptural advice to the effect that there was no evidence whatsoever that Herod had eventually stabbed Pilate in the back! So the charcoaled drawings had been wiped out and Huddle had begun again, a lovely vigorous painting of the Annunciation and birth of Christ. The church floor was swept and washed clean, thanks to Cecily the courtesan who had earned her pennies honestly by scrubbing every inch.

'Honestly, Father,' she confessed, leaning on her broom of brittle twigs, 'I've changed. I intend to change.'

Athelstan stared into her childlike eyes and wondered if the woman was a little simple. The friar was sure he had seen her lying in the graveyard amongst the tombs with Simon the tiler, and he a married man with three children.

'So, Father,' she had whispered, moving closer and swinging her hips suggestively, 'can I play the part of the Virgin Mary in the parish masque for Corpus Christi?'

Athelstan had hidden his smile beneath a stern look and said he would discuss it with the church council.

'Watkin the dung-collector,' he advised, 'takes his duties as church warden most seriously. He has his own thoughts in the matter.'

'I don't give a fig for what Watkin says!' Cecily had snapped. 'I could tell you a lot about Watkin, Father!'

'Thank you, Cecily,' Athelstan had said. 'Soon the church will look nicer.'

Cecily got on with her cleaning. Athelstan felt sorry. Perhaps he had been a little too harsh with her. Cecily was a good girl who meant to do well. He could see no objection to her playing the part of the Virgin. The only obstacle was Watkin the dung-collector, whose own ample wife also had her eye on the role.

On balance, decided Athelstan, he was pleased. All was well, apart from Godric, Bonaventure, and of course the pardoner. Huddle had told him about the rogue, turning up in his garish garments and standing on the church steps, offering to sell pardons to those who could afford them. Athelstan swore that if he got his hands on the fellow, Cranston would have another murder to investigate.

He leaned against the rood screen and stared up at his newly repaired roof. He wondered where Cranston was. Why had he allowed two days to go by? Was he sulking or just ill with drinking? Athelstan couldn't leave his parish and go into the city, but he wished he could speak to the coroner, apologise for leaving him so abruptly the night before last. He hadn't meant to, it was just that he had become so tired, so exhausted with the Springalls, the murders, the deceit and the lies. He felt Vechey and Brampton had not committed suicide. He also suspected that Sir Thomas Springall had not been murdered by Brampton. The real murderers now hid in the shadows, mocking both him and Cranston, believing they would never search out the truth. Athelstan smiled thinly. Cranston, when he gathered his wits, would soon prove the bastards wrong.

Athelstan heard a sound and looked round. The church door opened and Crim, the young urchin, scampered in. His mother had taken special care to remove the dirt from his face and hands at least.

'Good morning, Crim,' Athelstan called. 'Come!'

He took a taper and lit it from the large wax candle burning in front of the statue of the Madonna.

'Now hold that and, as I walk through the street, you go before me carrying the light. And here,' he went behind the altar and took a small bell, 'you ring this. Now, if the candle goes out, don't be afraid. Just keep on walking and ringing the bell. You know where we are going?'

The little boy, round-eyed, shook his head.

'To Hob the grave-digger.'

'Oh. He's dying, Father!'

'Yes, Crim, I know. And he must die with Christ, so it's important we get there. Do you understand?'

The little fellow nodded solemnly. Athelstan, taking the keys from his belt, went up beneath the winking red sanctuary lamp and opened the tabernacle door. He took out the Viaticum, placing it in a small leather pouch which he slung round his neck, then went into the sacristy to collect the church's one and only cope. A faded, red and gold garment, showing the Holy Spirit as a dove with one wing, sending faded rays down on an even more faded Christ. Athelstan wrapped the cope around him and, telling Crim to go forward, they left the church, processing down the steps and into the maze of Southwark streets. Athelstan was always surprised at the effect he caused; here he was in a place where men died for the price of a few coins, but at the sight of the lighted wax candle, the sound of the small tinkling bell and him swathed in a cope, the coarsest men and women stood aside as if they acknowledged the great mysteries he carried.

Hob's cottage was a dour, earth-floored building divided into three rooms; one a bedroom for Hob and his wife, the second for his four children, the third a scullery and eating-place. It was poor but swept clean, a few pewter pots and pans, scrubbed in boiling water, hanging from nails in the wall. Inside, at the far end of the hut, Hob lay on a bed, his face white, the red blood frothing at his lips. Athelstan blessed the man, holding his hand, reassuring his good wife that all would be well whilst trying not to look at the blood. He gave the man the Viaticum and blessed him, anointing him on the head, chest, hands and feet. Afterwards he had a few words with Hob's wife, the children cowering around her. Athelstan promised he would do something to help her and left quietly, the cope still round his shoulders, Crim jumping up and down in front of him all the way back to the church.

Ranulf the rat-catcher was waiting for him just outside the door, a sleek, well-fed Bonaventure in his hands. He waited until Athelstan had put the black pouch back into the tabernacle and Crim had taken his penny and fled like the wind, before putting the cat down and approaching Athelstan.

'I found him waiting, Father, but if you want to sell him?'

Athelstan smiled.

'If you want him, Ranulf, he's yours. But I doubt if he will leave.'

The friar knelt down and tickled the cat between his ears. He looked up at the lined, seamed face of the rat-catcher, framed by his black, tarry leather hood.

'He's a mercenary. If you took him away, he'd be back tonight!'

Bonaventure agreed, stretched, and walked back to his favourite place at the base of the pillar.

Once Ranulf had gone, Athelstan sat on the altar steps, his mind going back to the corpses he had seen: Vechey's lying cold amongst those dreadful heads on the tower gate of London Bridge; Brampton's sheathed in dirty canvas in the death house of St Mary Le Bow; Springall lying alone under its leather covering in the great four poster bed in his mansion. What eluded him still? He thought of Hob dying in his hovel, his wife frightened of the future. Surely he could get some money for her from somewhere? He lifted his hands to his face and smelt the chrism he had used on Hob's head, hands, chest and feet. The feet!

Athelstan jumped up. Of course, that was it, Brampton's feet! The manservant hadn't committed suicide. He couldn't have done. He had been murdered!

Athelstan looked around the church. He wished Cranston were here. The sun streamed through the horn-glazed windows and Bonaventure stretched out, relaxing after a good night's hunting. Athelstan turned from the familiar, domestic sight and knelt before the altar, his eyes fixed on the red light.

'Oh, God,' he prayed, 'help me now. Please!'

In his own private chamber at his house in Poultry, Sir John also was thinking as he leant over his writing desk, quill in hand. He was engaged in the great love of his life: writing a treatise on the maintenance of law in the city of London. Cranston had a love of the law and, ever since his appointment as coroner, had been engaged in drawing up his own proposals for law reform. He would put them forward in a specially written book, bound in the finest calf, to some powerful patron who, in Cranston's dreams, would see them as the solution to all of London's problems.

Sir John loved the city, knew every stone, every church, every highway, every alleyway. Immersed in London's history, he was constantly begging the monks of Westminster Abbey, or the clerks of the chancery in the Tower, to let him have access to manuscripts and documents. Some he would take home, copying them out most carefully before returning them in their leather cases to their proper places. In a sense, Cranston never wished to finish his labour. He believed that his survey would be of use, but privately thought of it as his escape. No one else knew. No one except Maude, of course.

Cranston put down the pen, a wave of self-pity suffusing his huge body. He looked out of the window and heard the cries from Cheapside, the clatter of carts, the rattle against the cobbles of iron-shod horses going towards Smithfield and the horse market. He drank too much, Cranston knew that. He must give it up. He must reform his life. Virtuously, he patted his great stomach. But not today. Perhaps tomorrow. He wondered what Athelstan was doing. He speculated whether he should speak to the friar, open his heart, tell him his secrets, get rid of the sea of misery he felt bathing his body, drowning his mind.

Maude came in and Cranston looked at her, hang-dog, for even in bed his tourney of love was failing. He watched his wife carefully out of the corner of his eye as she busied herself, stacking blankets, opening chests, replacing candles in their holders. He studied her comely figure, her small, full breasts, clear face, bright eyes, ready smile, the slight sway when she walked. Cranston got up. Perhaps there was some-thing wrong, but it was not that serious. He moved over and embraced his wife, pulling her close to him.

'Oh, Sir John!' she whispered, nestling against him.

'Bolt the door!' he murmured thickly. 'Bolt the door. I wish to show you something!'

She turned, her eyes round.

'I suspect I have seen it before.'

Nevertheless, the door was locked, the window casement shut, and Cranston proved to his own satisfaction, as well as his wife's, that perhaps age had not yet drained the juices of his body. As they lay on the great four poster bed, their bodies entwined, Maude almost lost in Cranston's great fat folds, Sir John stared up at the ceiling, brushing his wife's hair with his cheek, listening to her chattering about this and that.

'What was that?' He pushed her away sharply.

'Sir John, what is the matter?'

'What did you just say?'

Maude shrugged. 'I was talking about Agnes, the wife of David the waterman. You often hire him to take us across the river. Well, she says that the boatmen and wharfers are drawing up a petition which they would like you to look at. They wish some of the arches of the bridge to be widened, the starlings to be replaced. The water level is so high, it is dangerous and boats are dashed against the pier or the arches. Sir John, men have drowned. Children as well!'

Cranston sat up in bed, his fat body quivering with pleasure.

'That's what was wrong! Now I know what I saw on the bridge!' He turned and embraced his surprised wife, kissing her passionately on the forehead and cheeks.

'Maude, whatever would I do without you? You and your chatter. Of course! I wonder if Athelstan thought of that?'

Despite his huge bulk, Cranston leapt out of bed.

'Come, Maude! Come, wife, quickly! Fresh hose, a clean shirt, a cup of claret, a meat pie and a manchet loaf! I must be off! Come on!'

Lady Maude moved just as quickly, glaring at her husband. One minute he was embracing her, kissing her passionately, and now he was leaping around the bedroom like a young gallant, getting ready to get out. Nevertheless, she scurried around, putting on her dress and smock whilst muttering how, if other people had left her alone, she would have things ready anyway.

Sir John ignored her, dressing hastily; he now knew that Vechey had been murdered. Had to have been. The level of the river water would prove that. He would drag that bloody friar from his stars and they would go back to the Springall mansion and this time demand answers to their questions.

Chapter 5

As soon as Athelstan skirted the church, he saw the coroner standing beside Philomel. The old destrier was saddled and ready to depart. Cranston grinned.

'Good morning, Brother!' he bellowed, loud enough for half the parish to hear. 'Your horse is ready. Your saddlebags are packed.' He held them up. 'Quills, pens, writing tray, parchment, and I have ensured the inkhorn is well sealed, so if it spills, don't blame me.'

Athelstan, still feeling depressed after his visit to Hob's wife, ignored the coroner and pushed by him into his small, two-roomed house. Cranston followed like an unwelcome draught, sweeping in, filling the room with his broad girth.

'Really, Brother!' he boomed, as he looked around. 'You should live in a little more comfort. Do you have any wine?'

Athelstan gestured towards an earthenware jug and watched with delight as Cranston took a great gulp, then, his face puce as a plum, went to the door to spit it out.

'God's teeth, man! More water than wine!' he snapped.

'St Dominic and my Order,' Athelstan said tartly, 'have in their wisdom decreed that wine at full strength is not for monks.' He tapped Cranston's great girth. 'Perhaps not even for king's coroners!'

Cranston drew himself up to his full height and squinted at Athelstan.

'My orders, little friar, are that you are to accompany me into Cheapside to a tavern called the Bear and Ragged Staff. You have heard of it?'

Athelstan shook his head, his heart sinking. Cranston smirked.

'We are going to sit there. I shall remain sober and tell you how Vechey was murdered. He did not commit suicide.'

'And I shall tell you, my Lord Coroner, how Edmund Brampton, steward to Sir Thomas Springall, did not hang himself in the garret of that house in Cheapside!'

'So you have been thinking, Friar?'

'Coroner, I never stop.'

'Well, come on then!'

'Sir John, we could stay here and discuss our concerns.'

Cranston turned, shaking his head. 'Here? Where every little snot from Southwark can come knocking at your door, bothering you with their complaints. Oh, no, Brother. Our stop at the Bear and Ragged

Staff is only half our journey. We go then to Newgate, and perhaps elsewhere.'

So saying, he strode out of the house. Athelstan breathed a prayer for patience, made a sign of the cross over himself and followed suit. Cranston, now mounted, watched him.

'Aren't you going to lock your door?' he bellowed.

'What's the use?' Athelstan replied. 'If I do, thieves will break it down thinking there is something valuable to steal.'

Snorting at the friar's apparent stupidity, Cranston turned his horse and led them out of the main alleyways of Southwark. A group of urchins, recognising Sir John, followed from afar and, despite Athelstan's pleas, shouted insults about the coroner's ponderous girth. Garth the woodcutter, who also took the death carts round the streets, was drinking outside the tavern and joined in the noisy abuse.

'Sir John Cranston!' he bellowed, tapping his own round belly. 'You must be pregnant. What will it be, boy or girl?'

That was too much for the coroner. He reined in his horse and glared at his cheery-faced tormentor.

'If I was pregnant by you,' he shouted back, 'then it would be a bloody great Barbary ape!'

And, amidst the raucous laughter which greeted this repartee, Athelstan and Cranston continued on their way to London Bridge. They crossed over quietly enough, Athelstan smiling as he passed through the gateway at the far end on to Fish Street Hill. He wondered how the little man was coping, remembered the heads and concluded it was an acquaintance he would not wish to renew.

The fine day had brought the crowds pouring into London, varlets, squires, and men-at-arms accompanying knights north to the great horse fair at Smithfield, after which there would be tournaments and tourneys. The streets were packed with men, helmeted and armed, and great destriers caparisoned in all the colours and awesome regalia of war moved majestically along Fish Street Hill. High in the saddle rode the knights, resplendent in coloured surcoats, their slit-eyed helmets swinging from saddle bows, bannered lances carried before them by squires. Hordes of others followed on foot: retainers gaudy in the livery of great lords, and the bright French silks of young gallants who swarmed into the city like butterflies under the warm sun and blue skies. They thronged the taverns, their coloured garments a sharp contrast to the dirty leather aprons of the blacksmiths and the short jerkins and caps of the apprentices.

As Cranston and Athelstan turned into Cheapside, they saw the festive spirit had spread. Stalls were out and there were mummers performing miracle plays. Men shouted themselves hoarse proclaiming cock fights, dog battles, and savage contests never seen before between wild hogs and mangy bears. The crowds had impeded the dung carts, and the piles of rubbish and refuse were everywhere, the flies rising in thick black swarms.

'God's teeth!' Cranston said. 'Come, Athelstan.'

They had to dismount and force their way through, past the Conduit and the Tun and up a small alleyway which led into the Bear and Ragged Staff. They stabled their horses and did not enter the tavern but passed into a pleasant garden beyond. A private place with a chessboard garden, a square divided into four plots by small gravelled walks and paths. These were fringed by a hedge of varying shrubs and small trees – white-thorn, privet, sweetbriar and the occasional rose – all entwined together. They sat against the wall on turfed seats in the shade, looking out over raised herb banks of hyssop, lavender and other fragrant shrubs. A slattern brought a small table for Athelstan to rest his writing tray on, and of course a jug of wine and two goblets, though Athelstan shook his head and asked for water. They sat and enjoyed the fragrant smells and the coolness after their dusty ride through the city.

'I could stay here all day,' Athelstan said, leaning back against the wall. 'So quiet, so peaceful.'

'You would prefer to be back in your monastery?'

Athelstan smiled. 'I didn't say that!'

'But you do not like your work?'

'I did not say that either.' He turned and looked at Cranston, noting how the fat coroner's face was dewed with drops of sweat. 'Do you like yours, Sir

John? The murder, the lies, the deceits? Do you remember,' Athelstan asked, 'I once quoted Bartholomew the Englishman?'

Cranston looked expectant.

'He wrote a book entitled *The Nature of Things*,' Athelstan continued, 'in which he described the planet Saturn as cold as ice, dark as night, and malignant as Satan. He claims that the planet governs the murderous intent of men.' Athelstan squinted, watching the bees hover round a succulent rose. 'I often think it governs mine. You heard Fortescue refer to my own brother?' Cranston nodded. 'My father owned a prosperous farm to the south, in Sussex. I was intended for the religious life. My brother was destined to till the soil. Now there's a road which goes by our farm down to the coast. We used to see the men-at-arms, the crossbow men on their way to the ports for the crossing to France, then we'd watch them return laden with booty. We heard the legends and romantic stories about knights in shining armour, war horses moving majestically across green fields.

'One spring I left my noviciate and came back to the farm. The next party of soldiers which passed, my brother and I joined. We sailed from Dover, landing at Honfleur, joining one of the many bands plundering across France.' Athelstan stared up at the sky. 'We were under the command of the Black Prince with his general Walter de Manny and others. Our dreams soon died. No chivalrous knights, no majestic armies moving according to rules, but horrible deeds, towns gutted and burnt, women and children slain. Then one day my brother and I, serving as archers, were caught outside a town by a group of French horsemen. We took up our positions, driving stakes into the ground in the usual pattern. The French charged sooner than we thought. They were amongst us, hacking and killing.'

Athelstan stopped to compose himself before continuing: 'When it was over, my brother was dead and I had aged a hundred years. I might as well tell you, Cranston. I returned home. I'll never forget my father's face. I'd never seen him like that. He just stared at me. My mother? All she could do was crouch in a corner and sob. I think she cried till the day she died. My father soon followed her to the grave. I went back to my Order. Oh, they accepted me, but life was harsh. I had to do private and public penance, and take a solemn vow that, after I was ordained, I would accept whatever duties my superiors gave me.'

Athelstan snorted with laughter and leaned forward, his arms crossed, as if he was talking to himself and had forgotten the coroner sitting beside him. 'Whatever duties! Hard study and the most menial work the house could provide; cleaning sewers, digging ditches and, after ordination, I must go here, I must go there! Eventually I protested so Father Prior took me for a walk in the meadows and said I was to prove my worth with one final task.'

He leaned back against the wall. 'My final task was St Erconwald's in Southwark.' Athelstan stared across at Cranston. 'My father prior chose well. My parents accused me of the murder of my brother. Every day in Southwark someone dies. Men and women drenched with drink, quarrelling and violently fighting each other. In some alleyway or runnel, a man hacked to death for stealing ale. A woman slashed from jaw to groin found floating in a ditch. And then you, Sir John! Just in case I should forget, or withdraw, or hide behind my church walls, you are here, ready to lead me along the streets, remind me that there is no escape from murder, from witnessing the greatest sin of all – a man slaying his brother!'

Cranston drained his cup of wine and said, 'Perhaps your father prior is wiser than you think.'

'What do you mean?'

'I am writing a treatise, have been for years, on the maintenance of the king's peace in London. The most terrible crime is murder. The belief that a man can kill someone, walk away, and say, "I am not responsible". I am no theologian, Athelstan, nor a scripture scholar, but the first crime committed after Eden was one of murder: Cain plotting to slay his brother Abel and afterwards claiming he knew nothing about it.' Cranston grinned. 'The first great mystery – I mean murder. But nothing like what happened to your brother.' He turned and spat. 'That wasn't murder. That was young dreams and hot blood, minds crammed with stupid stories about Troy and Knights of the Round Table. No, murder is different. And why do men commit murder, Athelstan? For profit? And what will stop men murdering? Hanging, torture?' He shrugged. 'Go down to Newgate, as we will do later. The prison is packed with murderers, the gibbets are heavy like apple trees in the autumn, the branches bend with their rotten fruit.'

Cranston moved closer, his face more serious than Athelstan had ever seen it. 'What will prevent murder, robbery, arson, is when the perpetrator knows, believes, accepts in his heart, that he will be caught and he will be punished. The more vigilant we are, the fewer murders, the fewer deaths. The fewer women slashed from jaw to groin, the fewer men with their throats cut, hanging in a garret or swinging from some beam under a bridge. Your prior knows, Athelstan, that with your guilt and deep sense of justice, you are well suited to such a task.'

He laughed abruptly and went back to his wine cup. 'If your order produced more men like you, Athelstan, and fewer preachers and theologians, London would be a safer place. That's the reason I have brought you to this quiet garden, not to some tavern where I would drink myself senseless. No, I want to plot and catch an evil murderer. A man who has slain Thomas Springall and blamed it on poor Brampton, afterwards making his death look like suicide. I believe the same villain executed Vechey and strung his corpse up like carrion under London Bridge.'

Athelstan drank greedily from the water cup, refusing to look at Cranston. He had talked about his brother's death, and for the first time ever someone had not laid the blame at his door. Athelstan knew it would make no immediate difference, but a seed had been planted in his soul. The possibility that he had committed a sin but no murder. That he would atone for it and so the slate would be wiped clean. He put down the cup.

'You say Springall was murdered by someone else, not Brampton?' he asked abruptly.

'I do,' said Cranston. 'And so do you. And how can we prove that? The loose thread in this rotten tapestry is Vechey. Now, you may remember when we inspected his corpse, we noticed the water had soaked him up to his knees?'

'Yes,' Athelstan nodded.

'We also know that if Vechey committed suicide, he must have done it in the early hours, just before dawn. Correct?' Again Athelstan nodded.

'But that is impossible,' Cranston continued with a self-satisfied smirk. 'You see, after midnight, the Thames runs fast and full. The water rises and it would almost cover the arch. There would be, at the very most, a foot between the surface of the water and the beam Vechey used to hang himself.' He held up his stubby fingers. 'First, are we to accept that a man waded through water up to his neck to tie a noose to hang himself? Or that he hanged himself virtually under water? Yet when Vechey's corpse was found, somehow or other it had dried out except beneath the knees.'

Athelstan grinned. '*Mirabile dictu*, Sir John! Of course the river would be full. Vechey would have had to swim out to hang himself and that is a logical contradiction. So what do you think happened?'

'Vechey was drugged or knocked on the head, the corpse being strung up for others to find.'

'But why such contrivance?'

'I have been wondering about that,' Cranston replied. 'Remember, we know very little about the man. Vechey was promiscuous. He liked soft and perfumed flesh but, being a respectable citizen, he would hunt well away from his home in Cheapside. So I think he went down to the stews and bawdy houses along the river. Somehow or other he was trapped, knocked on the head or drugged, and his body taken down to London Bridge. The noose was tied around his neck and strung over the beam. The murderer was very clever, and the riverbank was deserted. The bridge, as the dwarf told us, was a favourite place for people to commit suicide. The murderer made one mistake. He probably inspected the area when the water had fallen well below the starlings. He forgot that when he came to hang up Vechey's corpse the river would have risen, covering any suitable platform for a suicide to stand on.'

'Yet he still went ahead. Why?'

'Because Vechey was probably dead, strangled before he ever reached that bridge, and what else could the murderer do with the corpse? Throw it in the river still bearing the noose-mark, or cart it round London and risk capture looking for a new gibbet!'

Athelstan smiled. 'Perfect, Sir John.'

'And Brampton?'

'You may remember, or perhaps not,' Athelstan replied, 'that Brampton's corpse was dressed in hose and a linen shirt. First, do we really accept that a man in the act of undressing suddenly decides halfway through that he will hang himself and goes up to the garret without his boots on to carry out the terrible act? Now, even if he had, the garret floor was covered with pieces of glass and dirt. However, when I examined the soles of Brampton's feet, there were no marks or cuts. Yet there should have been if he had walked across that floor without his boots on. In fact, there was very little dust on the soles of his hose. The only conclusion is that Brampton died like Vechey. He was carried up to that garret, probably in a state of stupor, drunk or drugged. The rope was tied round his neck. He fought for a while, hence the strands of cord found under the fingernails, but he was murdered and left there to hang so others would think he had taken his own life.'

Cranston pursed his lips and smiled. 'Most logical, Brother.'

'The other factor,' Athelstan continued, 'is that Vechey and Brampton supposedly hanged themselves. Now, I examined the bruise on each of the corpses. It is a remarkable coincidence that two men, relative strangers, put a noose knot in exactly the same place, Vechey copying Brampton in every particular when he hanged himself. I went down to the execution yard where I saw three corpses. The executioner himself said that each hangman has his own hallmark. The three corpses I studied there had the noose placed in the same spot. Vechey and Brampton also had the noose placed in the same spot. The only logical conclusion is that Brampton and Vechey were hanged by the same person.'

Athelstan picked up a quill with a modest flourish, uncapped the inkhorn and dipped in his pen. Cranston leant nearer. Athelstan found himself relishing the closeness. He felt as if he was back in time with his brother, plotting some mischief.

'As the good book says, let us start with the last. Vechey—' Athelstan wrote the name '—hanged by the neck under London Bridge. It appears he took his own life, but the truth is that he was murdered. By whom and how?' Athelstan drew a question mark and looked up at Cranston.

'Perhaps we will know soon,' Cranston observed. 'On my way down, I sent a message to the sheriff's office at the Guildhall and asked for two cursitors to make diligent inquiries amongst the taverns and stews along this side of the river. Perhaps they will discover something. Vechey was a fairly well-known man, a goldsmith. He would dress the part, even though he wore a cloak or hood. Such places tend to know their customers.'

'Secondly,' Athelstan continued writing, 'we have Brampton, steward of Sir Thomas Springall, who died apparently by his own hand in the garret of Springall's house.'

Cranston watched Athelstan's pen race across the page.

'We know it was murder not suicide, but how and by whom?'

Another question mark.

'Finally,' Athelstan concluded, 'Sir Thomas Springall was murdered in his own bed chamber by a cup of poisoned wine which was placed there by Brampton. But we have Dame Ermengilde's assurance that no one went up to Sir Thomas's chamber after Brampton had visited him. Nor did anyone enter the chamber after he retired. We know Sir Thomas drank the poisoned cup inside the room and not at the banquet, otherwise his death would have been public and in company.'

Athelstan wrote carefully. Cranston, craning his neck, followed the words forming quickly in the blue-green ink.

'So many questions, Sir John, so few answers. So where do we begin?'

Cranston jabbed one stubby finger at Athelstan's last few words.

'We will begin there. We have not fully scrutinised Springall's death. That is the key. If we solve that, the rest will unravel like a piece of cloth.'

'Easier said than done, Sir John, and you have only had one cup of refreshment!'

'Enough for the day is the evil thereof, friar. You should know that.'

Athelstan picked up his quill again. 'We have three riddles. First, Genesis, Chapter 3, Verse 1; secondly, the Book of the Apocalypse Chapter 6, Verse 8. And, thirdly, the shoemaker.'

'The shoemaker means nothing to me,' Cranston replied. 'But the verses... apparently Sir Thomas liked to tease his colleagues, and they would be curious. Vechey probably carried the verses around trying to solve the riddle. Oh,' the coroner grinned, 'my apologies for not telling you about Eudo the page boy but, according to my memory, there was nothing suspicious, just a fall from a window.'

The friar made a face. 'If Chief Justice Fortescue asked for a report, we could pose many questions and few solutions, Sir John.'

'That is why,' the coroner barked, getting up, 'we are off to Newgate to see Solper.' He grinned at Athelstan. 'Every morning the Guildhall send me a list of those indicted to hang. Young Solper was on this list, not before time. A rat from the sewer, but one of my best informants. Let us see if he wants to live!'

He strode away, leaving Athelstan scrambling to clear his writing tray, repack the leather bag and follow him out to the yard. Cranston had already ordered their horses to be brought out into Cheapside. They rode through the marketplace. The noise, clamour and dusty heat prevented any conversation. Cranston looked around him.

Yes, he would mention this in his treatise, he thought. There should be beadles placed at every corner, each covering his own section of the marketplace, and others mingling with the crowd. This would cut down on the number of naps, foists and pickpockets who plagued these places like the locusts of Egypt. His mind drifted and he let his horse find its path through the crowds. Athelstan pulled his hood over his head as he felt the heat of the sun on the back of his neck. He wondered what Sir John Cranston wanted at Newgate.

They moved out of Cheapside up towards the old city wall which housed the infamous gaol, past the small church of Nicholas Le Quern near Blow-Bladder Street and into the great open space before the prison. This was really no more than two huge towers linked by a high curtain wall. The area in front of Newgate, Athelstan thought, must be the nearest thing to hell on earth. There was a market down the centre, the stalls facing out, but the air and ground were polluted with the blood, dirt and ordure which ran down from the shambles where the animals were slaughtered and the gore allowed to find its own channel. Sometimes the blood oozed into great black puddles over which huge swarms of flies hovered. Athelstan was glad that Cranston had decided to ride.

The marketplace itself was full of people, jostling and fighting their way to the stalls, their tempers not helped by the heat, dust and flies. In front of the prison gate every type of disreputable under heaven was now thronging: pickpockets, knaves, and apple squires, as well as the relatives of debtors and other people trying to gain access to their loved ones. Cranston and Athelstan stabled their horses in a dingy tavern and walked back, forcing their way through to the great prison door. Outside, standing on a beer barrel, a member of the ward watch rang a hand bell which tolled like a death knell through the noisy clamour of the place.

'You prisoners,' the fellow was shouting, 'that are within for wickedness and sin, know now that after many mercies you are appointed to die just before noon tomorrow!'

On and on he went, shouting the usual rubbish about God's mercy and justice over all. Cranston and Athelstan pushed by him and hammered at the great gate. A grille was opened, revealing an evil, narrow-faced, yellow-featured man with eyes of watery blue and a mouth as thin as a vice.

'What do you want?' the fellow snapped, his lips curled back to reveal blackened stumps of teeth. Cranston pushed his face to the grille.

'I am Sir John Cranston, king's coroner in the city. Now open up!'

The grille slammed shut and they heard the noise of footsteps. A small postern door in the great gate opened. A guard stepped out with a club, forcing others back as Cranston and Athelstan were waved in. They shoved by, the stale odour of the gate-keeper's body making them choke. They stepped into the lodge or small chamber where the keeper always greeted new prisoners.

'I wish to see the keeper, Fitzosbert!' Cranston snapped.

The fellow grinned and took them along a dark, smelly passageway into another chamber where the keeper of Newgate, Fitzosbert, was squatting behind a great oak table like a king enthroned in his palace. Athelstan had heard about the fellow but this was the first time he had met him. Indeed, anyone who had any business with the law in London knew Fitzosbert's fearsome reputation. A very rich and therefore powerful man, as head keeper of Newgate, Fitzosbert had the pick of all the prisoners' possessions as well as the sale of concessions, be it beds, sheets, coals, drink, food, even a wench. Anyone who entered the prison had to pay a fee and Athelstan recollected that one of his parishioners, too poor to pay, had been beaten up for his poverty whilst Fitzosbert had stood by, smiling all the time. The keeper, Athelstan concluded, was not a pleasant man and on seeing him, the friar believed every story he had heard. He had a louse-ridden face, dirty blond hair and carmine-painted lips. Fitzosbert's sunken cheeks were liberally rouged and this made his bulbous grey eyes seem even more fish-like. The friar just stared at him and concluded that Fitzosbert would have liked to have been born a woman. Only that would explain his short lace-trimmed jerkin and the tight red hose. Athelstan smiled, revelling in fantasies of revenge, but Fitzosbert, however, had already dismissed him with a flicker of his eyes and was staring coolly at Sir John as if to prove he was not cowed by any show of authority.

'You have warrants, Sir?'

'I don't need warrants!' Cranston snapped. 'I am the king's coroner. I wish to see a prisoner.'

'Who?'

'Nathaniel Solper.'

Fitzosbert smiled. 'And your business with him?'

'My own.'

Again Fitzosbert smiled though Athelstan had seen more humour and warmth on the silver plate of a coffin lid.

'You must explain, Sir John.' The fellow placed two effete ring-bedecked hands on the desk before him. 'I cannot allow anyone, even the regent himself, to come wandering through my prison asking to see prisoners, especially such as Solper. He's a condemned man.'

'He's not yet hanged and I wish to speak with him, now!' Cranston leaned over the table, placing his hands over those of Fitzosbert and pressing down hard until the keeper's face paled and beads of sweat broke out on his brow.

'Now look, Master Fitzosbert,' Cranston continued slowly, 'if you wish, I will leave now. And tomorrow I will come back with warrants duly signed and sealed by the regent, and accompanied by a group of soldiers from the Tower. Then I will go through this prison, see Solper, and perhaps...' He smiled. 'We all have friends. Perhaps petitions could be presented in the Commons. Petitions demanding an investigation of your accounts. I am sure the Barons of the Exchequer would be interested in the profits to be made in the king's prison, and in what happens to money entrusted to you.'

Fitzosbert pursed his lips. 'I agree!' he muttered.

Cranston stood back. 'And now, sir, Solper!'

The keeper got up and minced out of the room. Athelstan and Cranston followed him, the friar fascinated by the man's swaying walk. He was about to nudge Cranston and congratulate him on his skills of persuasion, when he heard a sound and turned quickly. Two huge gaolers, with the bodies of apes and the faces of cruel mastiffs, padded silently behind them. Fitzosbert stopped and turned.

'Gog and Magog!' he sang out. 'They are my bodyguards, Sir John, my assistants in case I am attacked.'

Cranston's hand flew immediately to his sword. He pulled out the great blade, tapping the toe of his boot with it.

'This is my servant, Master Fitzosbert! May I remind you that I carry the king's warrant. If anything happens to me, it's treason!'

'Of course.' Fitzosbert's smile made him look more hideous than ever. They walked on, wandering through a warren of tortuous passageways where the noise and stench grasped Athelstan by the throat. He had heard that Newgate was a hellhole, but now he experienced it firsthand and understood why some prisoners went quickly insane. There were many who talked and sang incessantly, whilst others, particularly the women, who knew they were not there for too long, refused to clean themselves and lay about like sows in their own filth. Deeper into the prison they walked, past one open chamber where the limbs of quartered men lay like joints of meat on a butcher's stall, waiting to be soaked with salt and cumin seed before being tarred. Deeper into the hell, Athelstan shivered, folding his arms into the voluminous sleeves of his robe. Mad faces pushed against the grilles in the doors, tortured ones begging for mercy. The guilty baying their hatred, the innocent quietly pleading for a hearing. At last Fitzosbert stopped at one cell door and clicked his fingers. One of the giants shuffled forward, a ring of keys in his huge fist. A key was inserted in the lock and the door opened. Fitzosbert whispered something and the giant nodded and pushed his way into the cell. They heard screams, kicks, the sickening thud of a punch, and the ogre roaring Solper's name. He reappeared, grasping the unfortunate by the scruff of his shabby collar. Fitzosbert went up to the prisoner and tapped him gently on the cheek.

'Master Solper, you are fortunate. You have important visitors. Someone I believe you know, Sir John Cranston, and his—' he looked coyly at Athelstan '—companion.'

The friar ignored him, staring at Solper. The prisoner was nothing remarkable: young, white-faced, and so filthy it was difficult to tell where one garment ended and another began.

'We need a chamber to talk to this man,' demanded Cranston.

The head keeper shrugged and led them back up a passageway to a cleaner empty cell. The door was left open. Cranston waved Solper to a seat.

'Master keeper!' he called.

Fitzosbert came back into the room and Cranston laid some silver on the table.

'Some wine, bread, and two of your cleanest cups!'

The head keeper scooped up the coins as deftly as any tax collector. A few minutes later one of the

164

giant gaolers pushed back into the cell, carrying a tray with all Cranston had asked for. He placed it on the table and left slamming the door behind him. The young prisoner just sat nervously on a stool watching Athelstan. Cranston took one of the cups and a small white loaf and thrust them into his hands.

'Well, Solper, we meet again.'

The man licked his lips nervously.

Cranston grinned wolfishly. 'You have been condemned?'

'Yesterday, before the Justices,' the young man squeaked in reply, his voice surprisingly high.

'On what charge?'

'Counterfeiting coins.'

'Ah, yes! Let me introduce you, Brother,' Cranston said. 'Master Solper, counterfeiter, thief, footpad and seller of relics. Two years ago, Master Solper could get you anything: a piece of cloth from the napkins used at the Last Supper, a hair from the beard of St Joseph, part of a toy once used by the Baby Christ. Master Solper has tried his hand at – well, God only knows! You are marked?'

The young man nodded and pulled down his dirty jerkin. Athelstan saw the huge 'F' branded into his right shoulder, proclaiming him a felon.

'Twice indicted, the third time caught,' Cranston intoned. 'You are due to hang, and yet you may evade justice.'

Athelstan saw the hope flare in the young man's eyes. He squirmed nervously on the stool.

'What do you want? What do I have to do?'

'The Sons of Dives, have you ever heard of them?'

The young man pulled a face.

'Have you or haven't you?'

'Yes, everybody has. In the Guilds,' the young man continued, 'there are always small groups or societies prepared to lend money at high interest rates to the nobles or to other merchants. They take names and titles: the Keepers of the Gate, the Guardians of the Coffers.' He shrugged. 'The Sons of Dives are another group.'

'And their leader?'

'Springall, Sir Thomas Springall. He's well known.'

'Now, another matter.'

Cranston delved into a small leather pouch he had taken from his saddlebag, undid the cord at the neck and drew out a small vase containing the poison he had taken from Springall's house. He unstoppered the jar and handed it over.

'Smell that!'

The young man gingerly lifted the rim to his nose, took one sniff, made a face and handed it back.

'Poison!'

'Good man, Solper, poison. This is the real reason I came. I half guessed who the Sons of Dives were. But if I wanted to buy poison, a rare exotic poison such as belladonna, crushed diamond or arsenic, where would I go?'

The young man looked across at Athelstan.

'Any monastery or friary has them. They are often used in the paints they mix for the illuminated manuscripts.'

'Ah, yes, but you can't very well knock on a monastery gate and say, "May I have some poison?" and expect the father abbot or prior to hand it over without a question. Without taking careful note of who you are, why you asked and what you want it for. So where else? The apothecary, Master Solper?'

Cranston eased his great bulk on the table. Athelstan watched nervously. The table, not being the strongest, creaked and groaned in protest under his weight.

'Master Solper,' Cranston continued conversationally, 'I have come here offering you your life. Not much perhaps, but if you answer my questions, I can arrange for a pardon to be sent down under the usual condition: that you abjure the realm. You know what that means? Straight as an arrow to the nearest port, secure a passage and go elsewhere. Anywhere – Outremer, France, Scythia, Persia – but not England, and certainly not London! You do understand?'

The young man licked his lips. 'Yes,' he muttered.

'And if you do not satisfy my curiosity,' Cranston continued, 'I am going to knock on the door, leave, and tomorrow you will hang. So, if I want to buy a poison in London, where would I go?'

'Nightshade House.'

'Where's that?'

'It's owned by Simon Foreman. It's in an alleyway.' The young man screwed up his eyes, concentrating on getting the facts right. 'That's right, a street called Piper Street, Nightshade House in Piper Street. Simon Foreman would sell anything for a great price and not ask any questions. It is probable the poison in that phial came from him. He could tell you.'

'One further question. Sir Thomas Springall – you knew of him?'

The young man nodded his head towards the door.

'Like Fitzosbert, he liked young boys, the softer and more pliant the better, or so the whisper says. He went to houses where such people meet. Springall was also a moneylender, a usurer. He had few friends and many enemies. There was gossip about him.' The young man drained his cup and sat cradling it, eyes fixed on the wine remaining in the jug. 'It was only a matter of time before someone used that information.' He shrugged. 'But Springall had powerful friends at court and in the church. No bailiff or constable would touch him. He and all his kind meet in a tavern outside the city on the Mile End Road – it's called the Gaveston. You can buy what you want there, as long as you pay in good gold. That's all I know.'

Fitzosbert banged on the door.

'Sir John, are you finished?'

'Yes,' Cranston called. 'Listen!' he said to Solper. 'You are sure you know nothing else?'

The young fellow shook his head. 'I have told you all I know. The pardon, you will keep your word?'

'Of course. God keep you, Solper,' he muttered and went towards the door just as Fitzosbert threw it open. The coroner gently pushed the keeper out before him, took out his purse and clinked a few coins into his hand.

'I thank you again for your hospitality, Fitzosbert,' he said. 'Look after our friend here. Some more wine, a better cell. Letters will come down from the Guildhall tomorrow. You will act accordingly. You understand?'

Fitzosbert smiled and winked. 'Of course, Sir John. No problem. I will carry out any order given to me by such an illustrious coroner of the city.'

Cranston pulled a face and he and the friar walked as fast as dignity would allow from that loathsome place. When the great gate of Newgate slammed behind them, Cranston leaned against it, gasping for clean air, his great body quivering like a beached whale's.

'Thank God!' he spluttered. 'Thank God to be out of there! Pray to your God and anyone else you know that you never land up in the power of Fitzosbert, in one of those Godforsaken cells!'

He looked up at the great tower soaring above him.

'If I had my way, I would burn the entire place to the ground and hang Fitzosbert on a scaffold as high as the sky. But, come, Whitefriars and the Springall mansion await.'

Chapter 6

They collected their horses and made their way down Fleet Street towards the high white chalk store building of Whitefriars. As the press of people was so great, they walked their horses.

'Do you think Solper was right about Springall?' asked Athelstan.

Sir John nodded. 'I suspected as much. Many men have such inclinations. Yet, you know the sentence for such crimes: boiled alive in a great vat over a roaring fire at Southwark. Not the usual end for a powerful London merchant! Hence the secrecy, and hence perhaps the vicious quarrel with Brampton, the rather effete manners of Master Buckingham, as well as the fact that Sir Thomas did not sleep with his wife.' He looked slyly at the friar. 'Such a woman, such a body! It fair makes your mouth water. Why should a real man lock himself away from such pleasures, eh?' He stopped momentarily to watch a juggler. 'Springall, like many a man,' he said, pushing forward again, 'had his public life and his private one. I suspect if the drapes were really pulled aside, we would find a stinking mess.' He lifted his hand and gestured to the great houses on either side, soaring four storeys above them, blocking out the hot afternoon sun. 'In any of these buildings scandal, sin, failings and weaknesses are to be found. They even say,' he nudged Athelstan playfully, 'that vices similar to Springall's are found in monasteries and amongst friars. What do you think of that, Brother, eh?'

'I would say that priests are like any other men, be they lawyer or coroner, Sir John, they have their weaknesses. And, but for the grace of God…' Athelstan let his voice trail away. 'But why are we here?' he asked angrily, realising they were entering the area around the great Carmelite monastery.

Cranston touched him on the arm and pointed to the far corner, just past the huge gateway. An emaciated fellow with jet black hair, thin lips and large brooding eyes caught the friar's eye. The man was dressed completely in black, his dark cloak covered with the most fantastic symbols: pentangles, stars, moons, suns, and on his head a pointed hat. He had laid out a great canvas sheet before him, bearing different phials and small bowls. Now he stood still, his very appearance drawing the people around him.

'Watch this!' Cranston whispered. 'The fellow's our guide.'

The man took out two small whistles and, pushing one into each corner of his mouth, began to play a strange, rhythmic, haunting tune. He then put down the instruments and held up powerful hands.

'Ladies and gentlemen, knights, courtiers, members of the Guild!' He caught Athelstan's eye. 'Friars, priests, citizens of London! I am Doctor Mirablis. I have studied in Byzantium and Trezibond, and travelled across the land to the great Cham of Tartary. I have seen battle fleets in the Black Sea and the great war galleons of the Caspian. I have supped with the Golden Horde of Genghis Khan. I have crossed deserts, visited fabulous cities, and in my journeys, I have amassed many secrets and mysteries!'

His claims were greeted with roars of laughter. Cranston and Athelstan drew closer. An apprentice from a nearby stall took out a bullock horn, scooped some dirty water from a rain barrel and began to sprinkle the magician with it. Dr Mirabilis just ignored him and held up his hands, calming the clamour and good-natured catcalls.

'I will show you I have power over matter. Over the very birds in the air.' He turned, pointing up to the top of the monastery wall. 'See that pigeon there!' Everyone's eyes followed the direction of his finger. 'Now, look,' the fellow continued, and taking a piece of black charcoal, painted a rough picture of the bird on the monastery wall. He then began to stab the drawing, uttering magical incantations. The clamour grew around him, Cranston and Athelstan moved closer, their hands on their wallets as the crowd was infested with naps, foists and pickpockets as a rick of hay with mice and rats. Mirabilis continued to stab the picture, muttering low-voiced curses, looking up at the walls where the pigeon was still standing. Suddenly the bird, as if influenced by the magical incantations against the picture below, twitched and dropped down dead. The 'oohs' and 'ahs' of reverence which greeted this would have been the envy of any priest or preacher. Cranston grinned and gripped Athelstan by the wrist.

'Wait awhile,' he said.

Doctor Mirabilis's reputation now enhanced by this miracle, he began to sell his jars and philtres of crushed diamond, skin of newt collected at midnight, batwing, marjoram, fennel and hyssop.

'Certain cures,' he said, 'for any agues, aches and rheums you suffer from.'

For a while business was brisk, then the crowd drifted away to watch an old man further down the lane who cavorted and danced in the most fantastical way. Cranston handed the reins of his horse to Athelstan and went over to the 'doctor.'

'Most Reverend Doctor Mirabilis, it is good to meet you again.'

The fellow looked up, his eyes milky blue like those of a cat. He studied Cranston then stared past him at Athelstan.

'Do I know you?' he asked. 'Do you wish to buy my physic?'

'Samuel Parrot,' continued Cranston, 'I would not buy green grass from you in the spring.'

The fellow's eyes shifted to right and left.

'Who are you?' he whispered.

'Surely you have not forgotten me, Mirabilis?' Cranston murmured. 'A certain case before the Justices in the Guildhall about physic which was supposed to cure. Instead, it made men and women sick for weeks.'

The famous Doctor Mirabilis stepped closer.

'Of course!' His face broke into a gap-toothed smile. 'Sir John Cranston, coroner!' The smile was hideously false. 'Is there anything I can do for you?'

'Not here,' Cranston said. 'But Piper Alley, Nightshade House. You can lead us there?'

The physician nodded and, scooping up his philtres and potions into a leather sheet, led Cranston and Athelstan from Whitefriars down a maze of streets so narrow they continued to lead their horses.

'How does he do it?' Athelstan whispered.

'Do what?'

'The bird, the pigeon?'

Cranston laughed and gestured to where Doctor Mirabilis was now walking ahead of them.

'If you went to his little garret, you would find baskets of trained pigeons – you know, the type which carries messages. Every so often our friend here drugs one of them with nox vomica, a slow acting poison. The pigeon is released and takes up a stance nearby. The poor bird will remain immobile because of the effects of the poison. After a while it

will drop down dead, and there you have his magic!'
He laughed. 'Sometimes, of course, it does not work.
Doctor Mirabilis here is always ready to run, fleet as
a deer, fast as any hare!'

The learned physician, as if he knew his name
was being mentioned, turned and gave a gap-toothed
grin, waving at them to follow a little faster.

Athelstan now saw why Cranston had hired
Mirabilis. Southwark was bad but this area around
Whitefriars was worse. Even though it was still
daylight, the alleyways and runnels were dark, closed
off by the houses built on either side. A silent,
evil place, becoming more ominous the deeper they
went. The houses around them, built hundreds of
years ago, now derelict and unkempt, huddled close
together, blocking out the summer sky. Underfoot
the track was dirty, caking their boots and sandals
with ordure and mud. Most of the doorways were
empty. Now and again a shadow would slip out but,
seeing Cranston's long sword, retreat again. Mirabilis
twisted and turned, Athelstan and Cranston finding it
hard to keep up. Abruptly he stopped and indicated
an alleyway with a long, dark passage ahead.

'Piper Alley,' he whispered. 'Goodbye, Sir!'

And, before Cranston could object, Doctor
Mirabilis slipped up another alleyway and disappeared
out of sight.

Athelstan and Cranston walked cautiously down
Piper Alley. The houses on either side were shuttered

and closed. At last they came to one fitting Doctor Mirabilis's description of Simon Foreman's house. It had a huge, battered sign at the end of a long ash pole.

Nightshade House was separated from the street by a flagged courtyard, the general approach defended by iron railings. Even in daylight it had a sombre, suspicious air as if it wished to slink back from the adjoining houses. More like a prison than a private residence, the windows were grated and the huge door barred and bound with iron bands. There was no answer to Cranston's knock, so he banged again. Behind them a dog howled and a door opened and shut. Looking down towards the mouth of the street, they saw shadows gathering. Again Cranston knocked. Athelstan joined him, hammering on the door with his fist. There was a sound of soft footsteps, of chains being loosened and bolts drawn back. The door was swung open by an unprepossessing man of middle stature, creamy-faced, and merry-eyed. He constantly scratched the bald dome of his head. Mirabilis looked like a magician, while Foreman had the appearance of some village parson in his dark fustian jacket, hose and soft felt slippers. Like a host in some cheerful tavern, he told them to tether their horses and ushered them in, asking them to sit at the table and wait while he finished his business in his own secret chamber. They sat and glanced around. The room was surprisingly neat, tidy and well kept. A fire burnt merrily in the hearth. Around the room were tables and chairs, some covered with quilted cushions, and on the walls shelves of jars which were neatly labelled. Athelstan studied the jars, dismissing them as nothing but mild cures for ague, aches and pains. They contained herbs such as hyssop, crushed sycamore leaves, moss – nothing that could not be bought at any apothecary's throughout the length and breadth of the city. At last Foreman came back, pulling up a chair beside them like some benevolent uncle ready to listen to a story or tell a merry tale.

'Well, sirs, who are you?'

'Sir John Cranston, coroner, and my clerk, Brother Athelstan.'

The man smiled with his lips, but his eyes became hard and watchful.

'You wish to purchase something?'

'Yes, red arsenic and belladonna. You do sell them?'

The transformation in Foreman was marvellous to behold. The merry mask slipped and his eyes became more vigilant. He straightened in his chair, looking nervously over his shoulder. Athelstan sensed that, if he had known who they were before he answered the door, he would never have let them inside, or else would have taken measures to hide whatever he had in the house.

'Well, sir?' Cranston asked. 'Do you have these poisons?'

Foreman shook his head, his eyes never leaving the coroner's.

'Sir, I am an apothecary. If you want a cure for the rheum in your knee, an ache in your head, or your stomach is churned up by bad humours, I can do it. But belladonna and red arsenic are deadly poisons.' He let out a deep sigh. 'Very few people sell them. They are costly and highly dangerous in the hands of those who might use them for the destruction of life.'

Cranston smiled and leaned closer, his face a few inches from that of the apothecary.

'Now, Master Foreman, I am going to begin again. You do sell red arsenic, nightshade, belladonna, and other deadly potions to those who are prepared to pay. Look,' he lied, 'I have in my wallet a warrant from the Chief Justice and I shall stay here whilst my clerk hurries back to the city and brings men from the under-sheriff to search this house. If one grain of poison, red arsenic, white arsenic, the juice of the poppy or any other damnable philtre is here, then you will answer for it, not at the Guildhall but before King's Bench! Come, surely somewhere in this house there are records, memoranda of what you sell?'

The apothecary's face paled and beads of sweat broke out on his brow.

'There would be many,' the fellow whispered, 'who would curse you, Cranston, for dragging me into court! I have powerful friends.' His eyes flickered towards Athelstan. 'Abbots, archdeacons, priests. Men only too willing to defend me and keep my secrets – and theirs – hidden from the light the law!'

'Good!' Cranston answered. 'Now we understand each other, Master Foreman. I have no desire to stop your evil trade in whatever you sell, buy and plot, or to search out your secrets, though one day perhaps I will.' He stared up at the shelves above him. 'What I want now is to know who in the last month has been here to buy arsenic and belladonna? Surely you recognise this?' He took out the small stoppered jar of poison and Foreman's eyes rounded in surprise. 'This is yours, sir,' Cranston probed gently. 'Look, on your shelves, there are similar ones. Who in the last few weeks purchased this poison?'

He held up the jar. Foreman sighed, rose, and wandered back into the chamber. Cranston took out his dagger and laid it on the floor beside him. A short while later the apothecary returned, looked at the dagger and smiled thinly.

'There is no need for that, Sir John. I will give you the information. Anything to have you gone!'

He sat down on the chair, a roll of parchment in his hands. He unrolled it slowly, muttering to himself.

'One person,' he said, looking up, 'bought both poisons in that jar about a week ago, as well as a rare odourless potion which can stop the heart but not be traced.'

'What did he look like?'

The apothecary smiled. 'Unlike any man! She was a lady, richly dressed. She wore a mask to conceal her face. You know the type ladies from the court wear when they go some place with a gallant who is usually not their husband? She came and paid me generously.'

'What kind of woman was she?'

'The woman kind,' the fellow replied sardonically, now realising he had very little information to give this snooping coroner.

'Describe her!'

Foreman rolled up the parchment and sat back in his chair.

'She was tall. As I said she wore a mask, and a rich black cloak with white lambswool trimmings. Her hood was well pulled forward but I glimpsed her hair, a reddish chestnut colour, like some beautiful leaf in autumn. Stately, she was.' He looked at Cranston and shrugged. 'Another lady, I thought, looking for poison to make her love life that little bit easier.' Foreman tapped the roll of parchment against his thigh. 'That, sirs, is all I can and will tell you.'

Once they had left the shop and collected their horses, Athelstan and Cranston rode as fast as they could up Piper Alley back into the main thoroughfare. Once or twice they lost their way, but Cranston still kept his dagger unsheathed and soon they had reached Whitefriars and were back into Fleet Street.

'You know who the woman was, Cranston, don't you?'

The coroner nodded. 'Lady Isabella Springall.' He stopped his horse and looked across at the friar. 'The description fits her, Brother. She also had the motive.'

'Which is?'

'A surmise but I think correct: Lady Isabella is an adulteress. She did not love her husband but instead her husband's brother. But now is not the time to speculate. Let's ask the lady herself.'

When they arrived at Springall's mansion in Cheapside, Cranston acted with the full majesty and force of the law. He told a surprised Buckingham, who greeted them in the hallway, that he wanted to see Sir Richard and Lady Isabella and other members of the household in the hall immediately. The young clerk pouted his lips as if he was going to object.

'I mean now, sir!' Cranston bellowed, not caring if his voice carried through the house, out into the enclosed courtyard where craftsmen were working. 'I want to see everybody!' He swept into the great hall. 'Here!'

He then marched up the hall, climbed on to the dais and sat down at the head of the table there, snapping his fingers for Athelstan to join him. The friar shrugged and got out his writing tray, parchment, ink horn and quills. Buckingham must have realised something was wrong for he was quickly joined in the hall, first by Sir Richard and then by Lady Isabella. The latter's looks were not impaired by grief today. Her eyes were not so red, her cheeks blooming like roses. She was dressed in a dark blue gown, the white veil hiding her beautiful chestnut hair.

Sir Richard, in hose and open cambric shirt, wiped dust from his hands, apologising that he had been out with the craftsmen who were putting the finishing touches to their pageant for the young king's coronation. Cranston just nodded, accepting his explanation as something irrelevant.

The priest also came hobbling in, his long hair swinging like a veil round his emaciated face. He threw a look of deep distaste at the coroner but called out civilly: 'You are well, Sir John?'

'I am well, Sir Priest,' answered Cranston. 'And much better for seeing you all here.'

The young priest must have caught the new note of authority in his voice. He stood still a moment and stared at Sir John through narrowed eyes. Then he smiled as if savouring some secret joke and slumped at the end of the table so he could stretch his leg. Dame Ermengilde swept in, unctuously escorted by Buckingham. Dressed completely in black, she moved down the hall like some silent spider and stood over the coroner.

'I will not be summoned,' she snapped, 'here in my own house!'

'Madam,' Cranston didn't even bother to look up, 'you will sit down and listen to what I say. You will obey me or I will take you to the Marshalsea Prison, and *there* you can sit and listen to what I say.' He looked up at Sir Richard and Lady Isabella. 'I mean no offence. I appreciate that yesterday the funeral ceremonies were carried out, but Masses were also sung for the souls of two other men, Brampton and Vechey, and I have news of them. They did not commit suicide. They were murdered!'

Cranston's words hung in the air like a noose. Dame Ermengilde tightened her thin little lips and sat down without further ado. Sir Richard looked nervously at Lady Isabella. Ermengilde, seated beside Athelstan, also looked frightened, trying hard to hide it behind her mask of arrogance. Further down the table the priest tapped the table gently, singing some hymn softly under his breath. Buckingham sat, hands together, staring down at the tabletop, his face registering surprise and shock at Sir John's words. Allingham was the last to join them. The tall, lanky merchant was nervous and ill at ease, his hand constantly fluttering to his mouth or patting his greasy hair. He mumbled some apology and sat next to the priest. He seemed unable to meet the coroner's eyes, not daring even to look in his direction.

'Sir John,' the merchant mumbled, 'you said Brampton and Vechey had been murdered? But how? Why? Brampton may have been a quiet man, but I cannot imagine him allowing anyone to hustle him upstairs in a house full of people, tie a noose round his neck and hang him. The same is true of Vechey.' He looked down the table at Allingham. 'Stephen, you would accept that, wouldn't you?'

The merchant never looked up but nodded and muttered something to himself.

'What are you saying?' Cranston leaned over the table. 'Master Allingham, you spoke. What did you say?'

The merchant rubbed his hands together as if trying to wash them.

'There's something evil in this house,' the merchant said slowly. 'Satan is here. He stands in the corners, in quiet places, and watches us. I believe the coroner is right.' He looked up, his lugubrious face pale, and Athelstan saw it was tear-stained. 'Vechey was murdered! I think he knew something.'

'Tush, man!' cried Sir Richard. 'Master Stephen, you worry too much. You have spent too many hours on your knees in church.'

'What?' Athelstan asked, putting his quill down. 'What did Vechey know?'

The lanky merchant leaned forward, his face screwed up, eyes pinpricks of hatred.

'I don't know,' he hissed. 'And, if I did, I would not tell you, Friar. What can you do?'

'On your allegiance,' Cranston bawled, 'I ask you, do you know anything about the deaths which have occurred in this household?'

'No!' Allingham grated. 'They are a mystery. But Sir Thomas liked riddles and his own private jokes. There must be something in this house which would explain it all.'

'What are you talking about, man?' asked Sir Richard.

185

But the merchant rubbed the side of his face uneasily. 'I have spoken enough,' he mumbled, and fell silent.

'In which case,' Cranston began, 'let us make a brief summary of what we do know. Correct me if I am wrong but Sir Thomas Springall was an alderman and a goldsmith. On the night he died he held a great banquet, a feast for his household, and invited Chief Justice Fortescue. He drank deeply, yes?'

Lady Isabella nodded, her beautiful eyes fixed on Cranston's face. Sir Richard, however, watched Athelstan's quill skim over the piece of vellum.

'The banquet ends,' Cranston continued. 'Sir Thomas retires. You, Sir Richard, wish him good night whilst Lady Isabella sends down a maidservant to ask if he wishes for anything.'

Both of them acknowledged this.

'You, Dame Ermengilde, heard Brampton take a cup of wine up to Sir Thomas's room during the feast?'

'I did not just hear!' she retorted. 'I opened my door and saw him. Then he went down.'

'And how was he dressed?'

'In a jerkin and doublet.'

'And his feet?'

'He had on the usual soft pair of boots which he always wore.'

'Why do you remember this?'

'Brampton was a quiet man,' Dame Ermengilde replied, a touch of softness in her voice. 'A good steward. He moved slowly, quietly, like a dutiful servant.'

'And how did he seem?'

'As normal. A little white-faced. He knew I opened the door but he never looked at me. He went down the stairs. No! He went along the other gallery up to the second floor and his own room.'

'Did you ever see him again?'

'No, I did not.'

'And you say that only Sir Thomas, then Sir Richard and Lady Isabella's maidservant, went along the Nightingale Gallery?'

'Yes, I am certain of that.'

'And you are sure that Sir Thomas was not disturbed during the night?'

'Yes, I told you, man!' she snapped. 'I am a light sleeper. I heard no one.'

'And you, Father Crispin?' Cranston leaned sideways to catch a glimpse of the young clerk's face. 'You went up the next morning. Dame Ermengilde heard you go along the Nightingale. When you failed to rouse Sir Thomas you went for Sir Richard whose chamber is on the adjoining passageway. Sir Richard came back with you. You were unable to arouse Sir Thomas, so you asked the servants to break down the door?'

'Yes.' The priest nodded, his eyes bright. 'That is exactly what I did.'

'When the room was broken into, all of you here were present? You went in. Sir Thomas was sprawled

187

on his bed, a cup of poison on the table beside him. Nobody said anything…'

'Except Vechey!' Allingham broke in. 'He said, "There were only thirty-one!"'

'Do you know what he meant by that?' Cranston asked.

'No, I wish to God I did!'

'The physician was sent for,' Cranston continued. 'Master de Troyes. He came. He examined Sir Thomas's corpse, pronounced him to have been poisoned, and claimed the potion was placed in a half-drunk cup of wine beside Sir Thomas's bed. Now Brampton was last seen late in the evening taking a wine cup up to Sir Thomas's chamber and was not seen alive again. The next morning, after Sir Thomas had been discovered dead, Brampton's corpse was found swinging from a beam up in the garret. Master Vechey was here when Brother Athelstan and I came to the house for the first time. He went out late on the same evening, God knows where, and was found hanging from a beam under London Bridge. Now we have evidence which we will keep privy for the time being which will prove that neither Brampton nor Vechey committed suicide. Though, Lady Isabella, we are no further forward in resolving the mystery of your husband's death.'

'It could still have been Brampton!'

It was Buckingham who spoke. Cranston looked at him.

'What makes you say that?'

The clerk shrugged. 'I accept you have your own reasons for claiming Brampton did not commit suicide but that does not mean he is innocent of Sir Thomas's death.'

Cranston grinned.

'A good point, Master clerk. You would make a good lawyer. I shall remember that.' There was a sudden commotion at the door. A servant scurried in, leaned over Sir Richard's shoulder and whispered in his ear. The merchant looked up.

'Sir John, there is a messenger, a cursitor from the sheriff's office, who wishes to speak to you.'

'I will see him, Sir Richard, by your leave. Tell him to come in.'

The cursitor, a pompous young man, swaggered in. 'Sir John, a message from the under-sheriff.' He looked around him. 'It concerns Master Vechey.'

'Yes!' Cranston said. 'You may speak here.'

'He was seen in a tavern down near the riverside. The landlord of the Golden Keys said a man who fitted Vechey's description was there drinking late at night. He left with a young, red-haired whore whom he had never seen before.'

'Is that all?' Cranston asked.

'Yes, Sir John.'

Cranston dismissed the cursitor. Athelstan felt the mood of the company in the hall lift.

'See!' Dame Ermengilde cried exultantly. 'Vechey was seen with one of his whores. Master Buckingham

189

must be right. Brampton may still have killed my son, and Vechey's death be totally unconnected with this.'

Athelstan could see Cranston was not pleased by the news.

'Nevertheless,' he snapped, 'I have other questions. Lady Isabella and Sir Richard, I must ask you to stay. The others, I would prefer to leave.'

Dame Ermengilde was about to protest. Her son stretched across the table and touched her gently on the wrist, his eyes pleading with her. She rose, threw one withering look at Cranston and followed the others out. Sir John watched them go.

'Lady Isabella,' he said softly, 'have you ever been to Nightshade House in Piper Alley near Whitefriars?'

'Never!'

'And you have no knowledge of an apothecary called Simon Foreman?'

'I have heard of him but never met him.'

Athelstan saw the fear in Lady Isabella's eyes. Her face lost its golden hue, becoming pale and haggard.

'Sir Richard?'

'No!' As he leaned forward, he clapped his hand to his side, where his sword should have been. 'You come into this house!' he hissed. 'You insult both me and Lady Isabella, hinting we go amongst rogues and vagabonds. Don't be clever, Cranston! My brother was murdered by poison. I resent the inference in your questions that one of us visited that apothecary and secured the poison to carry the murder out.'

'Yet this afternoon,' Cranston said conversationally, 'both Brother Athelstan and myself went to that apothecary's shop. He claims he sold poison to a woman fitting your description, Lady Isabella. She was dressed in a black cloak lined with white fur, had chestnut hair, was of your height and colouring.'

'I have never been to Whitefriars! I have never visited an apothecary's shop!'

'You do have a black cloak lined with white fur?'

'Yes, like hundreds of women in the city!'

'Have you ever met Foreman?'

'I don't know. I could have done. My husband had many strange friends. Anyway, why should I kill him?' Lady Isabella cried, half rising from the chair. 'He was a good man. He gave me everything a woman could desire.'

'Lady Isabella,' Cranston said smoothly, 'it is well known that your husband had strange tastes and foibles. Did you love him?'

'That, sir, is enough!' Sir Richard grabbed Cranston by the wrist but the coroner shook him off.

'That will do!' Cranston was annoyed now by the arrogance of these people, thinking they could push him around whenever they wished. 'I am an officer of the king, and the crown is involved. These charges may involve treason, conspiracy as well as murder!'

Sir Richard sat down again, breathing heavily. Lady Isabella linked her arm through his. She looked at him and shook her head.

'My Lady,' Athelstan said softly, 'it is best if you tell the truth. You must! Your husband lies murdered. Two others have been brutally executed. The murderer may well strike again. Sir John and I go around London playing Blind Man's Buff in this deadly game. Your husband, Lady Isabella, had secrets – that is why he was murdered. Brampton was supposed to have been the culprit but, due to chance and circumstances, we have ascertained he was innocent, and he, too, was murdered, though it was made to look like suicide. Vechey saw or heard something so he, also, was silenced. Now, Lady Isabella, on your oath to the new king, have you ever visited the apothecary called Simon Foreman?'

'No!'

Athelstan stared back.

'Did you love your husband?'

'No! He was a gentle, kind man but he did not know me, not in the carnal sense. He had his own tastes...' her voice trailed away.

'A liking for young men?' Athelstan asked.

'He was a sodomite!' Cranston barked. 'He liked young men! He lusted after them!' Athelstan stared at him and shook his head. Lady Isabella put her face in her hands and sobbed bitterly. 'My Lady,' Athelstan pressed her, 'your husband?'

'He left me alone. I made no inquiry into what he thought or did.'

'You, Sir Richard, do you love the Lady Isabella?'

The crestfallen merchant pulled himself together. 'Yes. Yes, I do!'

'Are you lovers?'

'Yes, we are.'

'So you both had a motive?'

'For what?' Sir Richard had lost his usual ebullience. He slouched back in the chair, his face drawn as if he realised the mortal danger they were now in.

'For murder, sir.'

The merchant shook his head. 'I may have lusted after my brother's wife,' he muttered, 'but not his life!'

'In King's Bench,' Cranston barked, 'it would not appear like that. It would appear, Sir Richard, that you lusted after your brother's wife as well as his riches; that while he was alive you committed adultery with her and, with each other, you plotted together to carry out his murder and lay the blame on Brampton.'

'In which case,' Sir Richard replied meekly, 'I must also be responsible for the deaths of Vechey and Brampton. But I have witnesses. I stayed at the banquet with my brother the entire evening. I said good night to him, and the rest of the time I was with the Lady Isabella. We shared the same bed,' he confessed.

'And the night Vechey died?' Cranston asked abruptly.

'The same. We have servants here. Workmen in the yard. They will vouch that I stayed here, doing accounts, going out to look at the carvings which were being made for the pageant for the king's coronation.'

Lady Isabella drew herself up, resting her elbows on the arms of her chair.

'If we had murdered Sir Thomas,' she asked, 'how could we enter his chamber, force poison down his throat or into his wine cup, and leave the room, locking and bolting the door from inside? That, sir, is impossible.' Her eyes turned towards Athelstan, pleading with him. 'I beg you, sir, to believe us. If we were in bed together, how could we go down, seize Brampton, take him up to that garret and hang him? No, I did not go to Whitefriars. I did not visit Simon Foreman. I did not buy poisons. I am innocent, not of sin but of my husband's death and that of others. I swear before God I had nothing to do with them.'

'You sent wine up to Brampton?' Athelstan asked.

'Yes, as a peace offering.'

'And was Brampton in his room?'

'No, I found out later that he was busy taking the cup of claret to my husband's chamber.' She wiped her eyes. 'The servant left the wine in Brampton's chamber and came down. That is all, I swear!'

Despite the tears, Athelstan still wondered if her adultery made her an assassin or perhaps an accomplice to murder. The friar felt the frustration grow within him. How had Sir Thomas been murdered? And how had Brampton been hanged? And Vechey?

Athelstan dallied with the thought of tying each of the people in this house down to their exact movements during the night Sir Thomas died, as well as the following one when Vechey disappeared, but realised the futility of it. Moreover, there was no real proof linking the murderers with anyone in the house. Perhaps they had been carried out on the orders of someone else? But who? And how? Why?

Athelstan stood, walking up and down just beneath the dais, his fingers to his lips. Cranston watched him carefully. The clever friar would sift one fact from another. The coroner was quite prepared to let Athelstan use the advantage they had now gained.

'Lady Isabella, Sir Richard,' he began, 'I have no real proof to convict you. Nevertheless, we have enough evidence under the law to swear out warrants for your arrest and ask for your committal to Newgate, Marshalsea, even the Tower.' He held up his hand. 'However, we wish for your cooperation. We want the truth. The Sons of Dives... you belong to them, don't you, Sir Richard?'

The merchant nodded.

'Everyone in this household is a member, are they not?'

'Yes,' Sir Richard replied meekly. 'Yes, we are. The church condemns usury and the loaning of money at high interest. The Guilds also condemn it. However, in every guild, in every livery company in the city, groups of merchants get together in some society. They give themselves strange names. Ours is known as the Sons of Dives. We lend money secretly to whoever needs it but charge interest much higher than the Lombards or Venetians. The money is delivered quickly. Payment is over a number of years. We choose our customers carefully: only those who can underwrite the loan, give pledges that they are good for the money they have borrowed. A petty mystery, our guild is full of such covens.'

'And the riddles? The shoemaker?'

Both Sir Richard and Lady Isabella shook their heads.

'We don't know!' they murmured in unison.

'And the scriptural quotations from Genesis and the Book of the Apocalypse, you have no clue to their meaning?'

Again a chorus of denials. Athelstan returned to the table, rolled up the piece of parchment and put away his quills and inkhorn.

'Sir John, for the moment leave matters be. Sir Richard and Lady Isabella now know that perhaps we are not as stupid or as feckless as sometimes we may appear. You may rest assured, Sir Richard, that in the end we will discover the truth and the murderer, whoever he or she may be, will hang at the Elms for all London to see!'

Cranston pursed his lips and nodded as if Athelstan had said all there was to say. They bade both the merchant and his paramour adieu.

As they left the Springall mansion and waited in Cheapside for an ostler to bring their horses round from the stables, Athelstan sensed Cranston was furious with him, but the coroner waited until they had mounted and moved away from the house before stopping and giving full vent to his fury.

'Brother Athelstan,' he said testily, 'I would remind you that *I* am the king's coroner and those two,' he gestured in the direction of the Springall house, 'Sir Richard and that expensive paramour of his, are guilty of murder!'

'Sir John,' Athelstan began, 'I apologise.'

'You apologise!' Cranston mimicked. He leaned forward and grasped the horn of Athelstan's saddle. 'You apologise! If you had kept your mouth shut, Friar, we might perhaps have gained the truth. But, oh no! We established that Lady Isabella went to the apothecary's. We established that she and Sir Richard are lovers, adulterers, fornicators, and in only a matter of time we could have had a confession that they were guilty of Sir Thomas's death as well as the others!'

'I don't accept that, Sir John. There is no real proof of murder. Oh, they are guilty of adultery.' Athelstan felt his own anger rise. 'If that was the case, Sir John, we would hang half of Cheapside for adultery and still not discover who the real murderer is.'

'Now, look.' Sir John leaned closer, his face choleric. 'In future, Brother, I would be grateful if you would observe the courtesies and, before making any pronouncements, consult with me. As I said, I am the coroner!'

'Let me remind you, Sir John,' Athelstan retorted, leaning back in his saddle, 'that I am a clerk, a priest, and not your messenger boy, your little lap dog! In these matters I will say what I believe is best and if you find it so difficult to work with me, then write to my father prior. This is one burden I would be relieved of!' The friar's voice rose so loud that passersby stopped and looked curiously at him. 'Do you think I look forward to this, Sir John? Going around listening to the fat and the rich of the land confessing their secret sins, and secretly mocking us every time we reach a stone wall and can go no further? Do you?' Athelstan turned his horse. 'I suggest we both go back to our respective homes and reflect on what has happened. Perhaps tomorrow, or the day after we may continue our investigations?'

'You will go home when I say!' Sir John shouted.

'I will go when I wish!' Athelstan retorted.

And, without waiting for any reply, he urged Philomel down Cheapside, leaving the fuming coroner behind.

Chapter 7

By the time he reached St Erconwald's, Athelstan regretted his hasty words. Sir John was correct. He had pronounced on Lady Isabella and Sir Richard's guilt or innocence without any reference to the coroner. There might have been further questions Cranston would have liked to put. He wished he had taken Sir John aside, made his peace and offered some refreshment, some claret in one of the Cheapside taverns. After all there were other strands to the case, loose ends which needed to be tied up. Who was the red-haired whore who had lured Vechey to his death? Had it been Lady Isabella? But many whores wore red wigs.

After he had stabled Philomel, Athelstan remembered the verses from Scripture and studied the great leather-bound Bible that he kept chained in his house's one and only cupboard. Genesis 3, Verse 1: 'The serpent was the most subtle of all wild beasts in that garden God had made.' Athelstan translated as he read aloud: 'Did God really say you were not to eat any of this tree in the garden?' And the other text, the Book of the Apocalypse 6, Verse 8: 'I heard the voice,' Athelstan murmured, 'of the fourth animal shout "Come!" and immediately another horse appeared, deathly pale, and its rider was called Death and all Hell followed at its heels.'

What could they possibly mean? Somehow Athelstan knew these texts were the key to the mystery. And Sir John? Athelstan wondered whether he should eat a hasty evening meal and go back across the city and make his peace. But he felt tired, he'd had enough, and such matters would wait.

He went out and unlocked the church and checked that all was well. He took a pitcher of water for Philomel and a dish of creamy milk for Bonaventure. He'd bought the latter just after he had crossed London Bridge. Still feeling perturbed, he went back into his house, lay on his pallet bed and stared up at the flaking ceiling. He tried to compose himself, first with a psalm, '*Exsurge Domine, Exsurge et vindica causam meam* – Rise, oh Lord, rise and judge my cause.'

Athelstan let his mind drift, back to Cranston and the startled, frightened face of Lady Isabella. Athelstan shook his head free of such images. He wondered what the evening sky would be like and if Father Prior would send him a copy of the writings of Richard of Wallingford. Once Abbot of St Albans, Richard had invented the most wondrous instrument for measuring and fixing the stars. Athelstan had talked to another friar who had seen Wallingford's ingenious clock, the wheels within it fixed as if by magic, which not only measured the hours but indicated signs, the phases of the moon, the position of the sun, the planets and the heavens. Athelstan licked his lips. He would give a fortune for one of those. Everything he owned just to have it in his hands for a few hours. Perhaps Father Prior would help? He'd already asked for a copy of the calendars of the Carmelite, Nicholas of Lyn.

The ceiling reminded him about the church. The roof had been mended but really it was little more than a pig sty. He heard voices outside his door, rose in just his robe, peered out of the window and groaned quietly. Of course, he had forgotten, the meeting with his parishioners! They were to assemble in the nave and discuss the pageant for Corpus Christi.

Athelstan's premonitions about the occasion proved correct. The meeting was not a happy one. Foremost amongst his parishioners were Watkin the dung-collector and his wife, a woman built like a battering ram, hard-faced, with iron grey hair hanging down to her shoulders. Cecily the courtesan made constant barbed remarks, hinting she knew more about Watkin than his wife did. Ranulf the rat-catcher, Simon the tiler, and a host of others thronged the nave, sitting facing each other on the church's two and only benches with Athelstan sitting between them on the sanctuary chair.

The occasion was marred by bickering. Nothing was resolved and Athelstan felt he had failed to take a decisive role. The meeting ended with all his parishioners glaring up at him accusingly. He apologised, said he felt tired, and promised they would meet again when some decisions could be made. They all trooped out, mumbling and muttering, except Benedicta. She remained sitting on the end of one bench, her cloak wrapped about her.

Athelstan went to close the door behind his parishioners. When he returned, he thought Benedicta was crying, her shoulders were shaking so. But when she looked up, he realised she was laughing, the tears streaming down her face.

'You find our parish meetings amusing, Benedicta?'

'Yes.' He noticed how low and cultured her voice was.

'Yes, Father, I do. I mean—' She spread her hands and giggled again.

Athelstan just glared at her but still she could not control her mirth. Her shoulders shook with laughter, her alabaster cheeks flushed with warmth. Athelstan could not prevent his smile.

'I mean,' she said, 'Cecily the courtesan's ambition to act the role of the Virgin Mary! And the face of Watkin's wife!' She laughed so infectiously that Athelstan joined in and, for the first time since he had arrived at St Erconwald's, the nave of his church rang with laughter. At last Benedicta composed herself.

'Not seemly,' she observed, her eyes dancing with merriment, 'for a widow and her parish priest to be laughing so loudly in church at the expense of his parishioners! But I must say, never in my short life have I witnessed anything so funny. You must regard us as a cross to bear.'

'No,' Athelstan replied and sat down beside her. 'No cross.'

'Then what is it, Father? Why are you so sad?'

Athelstan stared across at the blue, red and gold painting now being formed on the wall. What is my cross? he thought. A large burden, a veritable mortal sin of the flesh, with balding head, shrewd brown eyes, and a face as red as a bloody rag. Sir John Cranston, lord of the stomach, master of the sturdy legs and an arse so huge that Athelstan secretly called it 'Horsecrusher'. But how could he explain Cranston to Benedicta?

'No crosses, Benedicta. Nothing, perhaps, except loneliness.'

He suddenly realised how close he was to her. She stared calmly back, her jet black hair escaping from underneath the wimple. Her face was so smooth. He was fascinated by her generous mouth and her eyes, beautiful and dark as the night. He coughed abruptly and got up.

'You stayed back, Benedicta! Do you wish to talk to me?'

'No.' She, too, rose as if sensing the sudden chill between them. 'But you should know that Hob has died. I visited his house before I came here and saw his widow.'

'God save him!' whispered Athelstan. 'God save us all, Benedicta! God save us all!'

–

The next day Athelstan refused to think about Sir John and the terrible murders in the Springall household. Instead, he busied himself about his parish duties. The new poor box was replaced and padlocked near the baptismal font. He tried to settle matters between Cecily and Watkin the dung-collector's wife and achieved some accord: Cecily would be the Madonna provided Watkin's wife could be the Virgin's cousin, Saint Elizabeth. Watkin would have pride of place as St George while Ranulf the rat-catcher eagerly agreed to put on a costume and act the role of the dragon.

There were other more serious matters. Hob the grave-digger was buried late in the afternoon and Athelstan organised a collection, giving what he could to the poor widow and promising her more as soon as circumstances allowed. He slept well that night, getting up early to climb the wet, mildewed stairs to the top of the church tower where he saw the stars clear in the skies, studying their alignment before they faded with the dawn.

Later in the morning he was down in the church preparing the corpse of Meg of Four Lanes for burial.

Meg of the flowing, black hair, white face and nose hooked like an eagle's beak. In life she had been no beauty, in death she looked ugly, her greasy locks falling in wisps to her dirty shoulders. Her face was mere bone over which the skin had been stretched tight and transparent like a piece of cloth. Her pale sea green eyes were now dull and sunken deep in their sockets.

Her mouth sagged open and her body, dirty white like the underbelly of a landed fish, was covered in marks and bruises. The corpse had been brought in just after the morning mass by members of the parish. Athelstan had borrowed a gown from an old lady who lived in one of the tenements behind the church and dressed Meg's corpse with as much dignity as circumstances would allow. The parish constable, a mournful little man, had informed him that Meg had been murdered.

'A tragic end,' he wailed, 'to a sad life!'

Athelstan had questioned him further. Apparently some villain, hot with his own juices, had bought Meg's body and used her carnally before plunging a knife between her ribs. Just after dawn that day her corpse, cold and hard, had been found in a rat-infested spinney. No one would come forward to claim the body and Athelstan knew the parish watch would bury it like the decaying corpse of a dog. However, the morning Mass had been well attended and the members of the parish had decided otherwise. Tab the tinker, who had come in to be shriven, had agreed to fashion a coffin of sorts out of thin planks of wood. He had built this out on the steps of the church and placed it on trestles before the rood screen. Athelstan blessed Meg, sprinkling the open coffin with holy water and praying that the sweet Christ would have mercy on her soul. Then with Tab's help he nailed down the lid, reciting the prayers for the dead, and entered her name amongst other deceased of the parish to be remembered at the weekly Requiem Mass.

After that, Athelstan gave Tab and his two apprentices some pennies to take the coffin from the church and out to the old cemetery. Athelstan walked behind, chanting verses from the psalms. Meg's coffin was lowered into a shallow grave packed in the dry, hard ground. Athelstan, distracted, vowed to remember to place a cross there and as soon as possible sing a Mass for her soul and that of poor Hob. He walked back to the church feeling guilty. He had spent time watching the stars whilst people like Meg of Four Lanes died horrible deaths, their bodies afterwards lowered into obscure graves. Athelstan felt angry and went to kneel before the statue of the Virgin, praying for Meg and the evil bastard who had sent her soul unshriven out into the darkness. He got up and was about to return to his house to wash the dirt from Meg's grave from his hands when Cranston swaggered in, throwing the door open as if he was announcing the Second Coming.

'It's murder, Athelstan!' he bawled. 'Bloody murder! Foul homicide!'

Athelstan knew Cranston loved to startle him, delighting in dramatic exits and entrances, and didn't know whether to laugh or cry. Cranston stood there, legs apart, hands on hips. The friar sat down on the sanctuary steps and stared into his fat, cheery face.

'What are you talking about, Sir John?' he said crossly.

The grinning tub of lard just stood there, smiling. 'The Springalls!' he bawled at last. 'It's happened again. This time poor Allingham's been found dead in his chamber, with not a mark on his body. Chief Justice Fortescue is hopping like a cat. By the way, where's yours?'

'Bonaventure probably left when he heard you coming!' Athelstan muttered. 'Why, what's wrong with the Chief Justice? What's he got to do with Bonaventure?'

'Fortescue is hopping like a cat on hot bricks, demanding something should be done, but he has no more idea than I what *can* be done. Anyway, we're off, Athelstan, back to the Springall house!'

'Sir John! I am busy with matters here. Two deaths, two burials.'

The coroner walked towards him, a wicked grin on his satyr-like face.

'Now, now, Athelstan. You know better than that.'

Of course, the friar did. He knew he had no choice in the matter but cursed and muttered as he filled his saddlebags, harnessed Philomel and joined Cranston who sat slouched on his horse on the track outside the church. They stopped for Athelstan to leave messages with Tab the tinker, now drinking away the profits of Meg's funeral at the nearest tavern, and began the slow journey down to London Bridge and across to Cheapside. Cranston was full of good cheer, aided and abetted by an apparently miraculous wineskin which never seemed to empty. Athelstan tried to apologise for his part in the quarrel at their last parting, but the coroner just waved his words aside.

'Not your fault, Brother!' he boomed. 'Not yours! The humours, the heat of the day. We all quarrel. It happens in the best of families.'

So, with Athelstan praying and cursing, and Cranston farting and swaying in his saddle, they cleared London Bridge and pressed on to Fish Street Hill. Of course, when the wine ran out, Cranston's mood darkened. He announced that he didn't give a rat's fart for mumbling monks.

'Orders were orders!' he roared, looking darkly at the friar, before going on to regale both him and the horses with an account of the meal his poor wife was preparing for the coming Sunday.

'A veritable banquet!' Cranston announced. 'Boar's head, cygnet, venison, quince tarts, junkets of apple-flavoured cream...'

Athelstan listened with half an ear. Allingham was dead. He remembered the merchant, long, lanky, and lugubrious of countenance. How unsettled and agitated he had been when they last had visited the Springall house. He glared darkly at Cranston and hoped the coroner was not too deeply in his cups.

On their arrival at the house in Cheapside, Athelstan was astonished to find how calm and collected Sir Richard and Lady Isabella were. The friar suddenly realised that Cranston's claim that Allingham was murdered was really a piece of pure guesswork on his part. Sir Richard greeted them courteously, Lady Isabella beside him. She was dressed in dark blue velvet, a high white lace wimple on her head. She recounted how they had gone up to Master Allingham's chamber and, finding the door locked, had ordered the workmen from the yard below to force the chamber.

'Allingham was found dead on the bed due to a stroke or apoplexy,' Sir Richard commented. 'We do not know which. We sent for Father Crispin.' He pointed to where the priest sat on a chair just within the hall door. 'He examined Allingham, held a piece of glass to his lips, but there was no sign of the breath of life. So he did what he has become accustomed to doing – gave the last rites. You wish to see the corpse?'

Athelstan turned and looked at Cranston, who just shrugged.

'So you think that Allingham's death was by natural causes?'

'Oh, of course! What else? There's no mark of violence. No sign of poison,' Sir Richard answered.

Athelstan remembered Foreman's words – how the lady who had visited his shop had bought a poison which could not be traced or smelt yet would stop the heart. He believed Sir Richard and Lady Isabella were speaking the truth, at least literally: in their eyes, and perhaps even those of a skilled physician, Allingham's death was from natural causes, but Athelstan thought differently. He agreed with Sir John. Allingham had been murdered.

The young clerk, Buckingham, now dressed more festively, the funerals being over, took them up to the first floor, then up more stairs to the second storey of the house. The middle chamber on that floor was Allingham's: the door had been forced off its leather hinges and a workman was busy replacing it. He pushed it open for them and they went inside.

The chamber was small but pleasant, with a window overlooking the garden. On the bed, a small four poster with the bolsters piled high, Allingham lay as if asleep. Athelstan looked round the room. There was a short, coloured tapestry on the wall depicting Simeon greeting the baby Jesus, two or three chests, a table, one high-backed chair, some stools and a cupboard with a heavy oak frontal pushed open. He caught the fragrant smell of herbs sprinkled across and stared down at Allingham's body. He said a short prayer. Cranston sat on the bed just staring at the corpse as if the man was alive and the coroner wished to draw him into friendly conversation.

Athelstan knew that Cranston, despite all his bluster and drunken ways, was quite capable of making a careful, perceptive study of the dead man. Athelstan leaned over to perform his own examination. The dead merchant's skin was like the cold scales of a fish. Rigor mortis had set in, but not totally. He pushed the mouth open and inhaled. A slight spicy smell but nothing unusual, and no discoloration of the skin, nails or face. He picked up the fingers. Again no smell except for chrism where the priest had anointed the dead man. Athelstan felt slightly ridiculous, he and Sir John sitting on the bed, Buckingham and Sir Richard looking down at them. Behind them, at the door, Lady Isabella peered on tiptoe over their shoulders, as if watching some masque or mummer's play. And then, behind her, the dull dragging footsteps of Father Crispin as he, too, came up to join them.

'Tell me,' Athelstan said, 'who found the corpse?'

'I did,' Sir Richard replied. 'We had all risen early this morning. Father Crispin here took one of the horses, a young one, out through Aldgate to gallop in the fields. He came back, stabled the horse and came in to break fast with us. We then noticed Allingham had not come down although he was generally an early riser. We sent up a manservant. He tried to rouse Stephen but, unable to, came down to tell us.

Father Crispin had unfortunately just knocked over a wine cup and was cleaning up the mess with a napkin. When the servant summoned me, I went up; Father Crispin, Master Buckingham and Lady Isabella followed me. Allingham could not be roused so we then sent for the workmen in the yard. They brought up a timber and forced the door.'

Athelstan went over to the door and looked carefully at it. Both the bolt and the lock were now broken beyond repair where the makeshift battering ram had forced a way in.

'Inside, Stephen Allingham was lying on the bed, as you see him now. Father Crispin examined him and said there was no sign of life.'

'What else happened?'

'Nothing. We arranged the body, which was lying half sprawled, legs on the floor, the rest on the bed.'

'Nothing suspicious?'

'No.'

'Except one thing,' Father Crispin spoke up, ignoring Sir Richard's warning glance. 'I could not understand why, if Allingham had been taken by a seizure, he had not tried to open the door, turn the key and call for help. I thought the lock might have stuck.' He shrugged. 'I went back and examined it. The handle of the door was jammed. I tried to free it, using the cloth I had brought up from the hall to gain a better purchase. I did not succeed, perhaps because of the way it had been forced. The lock itself seemed good, though wrenched away by the forced entry. The key was lying on the floor.'

'And how had Master Allingham been in recent days?'

'Morose!' Sir Richard snapped back. 'He kept to himself. On one occasion my mother, Lady Ermengilde, found him muttering to himself, something about the same number Vechey mentioned – thirty-one. And about shoemakers!'

'Yes, that's right,' Lady Isabella said. 'At table he would just glower at his food and refuse to talk. He said he must be more careful about what he ate and drank. He spent a great deal of time in the yard below with the carpenters and masons who were making the pageant cart for the coronation procession. He spent hours talking to them, especially the master carpenter, Andrew Bulkeley.'

'What was so important?' Cranston asked.

Lady Isabella shrugged her pretty shoulders, a movement which made even Athelstan's breath catch in his throat.

'I don't know,' she murmured. 'He used to go down there and stand and look at the frieze Bulkeley was carving; the one that will surmount the cart and later be hung in the chantry chapel at the other end of this house. Perhaps you should speak to him?'

Cranston looked across at Athelstan and nodded.

'Oh, one further question, Lady Isabella, and I ask it here in the presence of your household. Your husband's wealth – he made a will?'

213

'Yes, it's already with the Court of Probate in Chancery at Westminster Hall. Why do you ask?'

Athelstan noticed how her cheeks had become flushed and Sir Richard moved restlessly.

'Who were your husband's heirs?'

'Sir Richard and myself.'

'You are to receive all his wealth?'

'Yes, all.'

'And, Sir Richard,' Cranston continued, 'you have now been through all the memoranda, documents, household books and accounts in your brother's possession. Have you found anything suspicious? Loans made perhaps to powerful men who refused to pay?'

Sir Richard smiled. 'Nothing of the sort. Oh, the powerful lords owed my brother, and now me, monies but none of them would dare renege. Remember, they can only do it once. After that who else will loan them monies?'

Cranston patted his thigh and grinned. 'The world of finance, Sir Richard, escapes me – and of course Brother Athelstan here, with his vow of poverty. Come, Brother!' He rose and Athelstan followed him out.

'Where are you going?' Sir Richard hurried to catch up with them.

'Why, to see Master Bulkeley, of course! I would like to know what Master Allingham found so interesting in the yard.'

Sir Richard led them down through a flagstoned kitchen and scullery, out into the great yard around which the house was built. The place was a hive of activity. Dogs charged about like lunatics, scattering the chickens and geese, which pecked for food in the hard-packed soil. Grooms, farriers and ostlers were taking horses in and out of the stables, checking legs, hooves and coats for any injuries or blemishes. A few small boys, the children of servants, played hide and seek behind the carts, baskets and bales of straw. Servants hurried in and out of kitchens with pitchers of water while others sat in the shade whiling their time away with dice and other games of hazard. Outside the kitchen door scullions were bringing out steaming chunks of bloody red meat to throw into huge casks of pickle and salt to preserve them. At the other end of the yard, carpenters were busy around a huge, gaily decorated cart, the four sides now being covered with elaborate cloths and carvings. Sir Richard took Cranston and Athelstan over.

'Oh, by the way, Sir Richard. The Syrians, the beautiful chess set, what happened to them?' asked Cranston.

Sir Richard stood still, staring up at the blue sky, turning his face to feel the sun.

'Too precious to be left out on display. Master Buckingham has polished them and put them away, locked in a casket. They are safe. Why do you ask?'

Cranston shrugged. 'I wondered, that's all.'

The noise around the carts was terrible: the banging and the sawing and the moving of wood. The air was thick with sawdust and the sweet smell of freshly cut wood. The pageant prepared by Springall, which was only a small part of the vast coronation procession, looked even more magnificent at close quarters. The cart was huge, about nine feet high. The merchant explained there would be a tableau which would give honour to the king as well as reflect the glory of the Goldsmith's Guild, with huge screens on which the carpenters and masons had carved elaborate scenes.

'There are four,' Sir Richard explained, 'one for the front, one for the back and one for each side of the cart. These will be fastened on and above them a platform. On that will be set the tableau. Everything has to be correct,' he commented. 'We do not wish to bring any disgrace or dishonour on the guild from our cart collapsing as it rolls through the streets of Cheapside.'

No expense had been spared. Athelstan particularly examined each of the screens showing the four last things; Death, Judgement, Heaven and Hell. He admired the sheer complexity of the scenes as well as the genius of the craftsmen, in particular in their depiction of Hell. There was a representation of the devil carrying off the wicked to Hades. Each of the damned souls was guarded by a group of hideous demons. In the centre of the piece was a carving of a shoemaker resisting four shaggy devils who were dragging him from the embraces of what at first Athelstan thought was a young lady but, on looking closer, realised that with his tail and close-cropped hair, it was a depiction of a male prostitute. The profession of the Devil's captive, a shoemaker, was made apparent by the bag of tools clutched in one hand and the unfinished shoe in the other.

'Who carved this?' Athelstan asked Sir Richard.

'Andrew Bulkeley.'

'Where is he?'

Sir Richard turned and called the man's name and a small, bald-headed man wandered over. His vast form, more corpulent than that of Cranston, was swathed in a dirty white apron. He looked like one of the carefree devils he had carved, with his fat, cheery face, snub nose and large blue eyes which seemed to dance with wicked merriment.

'Master Bulkeley.' Athelstan smiled and shook the proffered hand. 'Your carvings are exquisite.'

'Thank you, Brother.' The voice betrayed a soft burr of warmer, fresher climes.

Athelstan pointed to the depiction of Hell. 'This particular carving, it's your work?'

'Yes, Brother.'

'And the idea is yours?'

'Oh, no, Brother. Sir Thomas himself laid down what we should do and how we should carve it.'

'But why the shoemaker and why the male prostitute?'

The craftsman wiped his mouth with the back of his hand.

'I don't really know. I have done such scenes many times. It's always the same. Someone being dragged from the warm embraces of a group of young ladies. But this time, I think Sir Thomas had some secret joke. He insisted that it be a shoemaker and the prostitute be male. That's all I know. He paid the money; I did what he asked. Have you seen the others?'

'Yes, thank you,' Athelstan said, and looked across at Cranston.

'Master Allingham came out to look at these carvings?' Cranston asked.

'Yes.'

'Do you know why?'

'No.'

'Any carving in particular?'

The craftsman shrugged.

'He'd look at them all, usually when we were not there, but he constantly asked why Sir Thomas had chosen certain themes. I gave him the same answer I gave you.'

Athelstan turned to the merchant. 'Was your brother fascinated by shoemakers?'

'I told you,' Sir Richard replied, exasperated, 'he liked riddles. Perhaps a shoemaker had offended him. I don't know!'

Athelstan touched Sir John gently on the elbow. 'I have seen enough. Perhaps we should go?'

The coroner looked puzzled but quietly agreed. They walked back through the kitchen and down the hallway to the front entrance of the house. They were about to leave when Sir Richard called out: 'Brother Athelstan! Sir John!'

They both spun round.

'You keep coming back here, yet you have not found any evidence linking the deaths, or the reasons for them. Is that not so?'

The merchant had regained some of his arrogance and Cranston could not stop himself.

'Yes, that's so, Sir Richard. So far, we have found nothing conclusive. But, I can tell you something fresh and you may tell the others.'

'Yes, Sir John?'

'Whatever the evidence, whatever you may think, Stephen Allingham was murdered. You should all take care!'

Before the startled merchant could think of a reply, Cranston had taken Athelstan by the elbow and steered him out into the sun-baked street.

'Last time we were here,' Athelstan quipped, 'you warned me, Sir John, not to open my mouth and say things I was not bidden to. Yet you have done so today. There is no evidence that Allingham was murdered.'

'Oh, I know that,' Sir John grunted. 'And so do you.' He stopped and tapped the friar gently on the temple. 'But up there, Athelstan, and here in your heart, what do you really think?'

Athelstan stared at the hubbub around them, the people oblivious to his dark thoughts of murder, fighting their way through the stalls, gossiping, talking, buying and selling, engaged in everyday matters.

'I think you are right, Sir John. Allingham's murder was well planned, and the murderer is in that house.' He pulled his cowl up against the hot midday sun. 'Shall we collect our horses?'

Sir John looked away sheepishly. 'Sir John,' Athelstan repeated, 'the horses, shall we collect them?'

Cranston let out a sigh, shook his head and gazed appealingly at Athelstan.

'I have bad news, Brother. We are summoned to Westminster. Chief Justice Fortescue believes that we have spent enough public money and time in the pursuit of what he calls will-o'-the-wisps. He wants us to account for our stewardship. But before I clap eyes on his miserable face, I intend to down as many cups of sack as I can! You are with me?'

For the first time ever, Athelstan fully agreed with Sir John's desire for refreshment. They walked quickly through Cheapside down to Fleet Street and into the Saracen's Head, a cool, dark place off the main thoroughfare. Athelstan was pleased to see that it was empty and insisted that this time he should be host. He ordered the taverner to bring two black-jacks of brimming ale and, since it was Friday, not meat but a dish of lampreys and fresh white bread for himself and Sir John. Cranston took to the food like a duck to water, smacking his lips, draining the black-jack, and shouting for the taverner's pot boy to come and fill it again. Once the first pangs of hunger had been satisfied, Cranston interrogated the friar.

'Come, Brother, what do you think? Is there a solution? You are the philosopher, Athelstan, though didn't one of your famous theologians say "From nothing comes nothing – *Nihil ex nihilo!*"'

'There must be an answer,' Athelstan said, reclining against the cool stone at his back. 'When I studied Logic, we learnt one central truth. If the problem exists, there must be a solution. If there's no solution, there's no problem. Consequently, if there is a problem, there must be a solution.'

Cranston belched and blinked at Athelstan. 'Where did you learn that?' he taunted.

'Logic will resolve this problem,' Athelstan persisted. 'That and evidence. The problem, Sir John, is that we have no evidence. We can build no premise without it. We are like two men on the edge of a cliff. A chasm separates us from the other side and now we are looking round for the bridge.' Athelstan paused before continuing. 'Our bridge will be evidence, the resolving of Sir Thomas's riddles about the biblical verses and the shoemaker.'

Cranston shook his head. 'We should have talked to Allingham.'

'We did try, Sir John, but he obstinately refused to confide in us though I agree that he knew something. I think he was either going to flee or perhaps blackmail the murderers, without telling us. He made one mistake. He underestimated the sheer malice of his opponents.'

'What makes you say that?'

Athelstan bit his lip, cradling the black-jack in his hands, enjoying its coolness.

'They relish what they are doing. They plot, they devise stratagems, they cause as much confusion as they can. They not only pursue a certain quarry, the mysteries and riddles of Sir Thomas, I think they enjoy the killing. They have insufferable arrogance. Satan has set up camp in their souls. In a word, Sir John, they enjoy what they do as much as you do a goblet of claret or a game of hazard or teasing me. To them murder is now part of their lives, a piece in the fabric of their souls. They will continue to murder for profit, to protect themselves but also because they want to. All the more to see us floundering around in the dark. The more we flounder, the more enjoyment we give them.'

Sir John shivered and looked around the tavern. He felt uneasy for the first time ever, a prickling at the back of his neck, a sense of personal danger. Had they been followed? He looked quickly across at Athelstan. The friar was right. Whoever had committed these murders planned them well. If Lady Isabella was not the woman who went to the apothecary's shop, then who was? And the harlot who had lured Vechey to his doom? And the secret poisoner of Sir Thomas and Master Allingham? Cranston suddenly blinked.

'You keep saying "they",' he said. 'Why?'

'There must be more than one. Either that or it's someone very clever. I did think that someone outside that house was using assassins, professional killers, but that would be too dangerous. You see, the more people you hire to carry out a plot, the greater the danger of betrayal; either through a mistake, or a bribe, or simply by one of your minions being caught red-handed.'

'And you have no suspects?'

'No. It could be Sir Richard, it could be Lady Isabella, Buckingham, Father Crispin, even Dame Ermengilde. Who knows? One of the murdered men may have been an assassin.'

Sir John drained his tankard and slammed it down on the table.

'You know, Athelstan, if it wasn't for you and your bloody logic, I'd put the entire mystery down to witchcraft. People moving about in the dead of night, poisons being administered in a locked room. How on earth can we resolve it?'

'As I said, Sir John, logic and a little evidence, some speculation, and perhaps some help from Mistress Fortune. In the end we will grasp the truth. I don't particularly mourn the four who died.

What bothers me, what's making me sour and evil-tempered, is that the murderers are here, laughing at us, watching us fumble. They shall pay for that enjoyment. We can all murder, Sir John.' He rose, dusting the crumbs from his habit. 'Cain is in each of us. We lose our temper, feel cornered and frightened, it can be the work of an instant. But to savour murder – that's not the prompting of Cain, that's Satan!'

Cranston, his mouth full of hot food, simply mumbled his reply. Athelstan felt the thick ale seep into his stomach, making him relaxed, even sleepy.

'Come on, Sir John. Chief Justice Fortescue awaits us and, as you know, justice waits for no man!'

Sir John glared, stuffed the rest of the food in his mouth and drained his tankard in one final gulp.

They hurried out into Fleet Street, Sir John wiping his mouth on the back of his hand, hitching his sword belt, shouting that he would revisit the tavern at his earliest convenience. They were halfway down Fleet Street when suddenly the Coroner's mood changed. He stopped abruptly and gazed round, staring back at the throng they had pushed through.

'What's wrong, Sir John?'

The coroner chewed his lip. 'We are being followed, Brother Athelstan, and I don't like that.'

He looked round and went over to a tinker's stall. Athelstan saw money change hands and Cranston came back with a thick broomstick.

'Here, Athelstan!'

The friar looked in surprise at the long, smoothly planed ash pole.

'I have no need of a staff, Sir John.'

Cranston grinned, his hands falling to the dagger and great broad sword he carried.

'You may have, Athelstan. Remember what your psalmist says: "The devil goes around like a lion seeking whom he would devour." I believe a lion or a devil, or both, are trailing us now!'

Chapter 8

As they hurried down Fleet Street Athelstan
wondered if perhaps Sir John had drunk too deep.
They turned abruptly into the long gardens of the
Inner Temple, fenced off from sightseers. The gate-
keeper, recognising Cranston, let them in without a
word. They hurried through the tranquil, fragrant-
smelling garden, past the Inner and Middle Temples,
and down Temple Stairs where they hired a wherry
to take them to Westminster. Cranston, despite his
bulk, jumped into the boat, pulling a surprised Athelstan along with him. He tripped on his staff and
nearly pitched head first into the water. The boatman
cursed, telling them to sit down and keep still, and
then, puffing and sweating, he pulled his craft out
midstream through the flocks of swans who arched
their wings in protest as if they owned the river.

They followed the Thames as it curved down
past the Savoy Palace, Durham and York House,
past the high-pooped ships scarred from long voyages
which were crowding in for repairs. At Charing Cross
the boatman began to pull in as the deep bend in
the river became more pronounced. They passed

Scotland Yard; Westminster Abbey came into sight; then the tower of St Margaret's and the roofs, turrets and gables, shop-dwellings, houses and taverns, which made up the small city of Westminster.

The boatman pulled in, allowing Athelstan and Cranston to disembark at the Garden Stairs and go through the courts, corridors and passageways which linked the different buildings of Westminster Palace. The place was thronged: gaolers with their prisoners, attorneys, lawyers and clients, as well as vendors of paper, ink and food. The ne'er-do-wells and the many sightseers mixed with the army of law clerks carrying rolls of parchment up from the cellar known as Hell where, Sir John explained, the legal records were kept. The smell was terrible, despite the fresh breezes wafting in from the river. Some of the lawyers and justices, resplendent in their silken robes, held nosegays to their faces to fend off the odour.

Cranston led Athelstan into the Great Hall, pointing out the painted walls, though some of the frescoes were beginning to flake. The famous ceiling, where the wooden angels flew face down through the dusty air above the crowd, was so high it could scarcely be seen in the gloom. Cranston stopped a beadle in his blue cloak, the shield of office on his breast and long staff tapping the paving stones proclaiming his sense of importance. Yes, the fellow assured them, with a nod of his head to the far end of the hall, the Court of King's Bench was now in session and Chief Justice Fortescue attendant upon it.

The beady, little eyes softened as Cranston displayed his warrant, a silver coin lying on top of it. However, the court had finished its morning session. Perhaps Chief Justice Fortescue was in his chamber?

The beadle led them through the gloomy rooms off the main hall where the Court of Common Pleas, Court of Chancery and Court of Requests sat, and down a warren of lime-washed corridors until he stopped in front of a door and rapped noisily with his wand.

'Come in!' Chief Justice Fortescue, his scarlet, fur-trimmed robe tossed over a chair, was sitting behind a table. The angry look on the judge's sallow face showed that either his attendance in court that morning or Cranston's arrival had put him in an ill humour.

'Ah!' Fortescue dropped the manuscript he was reading on to the table. 'Our zealous city coroner and his clerk. Please sit down.' He gestured to a well-cushioned window seat.

Cranston glared back at him and waddled over. Athelstan sat next to the coroner and wondered what was to come. The Chief Justice threw them both another ill-favoured glance.

'What progress has been made?'

In short, clipped tones Cranston told him exactly what had happened, and their suspicions. How the four deaths were linked. How Brampton and Vechey had probably not committed suicide but been murdered and that Allingham's supposed death from natural causes was probably the murderer striking again.

'You have no idea who it is?'

'No, My Lord.'

'Or why?'

'No, My Lord.'

'You found no great mystery that Sir Thomas Springall was hiding? Nothing which could endanger either the crown or the safety of the realm?'

'Nothing,' Cranston retorted. 'Why should there be?'

Fortescue dropped his glance, fiddling with the great amethyst ring on one of his fingers.

'Sir John, you hold your office from the crown. You could be removed.'

Cranston's face sagged and Athelstan felt a tremor run through the great, corpulent body. He spoke up.

'My Lord Chief Justice?'

Fortescue looked surprised, as if he had expected Athelstan to keep his mouth shut for the entire interview.

'Yes, Brother? You have something to add, perhaps? Something Sir John does not know.'

'No, I have nothing to add,' replied Athelstan. 'Except that Sir John and I have been most zealous in this matter. We could ask further questions – such as, My Lord, what you yourself were doing at the banquet on the night Sir Thomas died? You said to us that you left early in the evening, but according to other witnesses you left just an hour before midnight. It would help us, My Lord,' he said, ignoring the look of deep annoyance on the Chief Justice's face. 'If everyone spoke the truth, we might avoid future dangers.'

'Is that why you carry the staff, Brother?' The Chief Justice retorted, totally ignoring Athelstan's jibe. 'You fear something, don't you? What?'

'I fear nothing, My Lord, except perhaps that those who do not wish us to find the truth may intervene in a way we least expect. And that, of course, would help no one.'

'Meaning?'

'I mean, My Lord,' continued Athelstan, warming to his task, 'Sir John is a well-known and well-beloved coroner in the city. If he was attacked in public, people would be scandalised. The king's chief peace officer in the capital prevented from walking the streets! And if he was removed from office, questions would be asked. People would look very carefully at what matters Sir John was involved in when he was removed. There would be questions. There are aldermen who sit in the Commons, in St Stephen's Chapel, just a stone's throw away, only too willing to use any ammunition against the regent.' He spread his hands. 'Now, My Lord, I ask you to think again before you threaten Sir John. Remember, this task was given to us by you. If you wish, we can let the matter drop and others, perhaps more fortunate, can dig amongst the scandals, the lies and the deceit and possibly search out the truth.'

Fortescue took a deep breath to control the fury raging within him. How dare this friar, this bare-arsed Dominican in his dusty black robe and shoddy leather sandals, sit and lecture him, Chief Justice of the realm! Yet Fortescue was no man's fool. He knew Athelstan spoke the truth. He smiled falsely.

'True, Brother,' he replied, 'but there seems no answer to this conundrum in sight and the regent is most pressing. Indeed, he has invited both of you to a special tournament to be held at Smithfield the day after next and, following that, later in the evening, a banquet in the Savoy Palace. I may as well be blunt: Sir Richard Springall and all his household have also been invited. The duke does not care whether you wish to attend or not – he orders it. He wishes to inspect at close quarters all the actors in this drama. I take it you will attend?'

'Of course, My Lord,' Sir John spoke up. 'It's our duty.' He grinned slyly at his assistant. 'And both Brother Athelstan and myself would like some sort of respite, a short rest from tramping the streets on your work.'

On that parting note, Cranston belched noisily and left Chief Justice Fortescue, with Athelstan behind him. They made their way back to the river steps.

During their journey upriver, Cranston sat morosely in the bows of the boat, staring into the water. Only when they reached Temple Stairs and disembarked did he put one podgy arm round Athelstan's shoulders and press his face closer to that of the friar. His breath smelt as rich as a wine press.

'Athelstan,' he slurred, 'I thank you for what you said there, in the presence of that mean-faced bastard! I'll not forget.'

Athelstan stepped back in mock annoyance. 'Sir John, remember the old adage? "The devil you know is better than the devil you don't." Moreover, I always think that working with you will lessen my spell in Purgatory when I die.'

Sir John turned and belched as loudly as he could.

'That, Brother,' he retorted, 'is the only answer I can and will make!'

They continued through the Temple Gates into the alleyway which would lead them into Fleet Street and a new cook shop. They were chatting about the tournament and John of Gaunt's invitation when Cranston stopped as he heard a sound behind them: a slithering across the cobbles.

'Athelstan,' he whispered, 'keep on walking.' His hand went to the hilt of his sword. 'But grip your staff and be ready!'

They walked a few steps further. Athelstan heard a sound close behind him and spun round as Cranston followed suit. Two men stood there, one tall

233

and masked, the other a small, weasel-eyed individual dressed in a dirty leather jerkin, hose and boots which had seen better days. He wore a flat, battered cap on his head, pushed to one side to give him a jaunty air. Athelstan swallowed hard and felt a surge of panic. Both men were armed, each carrying a naked sword and dirk. What frightened him most was their absolute silence, the way they stared, unmoving, not issuing threats.

'Why do you follow us?' Cranston said, pushing Athelstan behind him.

'We do not follow, sir,' the weasel-eyed man replied. 'My companion and I merely walk the same path as you do.'

'I think you do follow us,' Cranston replied, 'and have been for some time. You followed us down to the river and waited until we returned. You have been expecting us.'

'I don't know what you are talking about!' The man took one step closer, sword and dagger now half raised. 'But you insult us, sir, and you must apologise.'

'I do not apologise to you, nor to the murderous bastard next to you! I am Sir John Cranston, coroner of the city.' He drew his sword and scrabbled behind his back to pull out the dirk. 'You, sirs, are footpads, which is a felony. You are attacking a king's officer and that is treason. This is Brother Athelstan, a member of the Dominican order, a priest of the church. Any attack on him would bring down excommunication on you. And that, sirs, is the least you can expect! I will count to three,' the coroner continued as if enjoying himself, 'and then, if you are not out of this alleyway and back whence you came, you will answer to me! One… two…'

That was as far as he got. The men rushed at them, swords and daggers raised. The coroner met both attackers, catching their weapons in a whirling arc of steel as he nimbly spun his own in self-defence. In those few seconds Athelstan realised the depth of his own arrogance. He had always considered Sir John a portly, self-indulgent toper, but at this moment the coroner seemed more at ease, sword and dagger in his hands, fighting for his life, than he had at any time since they had met. He moved with a grace and speed which surprised both Athelstan and his opponents. Sir John was a competent swordsman, moving only when he needed to, keeping both dagger and sword locked in constant play. Athelstan could only stand and watch, open-mouthed. The coroner was smiling, his eyes half closed, sweat running down his face. The friar could have sworn that Sir John was singing a hymn or a song under his breath. There seemed little danger. Whoever had sent these assassins had completely underestimated the fat knight. Sir John fenced on, parrying sideways, backwards and forwards, playing with his opponents. Cautiously, Athelstan joined the fray – not as expertly as Sir John, but the long ash pole came into play, creating as much confusion as it did harm. Athelstan now stood shoulder to shoulder with Cranston. Their two assailants drew back.

Cranston was loath to stop the fight. 'And again, my buckos!' he cried. 'Just once more and then a wound, an injury. If I don't kill you, the hangman will! Be sure of that.'

The small, weasel-eyed man looked at his companion, and before the coroner could advance another step, both men took to their heels and fled. Cranston leaned suddenly against the wall, wiping away the sweat now coursing down his face. His jerkin was stained with damp patches at the armpits and chest.

'You see that, Athelstan?' he gasped, resting his sword point on the ground. 'You saw me, didn't you? The sword play, the footwork. You will vouch for me with Lady Maude?'

Athelstan smiled. Sir John saw himself as a knight errant, a chevalier, and his little wife Maude as his princess.

'I saw it, Sir John,' he said. 'A born soldier. A true Saint George. You were in no danger?'

Cranston coughed and spat.

'From those? Alleymen, roaring boys, the dregs of some commissioner's levy! I tell you this, Athelstan,' sheathing his sword and dagger, 'I fought in France against the cream of French chivalry for the Old King, bless him! We were raging lions then and

England's name was feared from the northern seas to the Straits of Gibraltar. In my younger days,' he bellowed, pulling his shoulders back martial fashion, 'I was keen as a greyhound, fast as a falcon swooping to the kill.'

Athelstan hid a smile, looking at the sweat still pouring down the fat coroner's face, the great, stout stomach wobbling with a mixture of pride and anger.

Of course they had to stop at the nearest tavern for Sir John to take refreshment and go over his sword play, step by step, blow by blow. Athelstan, concealing his amusement, listened as attentively as he could.

'Sir John,' he interrupted finally, 'those men, the footpads, they were sent, were they not? They were waiting for us.'

'Yes,' Cranston stuck his fiery red nose deeper into his tankard, slurping noisily, 'they were sent after us. Which means, Brother Athelstan, that our final remark to Sir Richard as we left the Springall house hit home. The murderer now knows that we are on his trail. Vechey, Brampton and Allingham are dead, and the number of suspects shrinks. We have a greater chance of being able to flush this assassin out. But we must remain vigilant, Brother, for he may strike again.'

He stood up and gazed round the tavern. Athelstan wondered if he was going to describe to all and sundry the recent fray in the alleyway.

'You will come back with me, Athelstan, to Lady Maude?'

He shook his head. If he went back the day would be done. Cranston would drink himself silly, celebrating his triumph, and make Athelstan recount time and time again his great victory.

'No, Sir John, I crave your pardon but not this time. We shall meet the day after next. We have an invitation to a tournament which we must accept.'

Cranston reluctantly conceded his point and they both left the tavern and walked back to collect their horses. The coroner stood and watched Athelstan mount the ancient but voracious Philomel.

'My Lady Maude will come to the tournament,' he said, then looking up at the friar, tapped the side of his fleshy nose. 'You can always bring the woman Benedicta.'

Athelstan blushed. He dare not ask how Cranston knew about Benedicta. The coroner laughed and was still bellowing with mirth as Athelstan urged his horse forward out into the street. He still retained the staff Cranston had bought him. On the journey home he felt slightly ridiculous, like some broken-down knight preparing for a tournament. He tried to ignore the murmured whispers and laughter as he made his way through the streets across London Bridge and back into Southwark. He thought over the attack but felt no fear. The danger from the footpad, the silent assassin, was always present, here in his church or across the river. Athelstan stopped his horse outside St Erconwald's and thought about that further. Suddenly he realised he had no fear of death. Why? Because of his brother? Because of his priesthood? Or because his conscience was clear? Then he thought of Benedicta and felt a twinge of doubt.

That night, whilst Sir John roistered in his house like Hector home from the wars, Athelstan fed Philomel and Bonaventure. He promised himself he would not go up to the tower to observe the stars. Instead he went into his own church, secured the door, lit candles and took them to his small carrel where he placed his writing tray. He chose a piece of smooth parchment and began to write down everything that had happened since he first went to the Springall mansion. He was sitting there, half dozing over what he had written, when there was a loud knocking on the door. At first he refused to answer, then realised that no assassin would make such a noise so went down to the door and called out: 'Who's there?'

'Rosamund, Brother!'

Athelstan recognised the voice of the eldest daughter of Pike the ditcher. He unlocked the door and peered out into the darkness. A fresh-faced young girl burbled out her news. How her mother had just given birth to another child, her fifth, this time a boy. Athelstan smiled and mumbled his congratulations. The little girl looked at him solemnly.

'Mother wishes you to choose a name.'

Athelstan smiled and acknowledged the great honour.

'She wants a saint's name, Brother.'

Athelstan promised he would do what he could and hoped to see her and her family as soon as possible. He heard the girl run back down the steps and her footsteps faded in the distance. He locked the door and went back to the carrel. Athelstan picked up the piece of parchment and the candle, scrutinising what he had written. He shook his head. He was too tired for work but felt he must continue, otherwise he would think back to Cranston's words about Benedicta. Idly, he wondered if the widow would accompany him. After all, there would be nothing wrong in a day out for both of them. 'Christ had his friends,' he kept murmuring to himself. He thought of little Rosamund and went to the high altar where the great missal lay. The friar opened the book, turning to the back where a previous incumbent had written the names of all the saints, listing in a neat hand which guild, craft or profession they were patrons of. Joseph, Athelstan grinned, patron saint of undertakers and mortuary men. The friar laughed. Joseph of Arimithea – the only man he ever buried was alive and well three days later! Perhaps not the best saint the church should have chosen for such a profession. His eyes ran down the list, looking for a suitable saint's name. Suddenly he saw one and stopped, his heart pounding with excitement. He was fully awake. He looked at the name again and the craft and guild of which he was patron. Was it possible? Was it really possible?

Athelstan closed the missal, all thoughts of Pike the ditcher and his family cleared from his head. He went back to the carrel, seized his pen and continued to write out everything he knew. He tried to extract every detail from his memory, quoting to himself what he had said to Cranston earlier in the day: 'If there's a problem, logically there must be a solution.' For the first time ever, Athelstan had a piece of evidence, something that would fit, something which might unlock the rest of the secrets.

He fell asleep for a few hours just before dawn and woke cold and cramped, his head on the small desk, his body somehow wedged on the stool. He stretched, cracking muscles, and looked up at the small window above the high altar, pleased to see it would be a fair day. He prepared the altar for Mass, opened the door and waited for the small trickle of his congregation to enter. At last, when he thought he could wait no longer, he glimpsed Benedicta slip silently up the nave to join the other two members of his congregation, kneeling between them at the entrance to the rood screen. The widow's ivory face, framed in its veil of luxurious black curls, seemed more exquisite than ever and Athelstan said a prayer of thanks to God for such beauty.

As usual, after Mass, Benedicta stayed to light a candle before the statue of the Virgin. She smiled as Athelstan approached and asked softly if all was well.

Athelstan took his courage in both hands and blurted out his invitation. Benedicta's eyes rounded in surprise, but she smiled and agreed so quickly that the friar wondered if she, too, felt the kinship between them. For the rest of the day he could hardly concentrate on any problem, caught between contrition that he had done something wrong in inviting Benedicta and pleasure that she had so readily accepted. He could not really account for what he did, moving from duty to duty like a sleepwalker, so buoyed up he didn't even bother to study the stars that night, in spite of the sky being cloud free. His mind was unwilling to rest. Sleep eluded him. Instead he tossed and turned, hoping Girth the bricklayer's son had delivered his message to Sir John Cranston indicating where they should meet the next day.

The friar was up just before dawn and celebrated his Mass, Bonaventure and Benedicta being his only congregation. Athelstan's pleasure increased when he saw that Benedicta, her hair now braided and hidden under a wimple, had a small basket by her side in preparation for their journey to Smithfield. After Mass they talked, chatting about this and that, as they walked from Southwark across London Bridge to meet Cranston and his wife at the Golden Pig, a comfortable tavern on the city side of the river.

Lady Maude, small and pert, was cheerful as a little sparrow, welcoming Benedicta like a long-lost sister. Cranston, with at least three flagons of wine down him already, was in good form, nudging Athelstan in the ribs and leering lecherously at Benedicta. After Sir

John had pronounced himself refreshed, they made their way up to Thames Street to the Kirtle tavern which stood on the edge of Smithfield, just under the forbidding walls of Newgate Prison.

Athelstan remembered what he had learnt from his study of the Index of Saints but decided not to confide in Sir John. The puzzle had other pieces and the friar decided to wait, although he felt guiltily that Benedicta's presence might have more to do with his tardiness than it should have.

The day had proved to be a fine one. The streets were hot and dusty, so Cranston and Athelstan's party welcomed the tavern's coolness. They sat in a corner watching the citizens of every class and station go noisily by, eager to reserve a good place from which to watch the day's events: merchants sweltering under beaver hats, their fat wives clothed in gaudy gowns, beggars, quacks, story-tellers, hordes of apprentices, and a man from the guilds. Athelstan groaned and hid his face as a crowd of parishioners led by Black Clem, Ranulf the rat-catcher and Pike the ditcher, passed the tavern door, roaring a filthy song at the top of their voices. At last Cranston finished his further refreshment and, with Benedicta so close beside him his heart kept skipping for joy, Athelstan led them out into the great cleared area of Smithfield. Three blackened crow-pecked corpses still hung from a gibbet, but the crowd ignored them. The food-sellers were doing a roaring trade in spiced sausages and, beside them, water-sellers with great buckets slung round their necks sold cooling drinks to soothe the mouths of those who chewed the hot, spicy meat. Athelstan looked away, his gorge rising, after seeing Ranulf the rat-catcher sidle up beside one of these water-sellers and quietly piss into one of the buckets.

Smithfield had been specially cleared for the joust. Even the customary dung heaps and piles of ordure had been taken away. A vast open space had been cordoned off for the day. At one side was the royal enclosure with row after row of wooden seats, all covered in purple or gold cloth. In the centre a huge canopy shielded the place where the king and his leading nobility would sit. The banners of John of Gaunt, resplendent with the gaudy device of the House of Lancaster, waved lazily in the breeze. Marshalls of the royal household in their colourful tabards, white wands of office held high, directed Cranston and his party to their reserved seats.

All around them benches were quickly filling with ladies in silk gowns, giggling and chattering, who clutched velvet cushions to their bosoms as they simpered past the young men eyeing them. These gallants, with hair long and curled, and jerkins dripping pearls, proved to be raucous and strident. Cranston was merry, but some of these young men were already far gone in their cups. Athelstan ignored the lustful glances directed at Benedicta, trying to curb the sparks of jealousy which flared in his heart.

Once they were seated, he looked round, studying the tournament area. The field, a great grassy plain, was divided down the centre by a huge tilt barrier covered in a black and white canvas. At the end of this barrier were the pavilions, gold, red, blue and scarlet, one for each of the jousters. Already the contestants were arriving and around each pavilion scuttled pages and squires. Armour glinted and dazzled in the sun; banners bearing the gules and lozenges, lions, wyverns and dragons of the noble houses, fluttered in the faint summer breeze. A bray of trumpets stilled the clamour, their shrill so angry the birds in the trees around Smithfield rose in noisy protesting flocks. The royal party had arrived.

Cranston pointed out John of Gaunt, Duke of Lancaster, his face cruel under blond hair, skin burnt dark from his campaigns in Castile. On either side of him stood his brothers and a collection of young lords. In the centre of the group, with one of John of Gaunt's hands on his shoulder, stood a young boy, his face white as snow under a mop of golden hair, a silver chaplet on his head. Cranston nudged and pointed again: beside the royal party Athelstan glimpsed Chief Justice Fortescue in scarlet, lined with pure white lamb's wool, Sir Richard, Lady Isabella, the priest Crispin, Master Buckingham, Dame Ermengilde, and others of their household. Athelstan was sure that they all looked his way but again came the shrill bray of the trumpets. Gaunt raised his hand as if welcoming the plaudits of the crowd. There was clapping from the claque of young courtiers around him but the London mob was silent and Athelstan remembered Cranston's mutterings about how the expensive tastes of the court, coupled with the military defeats against the French, had brought Gaunt and his party into disrepute.

'Our quarry's in sight!' Cranston whispered to the friar, though his voice carried for yards around them. Athelstan looked sideways at Benedicta and his heart lurched. She had turned slightly, staring coolly back at a young, dark-faced gallant, resplendent in red and white silks, who lounged in his seat with eyes for no one but Athelstan's fair companion. Cranston, sharp enough under his bluff, drunken exterior, caught the friar's pained glance. He leaned over and tapped Athelstan on the arm.

'The tournament is about to begin, Brother,' he said. 'Watch carefully. You may learn something about combat.'

Another shrill blast of the trumpets. Banners were lowered, and behind the pavilions came a procession led by pages in tight quilted jackets, multi-coloured hose and gaudy feathered hats. They carried huge canvas paintings depicting scenes from the Bible and classical times. Hercules fighting with the python; the slaying of Hector; the Siege of Troy; Samson amongst the Philistines; and the serpent entering Eden. Such a tableau always preceded tournaments. It was followed by musicians with tambour, fife and viol. Behind them came squires and further pages and, finally, the knights themselves, not yet armoured, their colours carried before them. The procession wound around the whole tournament area, knights and men-at-arms acknowledging the cheers and cries of the crowd.

Athelstan looked more closely at one of the paintings, a scene from the Book of Genesis, remembered something he had glimpsed in the Springall house, and he gasped. The sounds around him died away. All he could see was that crude canvas painting being carried by two pages. Of course! His stomach churned with excitement. He turned to Cranston, grabbing him by the arm.

'The paintings! The canvas paintings!' he whispered hoarsely.

Cranston looked at him blearily.

'The paintings, Sir John, in the Springall house? The canvas ones on the walls. When we first went there, they were covered in black drapes because of the mourning. Don't you remember? Genesis Chapter Three, Verse One, the serpent entering Eden! There was a painting like that in one of the galleries in Springall's house. Maybe that is what Sir Thomas was referring to?'

Cranston blinked. Making sure his wife did not see him, he pulled a wineskin from underneath his cloak and took a generous swig.

'I am here to enjoy myself, man,' he said hoarsely. As he put the stopper back, Athelstan's words sank in.

'My God, of course, you're right! The paintings, the three riddles. They may hold the secret!'

Athelstan dare not tell him that he had already resolved one of them.

'What shall we do?' murmured Cranston.

'Go now!' Athelstan said.

'But we are here as the guests of John of Gaunt. I know the duke. If we leave, he will send some busy body squire or serjeant-at-arms after us.'

'Now is the best time,' Athelstan replied, drawing closer, whispering into Sir John's ear, conscious that Lady Maude was totally absorbed in the pageant before her whilst Benedicta, distracted, was still staring back at the admiring gallant.

'Sir John, the Springall house is empty now. Let us strike whilst the iron is hot!'

Cranston looked as if he was going to refuse but thought again. 'Follow me,' he said.

Cranston whispered to his wife, then waddled off with Athelstan in tow, pushing through the crowd towards the royal enclosure. Knight bannerets of the king's household stopped them but Cranston muttered a few words and they let him by. Athelstan, however, had to stand outside the protective ring of steel watching Cranston bow at the foot of the steps and fall to one knee. Athelstan looked behind him. The procession was still circling the arena. John of Gaunt came down the steps, laughing. He tapped Cranston on the shoulder and raised him up, whispering in his ear. The coroner replied. Behind Gaunt,

248

Chief Justice Fortescue glowered like some angry hawk. John of Gaunt looked up abruptly and stared like a hungry cat at Athelstan, his eyes yellow, hard and unblinking. He nodded and muttered something over his shoulder to Fortescue, then to Cranston. The coroner bowed and backed away. Athelstan looked to his left to where the Springall household sat. Surprisingly, no one seemed interested in Sir John's meeting with the regent.

Cranston himself said nothing until they had walked away from the royal enclosure.

'Brother,' he whispered, 'we have the Regent's permission to go down to the Springall house now, to examine and take anything we wish. The regent has said, even if it takes all day, we are not to appear at the royal palace or the Savoy until we have something more to tell him!'

Athelstan's heart sank. On the one hand he wished to examine those paintings and resolve the mystery. But on the other, he wished to be with Benedicta. He looked up. Fitful clouds were beginning to obscure the sun. He glanced across to where the women sat. Cranston's wife was making herself comfortable on the bench whilst the gallant who had been eyeing Benedicta had now moved closer and was talking quietly with her. He was teasing her, but Benedicta did not seem to mind. She seemed absorbed in the young man's conversation. Athelstan barely listened to Cranston's muttering. He fought to control a sense of panic and reminded himself that he was a priest, a man ordained, sworn to God. Had he not taken a vow of celibacy? Although he might have a woman as a friend, he could not lust, he could not desire or covet any woman, whether she be free or not. Athelstan steeled himself. Benedicta was courteous to everyone, whether it be Hob's wife, Ranulf the rat-catcher, or now a court gallant. Nevertheless, Athelstan felt a growing rage at his condition; a sense of jealous hurt that Benedicta could find someone else so attractive and entertaining, even though he dismissed the emotion itself as both childish and dangerous.

Chapter 9

They left Smithfield, taking a different route back into the city, past the ditch which smelt so rank and fetid that even Cranston, filled to his gills with wine, stopped to gag and cover his nose. The coroner made a mental note to include in his treatise a special chapter on the cleaning of the ditch. They hurried past Cock Lane. The mouth of the street was thronged with whores in scarlet, red or violet dresses; one of them, swaying her hips and making her breasts dance, shouted: 'Sir John! Sir John! See us now!'

Cranston turned, a broad smile on his expansive face, not caring about Athelstan standing beside him, writhing in embarrassment.

'All my girls!' he muttered. 'All my lovely girls!'

Then, urged on by Athelstan, they continued past Newgate into the Shambles and Westchepe. The city was fairly silent, quieter than usual due to the great tournament at Smithfield. The city authorities had taken care to use the day to process certain cases in the court. A number of whores caught and convicted at their second offence were being taken, their heads shaved, a white wand in their hands, down towards the Tun near Cornhill, the open gaol where they stood to be reviled by any passerby. They did not seem to mind, each patting her head and calling out that her hair would soon grow, which was more than could be said for the balding bailiffs escorting them. A liar or perjurer stood in the docks, a great whetstone round his neck, a placard proclaiming that he was a false perjurer and breaker of oaths; beside him a hapless youth who had stolen a leg of mutton and was standing there with the piece of meat, now well decaying and buzzing with flies, slung round his neck. Athelstan watched the scene around him and tried to keep his mind free of Benedicta and the petty jealousies which nagged him.

They found the Springall house deserted except for a few servants. By the looks of them, they had been playing whilst the cat was away. Most of them were well gone in their cups and offered no objection when Cranston knocked at the door and demanded entrance. The old retainer who had received them on their first visit tried to help but Cranston pushed him gently away, saying it was a holiday and besides he was here at Sir Richard's request to pursue his inquiries privately. Naturally, the fragrant smell of wine reminded Cranston of how long it had been since he had refreshed himself, so he ordered a large jug and the deepest goblet to be found in the kitchen.

He followed Athelstan as the friar went from one canvas painting to the next. Cranston showed himself surprisingly knowledgeable on the subject of the paintings they examined. He claimed that some were the work of Edward Prince, an artist who lived in the north of the city. Athelstan half listened to Cranston's chatter, trying to remember where he had seen the painting of Eve in the garden enchanted by the serpent. At last he recalled it was not in the Nightingale Gallery but in the one running to the left.

Followed by Cranston, who was now staggering, Athelstan went upstairs and removed the huge canvas painting from the wall. He cursed. It was apparent that someone else had realised the painting might hold the key to Sir Thomas's mystery. The wood at the back of the painting was deeply scored with a dagger as if someone had been searching for some secret crevice or compartment. Yet there was nothing.

'It is useless, Brother!' Cranston murmured, pouring himself another cup of claret. 'It is absolutely bloody useless! There is nothing here. And the other two? The reference to Death on a pale horse in the Apocalypse, and the shoemaker? We're wasting our time.'

Athelstan made him sit on the floor with his back to the wall and, crouching down beside him, told him quietly what he had learnt: how the wood carving being made for the coronation pageant might hold a clue to the killer's identity. Cranston, despite his befuddled wits, heard him out then bellowed in righteous indignation.

'Why didn't you tell me before? It makes sense. It's possible. But why didn't you tell me?'

Athelstan found nothing more amusing than Cranston portraying virtue outraged and let the coroner ramble on until he had exhausted his litany of complaint. Athelstan heaved the painting back on the wall. After that he went from chamber to chamber, from corridor to corridor, looking for other canvases which might fit the verse from the Apocalypse. Cranston staggered behind him, holding a wine cup in one hand and the jug in the other. They found nothing. Of course, certain chambers were locked: Sir Richard's and Lady Isabella's, for instance. With Cranston bouncing along the Nightingale Gallery, the whole house seemed to sing with noise. Sir Thomas's chamber, deserted except for a bed, table, and other sticks of furniture was, surprisingly, open. Cranston stared round. There was no painting here either. The walls were bare. Athelstan went over to the window and stared down at the chess table.

'You know, Sir John, if we find nothing this afternoon then I agree, we should record verdicts of suicide and murder and leave this matter alone for we are making little progress.'

He heard a loud crash behind him. Cranston had placed the wine cup and jug beside the bed, collapsed on to the mattress and was smiling beatifically at the ceiling, fast asleep. Athelstan sighed, went over, and with great difficulty arranged Sir John's huge body more comfortably on the bed. Then he sat beside him. He had not brought his writing tray or materials but mentally he went through each of the deaths he had investigated, trying to fix a pattern, with little success. Cranston snored gently like a child, muttering now and again and smacking his lips. Athelstan grinned as he heard the words 'Refreshment' and 'Some cups of sack!' Sir John burped noisily, rolled on one side and, if Athelstan had not been there, would have fallen completely off the bed. Athelstan let the coroner sleep. Why not? After all, there was only one painting which fitted the texts and that held nothing. His thoughts strayed to Benedicta. Was she missing him? Why had she talked so easily to that nobleman? Were all women like that? Had he done wrong in inviting her in the first place?

He picked up the wine cup and sipped from it and then sat on the bed next to Sir John, staring down at the great wooden bed posters. He dozed and was about to fall asleep when suddenly he woke with a start. The carvings! Especially the one on the right... He got off the bed and went around. Whoever had constructed the bed post had created a vivid scene. The serpent carved there seemed to writhe, its tongue darting, whilst its intended victim, Eve, stood like the personification of innocence with one hand covering her groin, the other raised to hold back her long flowing hair. In between them was the drooping branch of an apple tree. Even in wood the fruit seemed full and lush. Athelstan stood for a moment in disbelief, then he moved over to the other bed post: there, in the centre, the artist had etched a life-like horse. The dark brown of the wood made the creature seem real, one leg raised, head arched, and on its back a frightening, ghostly figure with a hood. Peeping out from beneath it was the skeletal face of Death itself. Athelstan gasped with excitement and went round to rouse the coroner.

'Sir John! Wake up!'

The coroner moved, snored and smacked his lips.

'Sir John!' Athelstan slapped him gently on the face. The coroner's eyes opened.

'My dear Maude…'

'I am not Maude!' Athelstan replied sharply. 'Sir John, I have discovered something.'

'A cup of sack?'

Athelstan refilled the goblet and held it to the coroner's lips. 'For God's sake, Sir John, wake up!'

The coroner sat up, shaking the sleep from his eyes, and stared blearily round.

'For God's sake, Friar, what has happened now?'

Athelstan showed him. At first, his mind dulled with sleep and wine, Cranston stared blankly but the significance of the friar's discovery gradually dawned on him. Without more ado, the coroner began to finger the carving of the figure of Death, probing and pressing it.

'There must be a secret compartment. I have heard of such in the Italian mode, built into chairs, tables

256

and desks. I have even heard of hiding places in beds but never seen one.'

Their search was fruitless, so they moved to the other bed post. They pushed different parts of the carving but nothing moved. Suddenly Cranston looked up and nudged Athelstan.

'Look, Brother!'

Athelstan stared across at the bed post where a small block of wood on which the carving had rested had now opened outwards like a door.

'The mechanism must be in this bed post, with a spring that runs here under the boarding and up into the other.'

Again they pressed, watching the small door close when Athelstan pushed the apple between the serpent and Eve. He pushed and it re-opened. Slowly they approached the cavity, each trying to control his excitement. Athelstan put his hand gingerly into the small, dark space and brought out two rolls of parchment. He ignored Cranston's excited pleas to hurry and went over to the window, unrolling them carefully. The first was a love poem written in a rough hand in Norman French. At first Athelstan thought it was addressed to a woman but realised it was written to a young man. He handed it over to Cranston.

'Make of that what you wish!'

The second was a small indenture or agreement. The top was perforated, so someone else must have a copy. Athelstan read and knew why John of Gaunt,

Duke of Lancaster, was so indebted to Sir Thomas Springall, and why the merchant had possessed secrets which could have brought him even greater wealth. Cranston had already dismissed the poem, but when he read the indenture, he sat at the foot of the bed stupefied, the parchment held loosely between his fingers.

'This was written fourteen months ago,' he said quietly. 'As the Black Prince, father of the present king, lay dying. If the Lord Edward had known this, he would have had John of Gaunt's head on a pole on London Bridge. If it was revealed now there would be a public outcry.'

'So we know the reasons for Springall's death,' Athelstan said, 'but not the hows, the wherefores, and above all the culprit or culprits. Look, Sir John, let's follow the method of the Schools at Oxford. You sit on the bed, I'll sit beside you. You will recite everything you know about each of the four murders, beginning with Sir Thomas Springall's. Though in fact there was another killing, making five in all.' He pointed to the parchment poem. 'The young boy who died here must also be regarded as a victim.'

And so they began, Cranston occasionally pausing for refreshment as he recited in an almost sing-song voice what they knew about Springall's death, and then Brampton's, Vechey's and Allingham's. Athelstan would correct him and make Cranston repeat the list of facts time and again until the coroner, not famous for his patience, shouted: 'Hell's teeth! What are you doing, Brother? We are wasting time! All we are doing is repeating what we already know.'

'Be patient, Sir John,' Athelstan replied, 'Remember, we are looking for a pattern. In logic when you have a problem, the very words of the puzzle contain the answer. There must be a pattern in each of the murders.' He saw Sir John set his mouth and glare from beneath bushy grey eyebrows. 'Look, there is one murder we know very little about – Vechey's. But three, Allingham's, Brampton's and Springall's, we do. There must be common factors, things which link all three. We have already established one: poison. I also suspect Vechey and Brampton were drugged. They would not have allowed people to pluck them up, take them prisoner, tie a noose around their necks and kill them. So we have some matching strands. Let us see if there are more.'

Once again Sir John grudgingly recited the facts they knew. Outside the day drew to a close. Athelstan, now listening with half an ear to Sir John's recitation, looked out of the window and wondered what had happened to Benedicta and Lady Maude. Should they return to escort the ladies? He broke Sir John's concentration by asking but the coroner just glowered.

'The Ladies Benedicta and Maude are well able to look after themselves,' he said. 'You started this,

Brother, so we'll see it through to the bitter end. Moreover,' he smiled, 'I asked the young gallant who was sitting by Benedicta to take care of both ladies. I am sure he will.'

Athelstan ground his teeth and glared at the coroner, but Sir John smiled sweetly back as if innocent of any devious stratagem. Athelstan again made him repeat all they knew, though this time excluding Sir Thomas Springall's murder. Then he walked over to the window and stared down at the chess board. Absentmindedly he began to count the squares, and his heart quickened.

'There is a pattern, Sir John,' he said softly. 'Yes!' He turned, his lean face bright with excitement. 'There is a pattern!'

'You know who the murderer is, don't you? Come on, you bloody friar!' Cranston roared. 'Tell me! I haven't sat here on this bed like a boy in a schoolroom reciting lists of facts for nothing!'

'Tush, Sir John, patience,' Athelstan replied. 'Let me work it into a pattern. Let me get the proper sequence of events, then I shall tell you what I know and the problem will be resolved. But for now you stay here, examine the indenture, reflect on what you have said. I won't be long!'

Before a bemused Cranston could reply, Athelstan had slipped out of the room, walking gingerly across the noisy Nightingale Gallery, down the stairs and out into Cheapside. Just in case he met any of the

Springall household, he went down Friday Street, turning into Bread Street and back up St Mary Le Bow. The church was open. Athelstan went into the nave and sat at the base of a pillar, legs crossed, whilst he stared up at the high altar behind the rood screen. He looked round the cool, beautiful church, at the frescoes on the wall, lectern, and pulpit of exquisitely carved oak. From the stalls in the sanctuary he heard the master assembling the choir, rehearsing the hymns and canticles for the feast of Corpus Christi. Athelstan leaned back, letting his head rest against the coldness of the pillar whilst he stared into the darkness, trying to rearrange what he knew, to make the pattern complete and trap the murderer. This was one occasion when the sons of Cain, the killers, would not turn round and claim with mocking innocence, 'Are we our brother's keepers? We are not responsible because we are innocent,' while the blood of five human beings stained their hands and darkened their souls.

The choir began the beautiful hymn 'Pange Lingua'. Athelstan let his mind and soul be calmed, moved by the rhythmical chanting. At one point the youngest boys, the choir's sopranos, took up the refrain, pure and lucid, filling the entire church with angelic sound.

'*Respice. Respice Domine.* Look back, oh Lord, look back on us!'

Athelstan muttered the words under his breath. 'Look back, oh Lord,' he prayed. 'Give me wisdom and light. Let me plumb the darkness, root out the wickedness. Let those things that were done in the dark of night be revealed for your justice and that of the king in the full light of day.'

Athelstan meditated for an hour. He saw the irony that here he was in a church, the house of God and gate to heaven, thinking about murder. But gradually the pattern was resolved. The culprits were identified, their motives revealed, and he reluctantly admired their deviousness, the sheer wickedness of their plan. He built his own traps, hedging them about, and, when he was ready, returned to the Springall house.

He found Cranston still resting on Sir Thomas's bed, a cup of claret in his hand, softly singing a lullaby. Athelstan could have sworn he was acting as if there was someone else there. As if he was singing to someone he loved. The friar noticed the coroner's eyes were brimming with tears. He looked away, pretending to stare out of the window as he began to summarise his conclusions. Behind him, Cranston regained control of himself. He listened to the friar describe the motive and the identity of the murderers. At first, the coroner rejected everything his assistant said.

'Too ingenious!' he cried. 'Too clever! Too diabolic!'

Athelstan turned. 'Diabolic, yes. But these murders were crafted in the human soul and decided upon by the human mind even if carried out for

262

malicious, devilish purposes. I think I speak the truth, Sir John.'

Cranston stared moodily down at the floorboards, scuffing his boots over the polished surface. Suddenly the Nightingale Gallery outside creaked and sang. Cranston's hand went towards his dagger and Athelstan rapidly approached the door. It was only the old servant, deeper in his cups than Cranston. He staggered and leaned on the door post.

'You have been here a long time, masters. Are you staying? Waiting for Sir Richard?'

'No,' Cranston replied, 'I have told you already. We are here on the regent's orders!' He lifted the wine cup and drained it. 'But I do thank you for your hospitality, sir. I shall remember it.'

'Oh,' Athelstan added, 'is it possible that I could speak to one of the laundresses?'

The servant looked surprised. He blinked but agreed, and some time later ushered a scared girl into the room. She became even more frightened as Athelstan outlined his request and asked her to bring the napkin as soon as possible. When she did, Athelstan poured the dregs of the wine over it, cleaned a dusty part of the room and put it beneath his cloak. The maid servant quickly left. Sir John looked bemused.

'What I have done is vital, Sir John,' Athelstan assured him. 'It may well trap the murderers.'

They left the deserted house, the old manservant locking the door behind them, and went down into a deserted Cheapside. Black rain clouds were scudding in over the Thames. It was dark and some of the merchants had lit the lantern-horns outside their doors, whilst Athelstan glimpsed the beacon light shining red and full in the steeple of St Mary Le Bow. They made their way down Friday Street, Old Fish Street and into the Vintry, and hired a wherry at Queenshithe Wharf to take them along the choppy river to the Savoy Palace. Viewed from the riverbank, John of Gaunt's palatial residence looked magnificent, and even more so tonight with the festivities going on. The windows were lit by the flames of thousands of beeswax candles and, as they approached the main entrance, they heard faint strains of music, chatter, and the sounds of merriment. A burly serjeant-of-arms stopped them, asked their business, and grudgingly let them through into the main courtyard where they were halted by a steward who took them up into the main hall.

Athelstan was dumbfounded by the magnificent spectacle awaiting them: the hall was long, the hammer-beam roof high, whilst every piece of wood-work and stone was covered in the most luxurious velvet and samite hangings, gorgeous banners and hangings of every hue. Down the hall on each side were long trestle tables covered in the costliest silk. Every few feet were huge eight-branched candelabra, each with its own beeswax candles. Above them in the loft the musicians played, though their music had to compete with the noise of the revellers sitting at table.

At the far end, on the dais, Athelstan glimpsed John of Gaunt. On the same table he saw the young king, Chief Justice Fortescue, and some of the leading nobility of the realm. At the table just beneath the dais, running parallel with it, they saw Sir Richard Springall, red-faced and deep in his cups. At his side was Lady Isabella who for that day had cast aside her mourning weeds and wore a pure gold dress with matching veil. Father Crispin and Master Buckingham were also visible, while at the other end of the table were Lady Maude and Benedicta, between them the young nobleman who had made his intentions so blatantly obvious earlier in the day. Lady Maude was looking down the hall, obviously looking out for her husband. Benedicta, cooler and more composed, was listening attentively to some story the nobleman was telling her, though now and again moving slightly away from him as if she had come to resent the young gallant's attentions. The steward was about to announce them, but Athelstan put a hand on his arm.

'No,' he muttered. 'Not now. The feast is in progress.' He looked down at the tablecloths splattered with grease and wine, the platters now cleared. The servants were bringing in bowls of fruit, junkets of cream, plates of thin pastries, sugar-filled doucettes, and jellies formed in exquisite shapes of castles, swans and horses. Soon the banquet would be over. He looked at Sir John. 'There's no point in joining the festivities. It is best if we have no dealings with Sir Richard and other members of his household.'

The coroner, gazing longingly at the jugs of claret, was about to protest.

'Sir John,' Athelstan reminded him, 'we have important business to attend to.'

Cranston sighed, nodded, and turned to the steward, asking him to take them to one of the duke's private chambers. The man looked askance but Cranston insisted.

'Yes, you will, sir,' he repeated. 'You will take us to one of the duke's private chambers here in the palace. Then you will tell your master and Chief Justice Fortescue that we have important matters to relate, matters affecting the crown. You will ask that Sir Richard and his household also join us as soon as the festivities are over.'

Cranston made the man repeat the message as he reluctantly took them out of the main hall and up the wide, spacious stairs to one of the duke's private chambers. Athelstan gazed around and nodded. Yes, this would do. A small fire had been lit in the hearth. The room, possibly used as a chancery by the duke, was dominated by a long table with chairs down either side and a high-backed, throne-like seat at the top. The steward left Cranston and Athelstan, who stood examining the exquisite hangings on the wall and a small cupboard full of manuscripts bound with the costliest leather and vellum. A servant brought them some wine and sugared pastries which Cranston immediately attacked. Another servant entered, a young page who announced in a high, shrill voice that the duke had received Sir John's message and would be with him as soon as dignity and circumstances would allow.

An hour candle placed on the table under the window had burnt a complete ring before Cranston heard footsteps outside. He and Athelstan rose as Gaunt swept into the room. Beside the duke was the young king, a silver chaplet around his head. Uncle and nephew were dressed identically in purple gowns edged with gold. The young king looked serene though Gaunt seemed angry and troubled, as if he resented Cranston's message. He slumped into the chair at the end of the table and ordered a servant to bring in a similar one for his nephew. Chief Justice Fortescue slid in like a spider, scuttling across to sit next to the Duke. He was followed by Sir Richard Springall and his household. The merchant was flushed with drink; he grinned at Cranston and Athelstan as if they were lifelong friends; Dame Ermengilde, her nose in the air, chose to ignore them. Father Crispin and Buckingham smiled wanly whilst Lady Isabella looked decidedly agitated.

'Are we all assembled?' Gaunt asked sardonically.

Chief Justice Fortescue glanced around and nodded. 'Yes, Your Grace, we are all here.'

Athelstan noticed that a burly serjeant-at-arms had just stepped into the room.

'I want this chamber guarded closely!' the regent ordered. 'No one is to leave or enter without my permission. Do you understand?'

The man nodded. Outside Athelstan could hear him shouting orders, the sound of running feet and the clash of arms. He gazed at the assembled company. Sir Richard Springall had sobered up surprisingly quickly. Lady Isabella was looking across at him, nervously twisting her fingers. Dame Ermengilde, even though she was in the presence of royalty, sat staring at the wall opposite her. The rest of them kept their eyes fastened on the duke, waiting to see what lay behind his summons.

Gaunt leaned forward, the jewels on his tanned hands flashing in the candlelight.

'Sir John, coroner of the city, I am pleased to see you. And even though you were not present at the banquet, it is obvious that you have drunk well. I hope your day was a fruitful one?'

Cranston caught the touch of menace in the duke's words and glanced at Athelstan.

The friar acknowledged the regent and the young king. 'My Lord of Gaunt, Your Grace, we were given a commission to investigate the true causes and purposes behind Sir Thomas Springall's death, and in consequence the truth behind other deaths equally unfortunate.' He rose to his feet. 'Your Grace, I ask your indulgence, but I would like us to perform a small mummer's play, a useful introduction to what we are about to declare.'

Gaunt gazed at the friar crossly. 'What is it, Brother?' he asked.

'A game, Uncle!' The young king suddenly spoke up, childish glee replacing the mask of royalty on his face. He clapped his hands.

'Your Grace,' Gaunt smiled thinly at his nephew, 'perhaps you should not be here?'

'Perhaps I should!' the young boy piped back. 'I want to be. It is my right!'

Athelstan was surprised at the precociousness of the child and, despite his tender years, the sway he held over his formidable uncle.

Gaunt sighed. 'Brother, we are in your hands. Though I warn you,' he gestured threateningly, 'don't waste my time or engage us in meddlesome, wasteful tricks. I am here for the truth!'

Chapter 10

Athelstan pointed to the chamber door.

'My Lord of Gaunt, let us pretend that behind that door lies someone you dearly love.'

Gaunt glared back at him.

'The door is locked and you are about to rouse them. What would you do?'

'A simple question! I would try the door, I would knock, I would hammer, I would shout!'

'Thank you, Your Grace. Lady Ermengilde, you heard Father Crispin come up to rouse Sir Thomas that fateful morning. What happened?'

The old dame had caught the drift of Athelstan's words, her face losing some of its haughty composure. She narrowed her eyes. 'I heard him come up. He tried the handle of the door of my son's bed chamber. Then he walked away. He went to find Sir Richard.'

'Now why was that, Father?' Athelstan asked. 'You went up to waken your master – he had asked to be roused early, remember? You went up as anyone would do, you tried the door, but then you went to get his brother. Why did you not try to rouse Sir Thomas Springall yourself? You tried the door but there was no sound from within. Anyone else would have pounded on the door, shouting Sir Thomas's name. You failed to do so. You immediately walked away to rouse Sir Richard. Why?'

'Because I thought that was the best thing to do.'

'It was not the logical thing to do,' Athelstan replied quickly. 'The logical thing was to pound on the door and shout Sir Thomas's name. You did not. It was as if you knew something was wrong.'

The priest swallowed quickly but gazed coolly around the room. 'What are you implying, Brother?'

'At the moment I am implying nothing. Let us proceed a little further. Sir Richard comes upstairs with other members of the household. The door is forced. And inside?'

'Why,' the priest replied, 'my master, Sir Thomas Springall, lying on the bed, poisoned.'

'And what happened then? Precisely?'

'I went across to look at Sir Thomas.'

'No, he did not!' Sir Richard thrust himself forward. 'I did that. You came into the room with me, but I did that!'

'So what *did* you do, Father?' Athelstan continued.

'I just stood there.'

'No, you did something else.'

'Oh, yes. I picked up the wine cup and smelt it. I took it over to the window to look at the contents because its odour was strange.'

'And when you went to the window, you passed the chess board. Then what?'

'I pronounced the cup was poisoned. The rest you know.'

'And how were you dressed?'

'I told you. I had been outside, visiting the stables.'

'You were wearing gloves? A cloak?'

'Yes, I was.'

'I will tell you this, priest,' Athelstan replied, 'you wore the gloves for a purpose. You see, you knew that Sir Thomas was already dead before you went into that chamber. You had arranged it that way. The wine cup was not poisoned. You took it to the window and poured in the potion which you had concealed in your glove. As you passed the chess board you took a piece from it, the bishop, the reason being that it was heavily coated with a certain poison.'

Father Crispin's face was marble white. He shook his head wordlessly.

'This is what happened,' Athelstan continued. 'On the afternoon of the banquet, you engaged Sir Thomas in a game of chess. You played with all your skill and finesse and managed to trap Sir Thomas. The game broke off just before the meal. You knew how Sir Thomas hated to be beaten, you admitted that yourself. He would be absorbed in the moves so that when the game recommenced, he could try to escape from the trap posed by your pieces. Now, I put this to you, sir. Just before the banquet, as people were coming down, you went up to Sir Thomas's room, unnoticed by anyone else and, choosing a chess piece, coated it thickly with poison. Some time later, Brampton took up the wine cup.

'After the feast was over, Sir Thomas retired to his chamber, locking the door behind him. Then he did what you intended him to do, what any good chess player would have done. He went across to the chess board, trying to work out the best method to escape the trap you had placed him in. He picked up the bishop, the piece under threat, moving it around the board, attempting to find a way out. Like anyone who is deeply puzzled, he would raise his fingers to his lips. Little did he know that every time he did so, he was poisoning himself. It would not have taken long. The poisons you had bought from the apothecary were potent. Sir Thomas may have felt strange from the first symptoms; he left the chess board and went to his bed where he later died.

'The next morning you came up to his chamber, gloved, because you knew you would have to touch the poison yourself. But you needed witnesses, you wanted to make it very clear that the blame lay with Brampton. Sir Richard entered the room with you, as did other members of the household. Like any people breaking into a room and finding someone unexpectedly dead, they gathered round the corpse. Meanwhile you had removed the chess piece, poisoned the wine cup and placed it back on the table.'

'The cup now seemed the bringer of death and the blame was placed on Brampton.'

The priest regained his wits. 'That's impossible!' he said. 'How could I know that Sir Thomas would touch the chess board after he had retired for that night?'

'Oh, but you did,' Cranston broke in. 'You did, you admitted as much yourself. You said that Sir Thomas could not leave the chess board alone. And the only people that touched the cup were Brampton, Sir Thomas and yourself. Only after that was the poison detected in it.'

'And I suppose that I am responsible for Brampton's murder?'

'Yes.' Cranston took up the tale. 'My good secret-arius here, my faithful clerk, has established that Brampton probably went back to his room after the banquet had begun. He felt hurt by Sir Thomas's accusation that he had been meddling with his private papers. Now, of course, Brampton had not. *You* had. However, we will return to that. You probably drugged Brampton.'

'Drugged!' the priest snapped. 'Brampton wasn't drugged! That's nonsense!'

He looked around the room, appealing for support, but Athelstan noticed how the others were beginning to distance themselves from the priest. Chief Justice Fortescue looked steadily at the tabletop. Gaunt had a smile on his twisted lips. The young king seemed totally absorbed. Cranston shook his head.

'It's no use lying, murderer,' he snapped. 'You know Brampton had drunk deeply that day. A servant told us as much. And you, Lady Isabella, didn't you say your husband had broached his best cask of Bordeaux and that you sent a cup to Brampton as a peace offering?'

'Yes, I did,' she murmured. 'No! I sent the cup up—' she pointed at the priest '—but you poured it, Father Crispin. Yes, it was *your* idea. It was drugged!' she exclaimed.

'That night,' Athelstan interrupted, 'after the rest of the household retired, Father Crispin went up to Brampton's room. You are a strong young man, Crispin. Brampton was small and light; he lived on the second storey of the house, very near the stairs to the garret. You took him off his bed and carried him up, half sat him on the table, fastened the waiting noose round his neck and left him to hang, God save his soul! But poor Brampton knew for a while that he was choking to death. He grabbed the rope, but it was useless. His breath was choked off and his unshriven soul fled into the darkness.'

Athelstan went and stood over the priest. 'You are steeped in mortal sin,' he murmured. 'Your soul is red, scarlet and wounded. You killed that man but you made a mistake! Why should Brampton walk up to the garret with his boots off. And, if he had worn them, he would have kicked them off in his death throes.' Athelstan bent down, his face only inches from Crispin's. 'But let us say he did go up without his boots. The garret was dirty, there was broken glass

276

on the floor, yet the soles of Brampton's feet, even after his corpse had been cut down, were clean and unscarred. Why? Because his feet never touched the ground.'

'Vechey was murdered too, wasn't he?' Lady Isabella stammered.

'Yes,' Athelstan replied. 'And do you know why? When the door to your husband's chamber was forced, Vechey came in. At one point he must have looked at the chess board after Crispin had removed the poisoned piece to clean it.'

'Of course,' Dame Ermengilde trumpeted. 'That's why Vechey kept talking about there being only thirty-one. He noticed the missing piece. Vechey always coveted the Syrians!'

'And then the piece was returned,' Athelstan answered, 'which only perplexed him further. Nevertheless, Vechey's sharp eyes cost him his life and he, too, was marked down for murder lest he voice his doubts.'

'God knows how you managed that murder!' Cranston bawled. 'The red-haired whore may have been a lure in your pay. It may, cunning priest, even have been you in disguise. I wonder, a thorough search being made, if we wouldn't find a red wig and dress in your possession. But, there again, you made a mistake. Vechey was probably drugged or knocked on the head. You hung him up under an arch of London Bridge, but the water level would have made such a death impossible. You hoped no one would notice that.'

'Wait!' Crispin cried. 'You allege I had the poison, but you know a lady very similar to our Lady Isabella in dress and appearance bought the identical poison from the apothecary, Simon Foreman!'

'Yes,' Cranston said, 'and that's your third mistake. I did ask Lady Isabella about that, but you were not in the room. Remember, we asked you to withdraw? Lady Isabella, Sir Richard, is that correct?'

Both nodded their heads.

'And did you ever tell the priest about my question?'

Again, both shook their heads wordlessly.

'You couldn't have overhead!' Dame Ermengilde snapped. 'Because I stood near the door of the hall. I tried to listen but I couldn't hear anything.'

'The only way you could know,' Athelstan murmured, 'was because you dressed in clothes secretly borrowed from Lady Isabella's wardrobe. Your head was hidden by a red wig as well as a hood. You went to Nightshade House and bought the poison.' Athelstan sipped from his wine cup.

'You would enjoy that, wouldn't you?'

The priest refused to answer.

'But such subterfuge!' Lady Isabella cried.

'Oh, Crispin planned well. One of Brampton's buttons was placed near your husband's manuscripts to start the tragedy. However, in case something went wrong and the poison was traced...'

'What better person than you to implicate, Lady Isabella?' Cranston observed. 'After all, you were playing the two-backed beast with your husband's brother!'

Lady Isabella looked away whilst Crispin placed his head in his hands. Dame Ermengilde turned to Cranston, her eyes full of malice.

'You are not such a fool, Master Coroner. But haven't you forgotten a few things? If my son had touched the poisoned chess pieces, his hands would have been stained. And how do you explain Allingham's death?'

Athelstan looked down at the priest. Father Crispin raised his head and stared unblinkingly back.

'Remember, our murderer also bestowed the rites of the Church. He made sure that the hands of both Sir Thomas Springall and Master Allingham were washed before he anointed them with holy oils.'

'That's right,' Sir Richard whispered. 'And the anointing took place immediately!'

'So there was no stain,' Athelstan continued conversationally, 'as in all his murders, no real evidence. You are a killer, Father. An assassin. And we know why. You remember the young page boy who fell from the window? Sir Thomas lusted after him, and found you wrote a love poem to him. We have seen it. I suspect you tried to seduce the boy. God knows what happened. Tell us, Father, did he jump because he was frightened or did you push him?'

The priest glared back at him but made no answer.

'I think Sir Thomas knew the truth but dared not accuse you openly. After all, he was guilty of the same sin of sodomy as you. Of course, being a chaplain, you were privy to the secrets of others. So what Sir Thomas did was take his revenge through the carving, the panel he was going to use in the coronation pageant and later hang in the chapel.' Athelstan glanced at Sir Richard. 'Do you remember the carving? What was it of?'

'A shoemaker being dragged away by devils.'

'Did you ever look at the shoemaker's feet?'

'No.'

Cranston banged the heel of his boot on the floor.

'Poor Father Crispin, always hobbling around, using his injury as a banner. But when he so chooses, he puts on his boots with their raised heel – and, behold, he can walk like any of us. That's true, isn't it, Priest? You were out riding the day Allingham died?'

Father Crispin dismissed Cranston's accusation with a flicker of his eyes.

'Sir John is correct,' Athelstan took up the story. 'A priest can go anywhere, be it in his master's chamber to poison a chess piece, around the house at the dead of night to comfort poor Brampton, to say prayers at St Mary Le Bow… whereas in fact on the night Vechey died, Father Crispin disguised himself as the red-haired whore and went hunting his prey amongst the riverside stews.' Athelstan paused and looked quickly at Fortescue. 'I told Sir John that there was more than one murderer. In a sense I was correct. You are two people, Father, the hobbling priest and the cunning assassin.'

Athelstan noticed how the Chief Justice's face had become so pale it looked as if he was going to vomit.

'Of course, Crispin,' Athelstan continued, 'you had your accomplice. Someone you had met at your master's table. Someone who could tell you where we went so you could have assassins lying in waiting. You remember the gospel, Father, and the man who claimed his name was Legion, so many devils possessed him? He would recognise you, Priest. You murdered for revenge, for profit, but also for the sheer malicious delight of plot and counter-plot.'

'What has that got to do with the carving in the Springall yard?' Gaunt sharply interrupted.

Athelstan looked at Sir Richard.

'You should have examined that carving,' he remarked. 'Especially the shoemaker. He is very like our Father Crispin. He has a clubbed foot.'

Athelstan ignored Lady Isabella's gasp. Instead he looked up at young King Richard, who seemed fascinated by the priest, whilst Gaunt was now staring at Fortescue out of the corner of his eye.

'And Father, who is the patron saint of shoe-makers?'

Athelstan admired the priest's composure. Not a muscle twitched in that gaunt, haunted face.

'Come, Father, you know. Crispin Crispianus! We celebrate his feast in October. Sir Thomas was mocking you. The insult would be carried throughout the length and breadth of London and afterwards it would ridicule you every time you entered the small chapel in Sir Thomas's house. Perhaps one day a more astute person might notice it. Allingham certainly did, didn't he, Father? He began to wonder, as well as to remember Vechey's absorption with the number thirty-one!'

Cranston belched and rose to his feet unbidden, as if he had forgotten he was in the presence of royalty.

'My clerk,' he announced grandly, 'is correct. So you, Father, the master poisoner, struck again. You bought your poisons from Foreman, mixing them deliberately so the wine cup smelt rank and offensive, to ensure Brampton got the blame. But Allingham was different. He took a poison which was more difficult to trace. After his mid-day meal, Allingham went back to his chamber and fell asleep. What he did not know was that the handle of his door had been smeared with poison. The same trick you had played on Sir Thomas, but you were sure it would work again.'

Cranston stopped to refill his cup, rather shakily so the wine spilled over on the table. But the coroner, in full flow and bent on refreshment, didn't give a fig.

'Brother Athelstan,' he announced expansively, 'will summarise my conclusions.'

Athelstan hid his smile. Cranston was amusing but the hard-faced priest, the wolf in sheep's clothing, was not.

'You see, first, Allingham had a nervous gesture. Do you remember? His hands were constantly at his lips, fluttering up and down like a butterfly. During his final sleep, Father Crispin here probably locked him in his chamber. Allingham wakes, and finds there is no key. Nervous and agitated, he tries the door; all the time his death-bearing fingers are going to his mouth. He feels ill, goes back to the bed where he collapses and dies. The door is forced, the priest makes sure he is there, the key is dropped on the ground. Naturally, people would think it fell due to the door's being forced. Of course, Crispin here acts the perplexed innocent. He poses the question, if Allingham had a seizure, why did he not try and open the door? Strangely enough, while trying the lock, our murderer holds a napkin which he had been using to mop up some wine he had spilt. He examines the handle, using the napkin to gain a better grip. Of course, what he is really doing is cleaning the poison off.' Athelstan dug beneath his robe and brought out the soiled cloth he had begged from the laundress. 'This is the cloth.'

'It can't be!' Fortescue suddenly shouted.

'Shut up!' the priest yelled at him, his eyes and face full of hatred. 'Shut up, you idiot!'

'Why can't it be?' Cranston asked softly. 'Isn't it strange that you should remember what happened to an innocent napkin?'

Athelstan held his breath. Would a confession come?

'I only did what he asked,' Crispin whispered.

'Who?' Cranston asked softly.

'Fortescue, of course!'

The Chief Justice looked up, his face white with terror.

'I asked the priest to get the secrets Sir Thomas held. I did not plan murder.'

'Perhaps not,' Athelstan replied. 'But your accomplice, Father Crispin, did. On your orders, Chief Justice Fortescue, he tried to find out Sir Thomas Springall's secrets. Sir Thomas, a canny man, knew his private accounts had been scrutinised and the blame was put on Brampton. However, Sir Thomas and Brampton may have reached an accord and questions been asked, so Father Crispin plotted Springall's death. Brampton would be blamed after his supposed suicide and the way left clear for you to search for Sir Thomas's secret.'

John of Gaunt suddenly stood up. 'Sir Coroner, do your duty!' he ordered.

Cranston waddled round the table. 'Father Crispin, I arrest you in the name of the king for the dreadful crimes of treason, homicide and sedition!'

The priest gazed stonily back and continued to do so when the burly serjeant-at-arms, summoned by Gaunt, tied his thumbs together behind his back.

'Wait!'

Athelstan walked over to Fortescue. He noticed how Buckingham was quivering with fright, his face drenched in sweat. The effete young secretarius would never forget this day.

'Chief Justice Fortescue,' Athelstan murmured, 'you are the king's highest law officer. Why did you act as you did? Was it the lust for power, wealth, or the desire to control the regent? You knew Springall held some great secret and, in one of your visits to his household, made a pact with this priest, this limb of Satan.'

Fortescue tried to reply but the words stuck in his throat.

'Don't you realise, my Lord Chief Justice, that when you make a pact with the devil, you lose your soul?'

'I am no murderer,' he muttered.

Athelstan turned back to the priest. 'You murdered the page boy, Eudo, didn't you? You sent the assassins after Sir John and myself. You were the red-haired woman, as well as the scarlet whore.'

Father Crispin laughed and, bringing his head back, spat full in Athelstan's face.

'Ask me in hell, Brother!' he shrieked. 'When we both dance with the devil!'

He was still laughing like a madman when the door closed behind him.

'I did not plan murder. I was curious but I am no murderer,' Fortescue proclaimed, half rising from his chair.

'In forty-eight hours,' Gaunt snapped, 'I shall send soldiers to your house. If you haven't abjured the realm by then, I will arrest you, Fortescue, for treason! You may well rot a long time before I gather the evidence to try you!'

Fortescue fled from the room.

Athelstan studied the duke, noting the beads of sweat on his face, the agitation in his eyes. He looked almost pleadingly at Cranston.

'Sir Richard Springall,' the coroner barked, 'and Lady Isabella, you had best leave now, together with your household. If you still wonder about the Bible texts Sir Thomas quoted, examine the posts of his bed which you desecrated!'

The merchant, Lady Isabella, a nervous Buckingham and the now not so proud Dame Ermengilde hastily left the room, cowed by the dreadful things they had seen and heard. Cranston followed them out and muttered a command to the guard there. He had no sooner re-entered than the young king rose to his feet.

'What was Sir Thomas's secret?' he asked.

'Nephew!' Gaunt's voice was harsh and brittle. 'Your Grace,' he stammered, 'I think you should leave. These matters are not for tender minds.'

286

King Richard turned, a stubborn look on his thin, pale face.

'Your Grace,' Gaunt repeated, 'these matters do not concern you. I must insist. Sir John, Brother Athelstan, you are to say no word!'

The young king walked towards the door. With his gloved fingers on the handle, he stopped and beckoned Athelstan over. The friar went and bent so that the king could whisper in his ear.

'Brother,' he hissed, 'when I grow up, I will make you an abbot! And you will take my side when...' The young king's voice trailed off.

'When what, Your Grace?' he murmured.

Richard put his lips closer against the friar's ears. 'When I murder my uncle!' he whispered.

Athelstan stared into those childlike yet totally chilling blue eyes. The young king smiled and kissed him on both cheeks before disappearing through the half-open door, a boy going out to play. Athelstan rose and closed the door.

'What did he say, Brother?'

'Nothing, My Lord, some childish game.'

Gaunt grinned to himself as if savouring some private joke and stretched out his hand.

'The indenture. You have it?'

'Yes, My Lord.'

Gaunt snapped his fingers. 'Give it to me!'

Cranston handed both it and the love poem over. Gaunt scrutinised them carefully, crumpled them up in his hand and watched the flames of the fire burn them to black feathery ash.

'You know what it said?'

Cranston chewed his lip, not replying.

'Yes, My Lord, we do.' Athelstan sat down uninvited, not caring for idle ceremony. 'My Lord, we are tired. We know what the document says, but it does not concern us. Fourteen months ago, your brother, the Black Prince, the young king's father, was dying. You drew up an indenture with Sir Thomas Springall in which he promised you vast sums of money to raise troops. As surety you offered the crown jewels, the ring, the orb, the sceptre, and the crown of Edward the Confessor. They were not yours to offer. If your brother had known, if your father, the old king, had even suspected, you might well have lost your head. If the Commons found out now, they would suspect you of plotting against the king. If your noble brothers and the other great lords, Gloucester and Arundel, even glimpsed that document, they would tear you to pieces!'

'I was worried,' Gaunt haltingly replied. 'My brother was dying, my father senile, young Richard sickly. This realm needs strong government. Yes, if necessary, I would have seized the crown.'

'And now, My Lord?' Cranston asked.

'I am the king's most loyal servant,' Gaunt answered glibly. 'I am indebted to you, Sir John. I will not forget it.'

'Then, My Lord, we bid you goodnight.'

'Sir John,' Gaunt called after them, 'I will see you later on this matter. Brother Athelstan, ask any favour you wish.'

'Yes, My Lord. I would like some silver for my church and, secondly, a pension for a poor woman, widow of Hob the grave-digger.'

Gaunt grinned. 'So little for so much! See my clerks. It will be done.'

Athelstan and Cranston strode out along the now emptying corridors of the Savoy Palace, down through the heavily perfumed garden and on to the riverside.

Athelstan rubbed his eyes wearily. 'The murderer made one mistake and so did we, Sir John. First, I suspect Father Crispin waited until the tide fell before stringing the hapless corpse up.'

'But he told us he was gone on errands?'

'And that's where we made our mistake, Lord Coroner. We didn't ask when he returned, not that it would have made any difference in the Springall house where Sir Richard and Lady Isabella were lost in themselves and Allingham led his own lonely exist-ence. Moreover, I am sure the priest had ways of sneaking in and out of such a large mansion without being noticed.'

'Do you think Crispin will hang?' asked Cranston.

Athelstan shook his head.

'Fortescue asked him to get the information but then, as we know, matters got out of hand. Fortescue will go abroad and gain employment in some foreign court. Father Crispin, being a priest, will probably be immured in a monastery for the rest of his life and eat the bitter bread of repentance.' He crossed himself. 'Gaunt would never dare bring either of them to trial. But I suspect, within a year, Fortescue and our evil priest will both suffer some "accident" and answer for their crimes before God's tribunal.' Suddenly he remembered Benedicta. 'Sir John!' he cried. 'Your lady wife? Benedicta?'

Cranston turned and looked slyly at him.

'I asked the captain,' he said, 'to have two of his men escort the Lady Maude home. Benedicta was invited to go with her, but whether she did or not...' His voice trailed off.

Athelstan stared up at the sky, now blood red as the sun began to set. He felt the evening breeze cool his face. He hardly spared a thought for assassins steeped in murder and ambition. How crimson was his own soul? Had not he too committed a secret sin?

'What shall we do, Brother?' Cranston interrupted.

Athelstan looked at that fat, friendly face, the good-humoured smile, the compassion in the bleary, drink-sodden eyes.

'You are a good man, Sir John.'

The coroner looked away.

'And I shall tell you what we shall do,' Athelstan continued, taking him by the elbow. 'We shall celebrate!'

He led Sir John along the waterside into the nearest tavern where he secured the best seats near the window. Athelstan raised a hand and called the landlord over.

'I want a jug of your best Bordeaux and two deep cups. My friend and I are going to get drunk!'

Sir John clapped his hands like a child, crowing with excitement. They drank like parched men. They heard the chimes of midnight and saw the stars come out before reeling back into the city and the warm security of Cranston's house. The Lady Maude screeched how she had heard of good seed falling amongst briars but never of good men falling from grace amongst friars! Cranston told her to shut up, announced he was going to give up ale and become a Dominican. He was still grinning beatifically when he passed out. Lady Maude knelt near her husband's porpoise-like body and made him comfortable for the night. She talked softly, keening over him as if he was Abelard and she Heloise. Love is strange, Athelstan thought, and has so many forms!

Late the next morning, thick-headed and a little wiser, Athelstan went back to his church. He said Mass with no congregation present and sang his matins, wondering what had happened to Benedicta. He had lacked the courage to question Lady Maude. He was just finishing a psalm when the door opened behind him. He knew Benedicta was standing there as she always did, leaning against the pillar at the back of the church. She called his name softly, once, twice, but Athelstan did not turn. He heard her footsteps and the door close behind her. The friar remembered the words of the poet: 'When a heart breaks, worlds shatter without a sound.'

–

Father Prior came to visit Athelstan, appearing suddenly like a thief in the night. He was courteous enough, for he had also visited Sir John Cranston to inquire how Athelstan was progressing, and the good coroner had escorted him across London Bridge to Southwark to see. Of course, Athelstan had had some warning: Cranston sent ahead Walt, son of Lionel the hangman, to advise him of the prior's intended arrival. Athelstan hastily rounded up some of his parishioners, a not too difficult task as they constantly loitered around the steps of the church, each involved in his or her own nefarious activities.

Cecily the courtesan brushed and scrubbed the porch, while Watkin did his best to clean some of the dirt from the nave and refilled the holy water stoups which the children always drank from. Athelstan had just preached a sermon on how men and women were all God's flowers, some being roses, others bluebells. He'd hoped to convince his parishioners that God loved their differences and that a garden full of roses might be very pleasant but also very boring. The sermon was difficult to give as Benedicta persisted in kneeling in front of him, staring up with those beautiful eyes. She would have resembled the holy Agatha had it not been for the laughter lines round her mouth.

At last Father Prior arrived with his clerks, secretarius, sacristan and other officials. Cranston was stone sober, sitting on his horse like a Solomon come to judgement. Athelstan's parishioners thronged round; Orme, one of the many sons of Watkin, thought Father Prior was the Pope but Cecily the courtesan loudly proclaimed he was the bishop. Athelstan shooed them away and brought his guests into the church whilst Crim and Dyke guarded the horses. Father Prior's retainers amused themselves by looking round. It didn't take them long and Athelstan saw the snotty-nosed sacristan laughing at his pathetic attempts to turn this church into a house of God. But who cared for his opinion? thought Athelstan. Perhaps someone should remind him that it all began in a manger, and the stable in Bethlehem had no fine paintings. Father Prior, however, was kind; he sat opposite Athelstan on the other of the church's two benches and gently questioned him on his doings over the last few months. Cranston sat beside him, staring up at the ceiling. Father Prior heard the friar out before taking him by the hand.

'Brother Athelstan,' he said, 'if you wish, you may come back to the Mother House. Your work and your penance are over.' He turned to the coroner. 'What do you think, Sir John?'

Cranston smiled and shrugged. 'He's a better priest,' he quipped, 'than he is a coroner's clerk! I think it best he should return.'

His eyes refused to meet Athelstan's.

The prior nodded, rose, and patted Athelstan on the shoulder.

'I have to go somewhere else,' he said. 'Sir John has kindly agreed to escort me. It's only a short distance. We shall return within the hour and receive your answer then.'

He walked out of the church, his black and white robe billowing behind him. Cranston did not spare Athelstan a second glance as he waddled out. A moment later Athelstan heard him roaring to Cecily the courtesan that he didn't care how pretty her arse was, she was to get out of his saddle! Father Prior's retainers, eager to leave, needed no second invitation. Athelstan heard their horses clatter off and told Watkin to guard the church door and leave him alone.

'Are you leaving us, Father?' the man asked anxiously.

Athelstan couldn't answer. He shut the door, barred it, and went to sit on the sanctuary steps. What should he do? On the one hand, he was glad Father Prior had come to take him back, but on the other, what would happen to his parishioners? Watkin's bevy of children? The youngest, Edmund, seemed a clever boy. If schooled properly, he might become a clerk. And Cecily the courtesan? What would happen if he no longer gave her pennies for cleaning the church? And Benedicta? He shut his eyes and tried to expunge her face from his mind. He prayed for a sign. The good Lord would surely guide him. He opened his eyes, got up and noticed the candle, the one Benedicta always lit in front of the Madonna. Athelstan went across and stared down at it. Only then did he notice the rose, a small white one, placed at the foot of the statue. He had his answer.

Athelstan was waiting for Father Prior when he and his party came up the lane and stopped outside the church. Athelstan took his superior's horse by the bridle and looked up into the prior's kindly face. He ignored Cranston's glare.

'Do I have your answer, Brother Athelstan?'

'Yes, Father Prior,' he replied. 'I would like to stay here until I am as good a coroner's clerk as I am a priest!'

'You are sure, Brother?'

'Yes, Father, I am sure.'

The prior smiled.

'So be it,' he murmured. He sketched the sign of the cross in the air above Athelstan's head, bade him adieu and urged his horse forward. Athelstan waited till the sound of the horses faded before staring at Cranston, who was surreptitiously wiping his eyes on the cuff of his jerkin.

'God's bones, Athelstan!' he bellowed. 'I have never been so sober for so long in my life! Now I am so hot, even my eyes are sweating.'

He looked at Athelstan mischievously. 'Perhaps a little refreshment?'

'God save us all!' Athelstan muttered, and walked back up the steps of his church, leaving Cranston bellowing after him.